Double Take

Also by Elizabeth Breck

The Madison Kelly Mysteries

Anonymous

Double Take

A Madison Kelly Mystery

ELIZABETH BRECK

NEW YORK

This is a work of fiction. All of the names, characters, organizations, places and events portrayed in this novel are either products of the author's imagination or are used fictitiously. Any resemblance to real or actual events, locales, or persons, living or dead, is entirely coincidental.

Published in the United States by Crooked Lane Books, an imprint of The Quick Brown Fox & Company LLC.

Crooked Lane Books and its logo are trademarks of The Quick Brown Fox & Company LLC.

Library of Congress Catalog-in-Publication data available upon request.

ISBN (hardcover): 978-1-64385-766-4
ISBN (ebook): 978-1-64385-767-1

Cover design by Nicole Lecht

Printed in the United States.

www.crookedlanebooks.com

Crooked Lane Books
34 West 27th St., 10th Floor
New York, NY 10001

First Edition: October 2021

10 9 8 7 6 5 4 3 2 1

To Hope, Faith, and Courage: Thanks for getting me through the tough times.

Life starts all over again when it gets crisp in the fall.

—F. Scott Fitzgerald

Chapter One

Monday 1:05 PM

The girl was fifteen, but she looked twelve.

"Step over here next to me," Madison said.

The girl stared at Madison with huge brown eyes that were filling with tears. When she tipped her head back to look up at the man standing next to her, a fat tear escaped and rolled down her chin, onto a T-shirt that was too tight and low cut for a teenager. The man was smirking at Madison, confident. The girl looked back at Madison and almost imperceptibly shook her head. *No.*

Madison ignored her response. "Don't look at him. Just walk over here next to me." Madison stood easy, her five-foot-eleven frame balanced evenly on her Doc Martens, her purse hanging from the crook of her arm. She took slow, deep breaths.

The man's deep voice boomed in the quiet neighborhood. "She *better* look at me. And *you* better mind your own business."

Madison glanced around. October in Idaho was freezing. Colder than a Southern California girl thought a place could be. Her lungs felt like they were bleeding. She'd been tracking Alicia and her boyfriend for the past month. Well, Alicia probably thought he was her boyfriend. But boyfriends don't take you away from your parents in California and drive you to another state, hiding your whereabouts so that your parents have to hire a private investigator to find you. And boyfriends don't make you do things for money, things which no fifteen-year-old should even know about. But sex traffickers did.

The tableau Madison found herself in had as its backdrop the University of Idaho on-campus apartments, and there wasn't a soul around. All of the students were in classes in the middle of the day. The couple had moved in with actual students, something the university wouldn't have allowed had it known. Madison didn't think the student residents even knew what had moved in. It was a great place to hide in plain sight. Madison had found them anyway. Now it was a secluded place for a confrontation that favored the bad guy. Madison was on her own with a very large man and a very scared girl.

"Your mom is worried about you. She misses her little girl," Madison said.

"You need to stop talking," the man said.

The tears started flowing again at the mention of Alicia's mother. *This girl wants to go home,* Madison thought. *She has wanted to go home for a while.*

"We're leaving," he said. He turned and started to walk, and Alicia pivoted like she was attached to him with an invisible piece of rebar. But suddenly she stopped, frozen like the ground on which she stood.

Madison still had a chance. "Come back, Alicia." Madison spoke quietly, encouraging Alicia to do what she wanted to do. Alicia turned toward Madison's voice.

"What are you doin'?" The man grabbed Alicia's arm and yanked. She made a whimpering sound and crouched low, as if to avoid a fist. *How many times has that happened?* Madison wondered. Alicia tried to pry his hand off her arm; his fingers were digging into her flesh and would certainly leave a bruise. His height gave him leverage, and he pulled her close and started to drag her down the sidewalk.

"Stop walking." Madison said it with authority, as if she had a gun trained on his central mass. Which she did.

He turned, saw the gun, and stopped. Slight surprise registered on his face, like he hadn't thought Madison had it in her. "You gonna shoot me out in the open like this?"

Madison knew that her concealed carry permit from California was recognized in the state of Idaho, but she didn't think the university would appreciate her having a gun on campus grounds. But she was a private investigator hired to find a kidnapped girl, and she wasn't leaving without her.

"You've already committed a federal crime: 'transporting a minor across state lines with the intent to engage in prostitution or any sexual activity for which a person could be charged with a criminal offense.' But let me dumb it down for you: she's jail bait and you took her across state lines. And now you're kidnapping her right in front of me. Hell yeah I'll shoot you. I'll get a fucking medal. People will volunteer to come clean your blood off the sidewalk. Now walk away before I have to waste a hollow-point pink-tipped .38 bullet on you."

The guy appraised Madison, using his experience and limited IQ to decide if she would really shoot him. She figured he knew bullets, and so he would know she'd just named one that would kill him with one shot, piercing his leather jacket and then expanding and exploding inside his chest, destroying every major organ, while staying inside his body so as to avoid collateral damage to the people around him. He couldn't know that she was a crack shot, but the way she was holding the gun probably gave him an idea. Madison could hear the wheels grinding in his tiny little mind.

"Shit, she ain't worth this. Beat it, bitch." He shoved Alicia, hard, and she flew to her left and went down. She started sobbing out loud. *Because he's dumping her?* Madison wondered. The girl started to crawl on her hands and knees toward Madison. *No, because she's relieved.*

Madison waited until he'd walked away, far enough to no longer be a threat. She put her gun back in her purse and went over to Alicia. "Get up, honey, and let's go call your mom."

Chapter Two

Monday 6:12 PM

Madison looked at Balboa Park from nine hundred feet above. The cars and people looked like little toys, weaving through the landscape on a beautiful San Diego evening. With seventeen museums and one of the largest zoos in the world, Balboa Park was bigger than New York's Central Park. The architecture in the park was spectacular: the California Tower looked majestic, with its colorful tile visible even from Madison's airplane seat. She gripped the arm rests. For someone who didn't like flying, she sure did it a lot.

Alicia was back with her mom, the campus police had taken the kidnapper into custody before he'd gotten away (thanks to Madison disabling his vehicle beforehand), and Madison was on her way home. She took a deep breath and let it out, resting her head against the plane seat. The last few months had been a whirlwind of activity. In the beginning she'd enjoyed the interviews and speaking engagements, and so many requests for her services that she'd had to turn down work—a first for her. But then it had started to wear on her. Madison was an introvert. She'd learned she had a limit to how many people she could talk to in a day. Yes, she had pulled off an amazing feat with her last investigation, and it was great that it looked like she would be able to have her pick of lucrative assignments. But she could never shake the feeling, likely because it was true, that she was only as good as her last assignment. When she used to do insurance fraud investigations exclusively, she'd had the problem of having to keep the client happy or it would be her last assignment. But working in her new specialty was worse: not only did she have to keep the client happy, now if she made a mistake someone might die. These cases involved people whose lives were dependent on Madison's luck and skill—she wasn't just protecting an insurance company's money. The pressure got to be too much. Finally she had put a vacation message on her email, turned off her phone, and spent a month doing yoga, running on the beach by her apartment, and spending time with Dave, the surfer who was her on-again, off-again boyfriend and all-the-time love of her life.

The trip to Idaho had been her first assignment back. She was frugal in her living, but not working for a month had put her in a pinch. Even though she needed money, she wanted to pick cases based on what value she could give to the world—getting a teenager away from a trafficker and back home was valuable. Sure, the stress of knowing she could be responsible for a death was immense. However, she wanted to make a difference, and she'd decided to only pick cases where she could. Her father, whom she missed every day—*does the pain ever go away?*—used to say, *Everything in life is a trade-off.* She could do small jobs whose outcome wouldn't matter in a hundred years and thereby have no stress, or she could do something that would change lives, and deal with the stress that came with it.

Madison closed her eyes as the plane touched down. As soon as the plane was safely on the ground, she grabbed her phone out of the seat pocket in front of her. The flight had been two hours and forty minutes, and in that time she'd received ten voicemail and fifteen text messages. As she glanced through the texts, one of them caught her eye:

I've left you a few messages, sorry to blow up your phone. My girlfriend has been missing for five days. The police aren't taking it seriously. Can you help me?

Five days was an eternity with a missing person; forty-eight or even seventy-two hours was the cut-off for a good chance of finding the person alive. But five days was still something to work with. Madison could help bring another person safely home. Finding someone who was kidnapped or lost or just needed help to get home was so fulfilling, it was like having a life's purpose she'd never known she'd been without.

She didn't believe that the police weren't taking it seriously—a lot of times loved ones didn't understand that just because the police were being tight-lipped, it didn't mean they weren't doing anything. But Madison could help. After all, she'd gotten her reputation by solving crimes that the police had been unable to solve. A combination of skill and good luck had been Madison's winning combination, and maybe it could be used to find another missing girl.

Madison's attention went back to her phone, and she read a few of the voicemail messages that had been converted to text. One of them she'd been waiting for, but also dreading:

Hi, it's Megan from Dr. Schultz's office. Dr. Schultz got your message and would like you to come in as soon as possible. Give us a call so we can schedule you.

The flight attendants opened the cabin door, and Madison stood. She had to stay slouched under the overhead compartments while she waited for the aisle to clear of passengers. The woman in the seat next to her was able to stand up to her full height under the compartment, and they smiled at each other ruefully as Madison leaned over the seat, trying to rest her back from the strain. Finally a man paused to let Madison into the aisle, and she stood up and grabbed her carry-on from above, pulled out the handle, and wheeled it toward the airplane door. As she joined the throng of passengers in the jetway, she could feel her phone vibrating in her pocket as another call came in.

Chapter Three

Monday 6:28 PM

"Thanks for calling me back. I must've sounded desperate in my messages. Well, I am desperate." He sounded around Madison's age, like mid-thirties maybe. "You've got to find her."

Madison rolled up the window in the back of the rideshare so she could hear him better. The driver pulled out of the airport proper onto Harbor Drive. Madison was treated to the last of a beautiful sunset behind the sailboats lined up in the harbor to her right and reflected in the windows of the city skyline ahead of her. She had been to a lot of airports, and she'd never seen one that could beat the view you got after landing at San Diego International Airport. Just ocean and boats and skyscrapers and more ocean. She normally liked to have the window down to breathe in the fresh air after being away, but she couldn't hear him with the window open.

"My name is Travis Moore, by the way. I'm not sure I said that in the messages. I've been sort of . . . beside myself I guess."

"That's understandable."

"Do you think you can help me? I heard about you on the news, and you seem like you're really good at finding people."

There was that double-edged sword of recognition. She was known for finding people; that could change on a dime if she failed to find someone in time. *Everything in life was a trade-off.*

"I'd like to help you." The driver of the rideshare honked at a car coming into their lane as they made the turn onto Grape, heading to the freeway. Madison was jostled in the seat and grabbed the armrest to steady herself. "But I need to hear a bit more about the case. When can you meet?"

"I'm available right now. Can you meet right now?"

Madison was so tired. She'd been gone for a week on Alicia's case, and all she wanted was to take a shower and go to bed. But a girl was missing. And Madison could save her. "Yes, I can meet now. Can you meet me at Su Casa in La Jolla in two hours?" At least she could have him come to her neck of the woods. And then she could eat, too.

"Yes. I know it. I'll be there."

"I'll require a retainer." It was a bad segue, but she couldn't help it. Madison hated talking about money. However, she'd figured out a while ago that it was a girl thing. In general, women were uncomfortable discussing money, asking for what they were worth, demanding payment. She observed men discuss money, and she was shocked to see absolutely no discomfort. Men had no emotion about it. They just baldly discussed money as if it were . . . business. Madison still felt awkward and uncomfortable, but she made herself act like a man. She even said it to herself each time: *Talk about money like you're a man.*

Travis either hadn't noticed the bad segue, or he was responding like Madison expected a guy to respond. "Of course. I work hard and I have money, and I have nothing better to spend it on than finding Barrett."

So Barrett was the girl who was missing. It was a great name. Madison had a million questions but she wanted to ask them in an orderly fashion; she would wait until she met him in person.

"Great. I'll tell you how much once I've heard more about the situation. I'll see you soon."

They disconnected the call and Madison set her phone in her lap and looked out the window. She was jumping right into another case, and it could be a big one. So many clichés came to mind: *No guts no glory, No pain no gain, Fortune favors the bold.* So many clichés had to do with taking risks in order to have the big payoff. She didn't want the glory; she wasn't good at being famous. But she did want to make a difference. Who knows, she might be Barrett's only hope. This is where her motto *Will it matter in a hundred years?* came into play. Finding someone like Barrett, maybe saving her life, would mean that Barrett had a chance to have kids, to be kind to a stranger, to make someone's day, to make a difference in someone else's life, maybe even to save someone else's life. The ripple effect of a person's existence was immeasurable. All Madison had to do was find her.

It was dark now, the sun having completed its descent to light up other worlds in other places, far away. Madison put her head back against the seat and closed her eyes. She reached for the button on the door, rolled down the window, and felt the air swirl in, blowing her hair back and rushing up and over her face. The air felt different at night. It was full of hope.

Chapter Four

Monday 7:03 PM

Madison used her key on the huge deadbolt installed in her front door. After what had happened during her last case, she'd had a service come out and install it. She'd said, "Make it impenetrable," and the guy had taken it as a challenge. She wasn't sure of everything they did, but it involved new hardware in the door jamb and a huge deadbolt. She also had a new alarm system, which started beeping its warning as she crossed the threshold. She disengaged it and dropped her purse on the big oak dining table that served as her desk. She let go of the handle of her carry-on bag and took a deep breath, spreading her arms high.

"Hello home."

Her huge lock and alarm system were pretty fancy for a 1929 nearly decrepit carriage house, built to service the Craftsman cottage in front. Her studio was on top of what became a garage in later years, and she had an ocean view over the tops of the houses lining Neptune in the Windansea section of La Jolla. She was in a cluster of small cottages and slightly bigger homes that were the last vestiges of charm in this neighborhood. She had a sweet garden with grass and flowers out her living room window, and beyond the grass was the front house where her neighbor Ryan and his roommates lived. They didn't talk much. They were polite when they saw each other, and that was all Madison wanted. They coexisted peacefully in their little oasis just a quarter block from the beach.

Madison was dismayed by the gentrification occurring in the town: adorable homes torn down to make way for million-dollar condos, completely changing the feeling of Windansea. The section of La Jolla called Windansea had been named in 1909 after a hotel that had long since been torn down. Windansea was listed as one of the finest surfing spots in the continental United States, and the Windansea Surf Club was difficult to get into unless you could show surfing prowess and dedicated community service. Dave had done both and was a longtime member of the club.

When Madison couldn't think how to classify Dave in her life, she called him her "love interest," and that always made her laugh. Dave was a throwback to old La Jolla: that feeling of the surfer, beachy, laid-back lifestyle—even commemorated in the Beach Boys song "Surfin' U.S.A.": *All over La Jolla . . .* But that feeling was being ruined by the young urban professionals who pulled their BMWs into their newly-built steel and concrete monstrosities they called home. Madison was jealous of the BMWs, but other than that she resented them for destroying the small-town charm of Windansea.

She needed to keep moving or she'd lie down, fall asleep, and miss her appointment with Travis. She grabbed her suitcase and rolled it into the bedroom area. Her tiny studio apartment made her happy. The desk chair, the wingback chair from her great-great-grandmother, the bookcase that separated the living area from her bed, and the tiny kitchen and bathroom were all she needed. So what if she had to turn sideways to get into the shower—at night she could hear the waves. The waves were always louder at night, and they could be both ominous and comforting.

"Alexa, play reggae music."

Madison pulled off her clothes and stood in front of the mirror, which was part of her antique oak vanity. She traced the scars across her chest with her finger. It had been just over three years since she'd had the bilateral mastectomy, removing both breasts and nipples, and replacing them with silicone implants placed under her pectoral muscles. In her clothes, her chest had normal-looking, breast-shaped mounds, but standing naked it was clear there had been a surgery and things were missing. Dave called them Barbie boobs, since they were firm and high and had no nipples; it made her laugh every time. She'd loved playing with Barbies, and in fact she still had all of them, carefully saved in a suitcase with their couture clothes that her great-aunt had made. When Dave said he didn't care that she had huge scars across her chest and no nipples, she tried to believe him.

She leaned into the mirror to get a better look at the new red bump sitting on her mastectomy scar. It had popped up next to the other red bump that had been there for a month. Two new growths. The cancer might be back.

She would return the doctor's call tomorrow. Meanwhile, she jumped in the shower to wash the airplane off of her, and changed into jeans and a vintage Rolling Stones concert T-shirt.

She had a little time before she needed to walk over to Su Casa, so she sat at her desk and turned on her computer. She had another motto: *Trust everyone, but cut the cards.* She wasn't going to go to work for a guy that she knew nothing about; he could be a domestic abuser and his girlfriend, Barrett, might be trying to get away from him. Madison pulled up her private investigator's database, a paid service that you had to have a PI license to use, and entered "Travis Moore." She quickly found him. The name wasn't unusual, but there weren't that many in San Diego, so she easily found the one that was in his mid-thirties. Madison knew the average person would be shocked by how much she could find out about them with just a name, in under thirty seconds. But that was why California made it so difficult to get a PI license—they didn't want stalkers and freaks having access to this database.

Travis lived in Lakeside, and Madison Google-mapped his house. A decent ranch-style house. Lakeside could go from nice to bad really fast, so it sort of depended where you lived. Travis was in a nice neighborhood in this rural part of San Diego. Inland. She could never live inland.

She tried to find some social media for him but only found a LinkedIn account: he was a pharmaceutical sales rep. Madison knew they could make decent money, so that was probably why he wasn't concerned about her retainer. She wondered about the no social media, but then again Dave didn't have any social media either. Some guys were like that.

She checked the time and saw she'd better run. She put on her Ralph Lauren flak jacket—she'd decided to stop resisting her obsession with all things Ralph Lauren and bought his clothes on sale whenever possible—and laced up her Doc Martens. She paused and thought about the gun that she had put in the safe on her return from Idaho. She didn't always carry it; in most cases, she would prefer to get herself out of a situation rather than shoot her way out of it. Meeting a new client at the local restaurant was not an occasion to whip out the Smith & Wesson. She turned off the music, set the alarm, and walked out the door.

It was windy, as it often was in the fall in Southern California. The waves were deafening as she walked out onto Bonair and then made the hop onto Neptune Place. She checked the ten-car parking lot to see if Dave's jeep was there, and she was surprised to see him there too, loading up his car. The rest of the lot was empty. He must've surfed sunset and hung out in the lot talking to his friends afterward. He'd already changed out of his wetsuit into sweatpants and a sweatshirt.

"You're back!" he yelled across the street to her. Even after all these years, Madison felt a thrill go through her when she saw him. He was six feet tall, with blond hair, piercing blue eyes, and sun-damaged skin—but on a guy it just made him look more handsome and rugged.

She crossed the street, and he walked to meet her at the edge of the lot. He grabbed her and swung her around in a circle, which gave an indication of his strength since she was no lightweight. He smelled like the sea.

"I'm back." She buried her face in his neck and squeezed. She felt safe with him. It made her want to tell him everything about her cancer fears. But she was afraid if she did, she would start crying.

Sometimes if you start crying you'll never stop.

"But I have to run—I have a new case and I'm meeting the client at Su Casa."

"Yum I'm starving." Dave placed his surfboard gently on the passenger seat of his Jeep. Surfboards looked tough, but they were made of fiberglass and could get dinged easily.

"Okay well don't come bother me, I'm working."

"It's nice to see you, too." He finished with the surfboard and came back around to her side of the car. "Okay, maybe I'll come bother you later?" Dave did his best impression of a creeper, and it made her laugh.

"Sounds tempting, but I'm so tired I just want to go to sleep, if that's okay?"

Dave paused and looked at her. He waited without speaking for just a beat too long. "That's cool. Text me later." He put his knit cap on and got into the driver's seat of the jeep. Madison felt an ache in her stomach.

Madison turned to walk away, and Dave called after her: "What's the case?"

She turned back. "A missing girl." It was awkward now, and she didn't know how to fix it.

"I hope you find her." He started the Jeep, which was extra loud because of something he'd done to the engine, and pulled out of the lot.

Madison stood for a moment, trying to figure out how that exchange had gone so bad so fast. Well, it was simple: he knew she wasn't being truthful about wanting to go to bed early. He probably thought it had to do with the guy she was meeting at Su Casa. She could've just told him what was going on, but she wasn't ready. His coming over would certainly result in her shirt coming off, and then he would see the new red bump. And he would ask questions. She wasn't ready to ask those questions of herself even. She wanted to see the doctor, find out what it all meant, and go from there. Maybe it was nothing, and she needn't worry him at all. She would text him later and try to smooth things over.

She turned and walked along the bluff overlooking the beach. The waves were thundering down below. The searchlight hanging from the apartment building on the corner lit up the boulders and the waves breaking on the shore, and the light cast eerie shadows on the shack made of palm fronds that had been a Windansea landmark since it was erected by surfers in 1946. The searchlight had been lighting this stretch of beach forever, and Madison wondered if it had been placed there for security reasons: a series of rapes had occurred along the beaches in San Diego in the early 1990s, including at Windansea. Young women were ordered at gunpoint to tie up their male companions, and then the women were raped, and their belongings stolen. Dave had said if it had happened to him, he would've died trying to take the guy down rather than lie there while a friend was raped. In Dave's case these weren't empty words. While having the clichéd passivity of a surfer, that passivity belied an eager willingness to take down a foe, using the unusual strength formed from paddling out against waves on a daily basis. The surfers she knew were kind and community serving, but freakishly strong—and willing to fight if the occasion required it, which for some reason didn't get portrayed in the movies. Windansea Beach could be territorial. The surf break was notoriously dangerous, and a *kook*, or inexperienced surfer, could get himself—or worse, someone else—killed; risking lives would get you met in the parking lot after your surf session with a strong, and sometimes violent, suggestion that you not return.

Madison took a deep breath of ocean air and turned the corner to walk up the one-way street, past the gentrified monstrosity on the corner and what remained of the cute cottages and apartments, to Su Casa at the intersection of La Jolla Boulevard. It had been serving delicious food, and margaritas that could put hair on your chest, since 1967, but she'd heard they were closing soon because the owners wanted to retire. Madison figured she was an old soul: she didn't like all this change. They were going to tear down this historic building and put up another strip mall.

She pushed open the heavy door at Su Casa and smelled the familiar mix of mustiness and stale beer, burnished into the carpet and walls from years of good times. Madison loved walking into a place where you could feel the history. It was dark, with red leather booths and a huge aquarium. She didn't know whether to walk into the restaurant proper or go left toward the bar. The door opened behind her and she didn't have to decide.

"Are you Madison?" he said.

He was probably six foot three, with curly brown hair and hazel eyes. Madison had to tip her head back slightly to look into his face; as she did so, she started to lose her balance and reached her hand out to steady herself on something, but there was nothing there and she started to fall to the side. He caught her and laughed.

"You okay there?"

Madison was feeling something she hadn't felt in a long time—frankly, not since she'd first met Dave. The power of attraction had something to do with it, but it was also meeting someone for the first time whom you feel you've known all your life. It was comforting and disorienting all at the same time: like coming home, but all of the furniture has been moved. *Jesus,* she thought. *That only happens a few times in a lifetime.*

She finally found her voice. "Yes, I'm fine. Sorry. I'm Madison. You must be Travis."

"That I am." He looked around. "Hey, this is quite a place."

"It is indeed. Classic Windansea. There'll never be another like it."

Travis had finished his examination of the restaurant and was now staring at Madison. "You seem . . . familiar."

"Really?"

"Yes. Is it possible we've met before?"

I'd remember you. "I don't think so."

He looked into her eyes like he could find the answer there. "It's sort of uncanny. I don't seem familiar to you?"

"Not in a we've-met-before kind of way."

"Is there another kind of way?"

The hostess came up and offered them a booth in the back. They dropped the familiarity discussion as they got seated and ordered drinks. Madison ordered club soda, and Travis asked for water. Madison told the waitress to bring guacamole and chips, and they would look at the menu and decide on the rest.

"I guess it's just one of those things," Travis said. "My friend says, 'There are really only four hundred people in the world—they just travel a lot.'"

Madison laughed. He had broken the tension. "We'll just chalk it up to that."

"Okay. Well. Let me dump some information on you, to bring you up to speed quickly."

"Good idea." Madison shook off the episode and got ready to focus on the matter at hand. This guy's girlfriend was missing. It was no time to get the vapors. "Just tell me everything you know."

Travis reached into his coat. "I brought you a photo. Her name is Barrett. Barrett Anna Brown."

Barrett looked tall, with blonde hair, like Madison, but about ten years younger; maybe twenty-five. She was laughing in the photo, reaching for the camera like you do when you don't want your photo taken. It was in a bar, and she was wearing a halter bathing suit top underneath a T-shirt. She was surrounded by other laughing people, some facing the camera and some facing away, involved in their own conversations. They all had bathing suits and beach-going attire on, shorts, tank tops. Barrett was tanned with straight white teeth. She looked happy. Frankly, she looked like Madison. "When was this taken?"

"Last year." Travis took a sip of his water. He hadn't touched the chips. "She went on a girls' vacation to Cabo. She told me how much fun she'd had. I was glad because she works really hard and she needed to get away. She always works so hard."

Something in his voice made Madison look up from the photo. Was he going to start crying? He took another sip of water.

"Okay so tell me everything. When was the last time you talked to her?"

"I called her on Wednesday night." Madison forcing him to get down to business seemed to have knocked him out of his slide into grief. "I called her, and she said she was going to bed early and we'd talk tomorrow. But then I didn't hear from her. I called her all day Thursday, tried her at work, nothing. Then I started calling hospitals."

"Does she have a car?"

"No, she's eco-conscious. She lives in Hillcrest, works at a small newspaper there, and she just rides her bike or walks. But I went to her house and her bike was there. It was like she walked out of the house and disappeared off the face of the earth."

Madison thought about that for a minute. Barrett might be the only person Madison knew in California without a car. It was hard to get around without a car, but then again people did it.

"And what do the police say?"

Travis made a scoffing sound. "Not much. 'She's a grown woman. She's allowed to not talk to you. Did you ever consider she's ghosting you?' Then the desk sergeant laughed. No, I haven't considered that. We have a great relationship. We've been going out for two years. She wouldn't just ghost me. They took a report, but they said they couldn't promise anything."

Madison wasn't part of the "all police are bad" club, but she knew the police had their shortcomings, usually based on their being weary of having seen it all. Women did ghost men. Women are allowed to stop answering the phone when a guy calls. But Travis seemed generally distraught over his missing girlfriend. Madison could check with her friend Tom, who was a homicide detective, but at the same time, if she could avoid a conversation with the police about her possible interference in their case, it would be better. She might just quietly start working on this. The more people trying to find Barrett, the better. If she got to the point where she thought she needed to coordinate her actions with the police, she would do so. Anyway, it was always easier to ask forgiveness than it was to get permission.

"Does she have family here?" Madison asked.

Travis had finally started eating the chips, which allowed Madison to relax a little. He was so on edge he was making her nervous. "Her parents died when she was young. She doesn't have any other family."

Madison brought up a new note on her iPhone, and named it *Barrett.* "Can you describe her to me, as far as height, weight, and notable markings? Any tattoos?"

"She's about five foot seven, blonde hair, green eyes, fit, and she has a tattoo of the Harley Davidson symbol on her shoulder."

Dang, Madison thought. *Harley Davidson?* There was more to this girl than met the eye. She looked back at the photo. She could see some ink just peeking out from underneath Barrett's T-shirt.

"Okay. What about other friends who she might've talked to about plans?"

"All she does is work. She works at *The Hillcrest Holler*, a cute little newspaper that is more event announcements and 'things to do this weekend' than a real newspaper. She might have some friends there, but mostly she just works, goes home and watches *Friends* reruns on TV, and then hangs out with me."

Again, this sounded strangely like Madison. A loner who liked to work and then go home and watch *Friends.* Other than Dave, there wasn't really anyone that Madison spoke to regularly. And even with Dave she might go a few days without talking to him. She sometimes wondered: If she died in her sleep, how long would it be before someone found her body?

"Who did she go on the Cabo trip with?"

Travis finished chewing before answering. "It was some Facebook group of book lovers. It was like, 'Let's go to Cabo and read books and drink margaritas,' or something, and there was a group of ten women from all over the country who'd met on Facebook. When the trip was over they all went their separate ways."

That sounded perfect to Madison: read books, have some laughs, never have to see each other again.

"Do you by chance have access to her apartment and anything like her cell phone bills or credit card bills?" Even though they were just boyfriend–girlfriend, sometimes a boyfriend would pay for the phone. Having access to her last phone calls would be helpful, and those would be listed on the bill.

Travis reached into his pocket and pulled out a shiny new key. "She had just given me this. It was in a box with a bow on it."

Madison smiled and took the key. "What about cell phone or credit card bills? Does she have location services turned on so you can find her phone?"

"No. I thought you'd be able to handle all that?"

Madison sighed. Sometimes people thought PIs were magicians. She actually only had access to public records, things the average person had access to. Sure, she had special access to a database that compiled a bunch of public records into a single report in seconds, but the fact remains they were *public* records. Cell phone records were not public records. Credit card information was not a public record. And the police needed a search warrant to get a triangulated location of the last place a phone pinged—even they couldn't get the exact location.

"I'll do what I can. Does she have an iPhone or another kind of phone?"

Travis paused to finish swallowing. He took a sip of water. "She has an iPhone."

That could help. A lot of people activated the "Find My iPhone" location service. But Madison would need access to Barrett's computer, and then she'd need access to her Apple account. "Do you have the password for her computer by any chance?"

"No, we didn't really get into sharing that kind of information."

That wasn't unusual. Madison wouldn't give anyone the password to her computer. "Do you have identifying information, like her Social Security number, date of birth, things like that?"

Travis pulled a piece of paper with chicken scratch on it out of his pocket and handed it to Madison. She took it and glanced at it briefly. It had all the particulars.

So it was time to discuss money. Madison took a deep breath and reminded herself to act like a guy. "I will need a five-thousand-dollar retainer. I charge seventy-five dollars an hour, and I will keep close track of the hours that I use. I will not go over five thousand dollars without checking with you first."

Travis pulled out his phone as she was speaking. "PayPal okay?"

Madison was relieved. He wasn't going to be difficult about money. She pulled up her PayPal and gave him the QR code to scan. Within seconds her phone pinged with a notification: *Travis Moore sent you $5000.*

The waitress appeared and asked if they were going to order dinner. Madison was starving; she hadn't eaten anything but the chips since she was in Idaho. Madison ordered enchiladas, but

Travis said he couldn't eat. She asked the waitress to pack them to go.

"Tell me what she's like," Madison said.

Travis cleared his throat. "She's so funny and smart. You can see she's beautiful from the photo, but what you can't see is how smart she is. And determined. She wants to be a hard-hitting journalist, even though she works at that tiny paper."

"Did she go to college?"

"Yeah, she went to UC San Diego. She graduated just a few years ago. She's twenty-four."

Madison, too, had graduated from there. The similarities were getting weird.

"Can you think of anyone that would want to take her or hurt her in some way?"

"I can't. All I can think is that it is something random, like she met with a bad person or . . . I don't know. I just want you to find her before it's too late. What if she's being kept somewhere?"

Madison thought about that for a minute. There were cases you hear about on the news, where some girl was kept chained up somewhere for years. If that were Barrett, and Madison had a chance to save her . . . Madison couldn't think about it, or she'd be paralyzed with the fear of a girl being tortured while waiting for Madison to save her. Madison just needed to find her, no matter what was happening.

The waitress brought Madison's food, and Travis insisted on paying. They walked out to the parking lot and the wind caught Madison's hair and flung it across her face. Her hands were full so she dipped her head and cleared her vision. The wind was blowing the clouds swiftly across the ocean. They walked in silence until Travis reached his car; Madison saw then that he had her dream car, a black BMW 540i. They faced each other and the silence went on a bit too long.

"So, anyway, I'll do everything I can," Madison finally said.

"I'm counting on it." He looked down at her, and Madison suddenly felt like they were on a date and he was about to kiss her.

She jumped in to cover her discomfort. "Travis, let me ask you something: What do you feel in your gut? What happened to her?"

They were both startled by a plastic shopping bag that flew up next to them in a tiny twister, swirling higher and higher, before an unseen hand whisked it haphazardly across the lot. Travis's attention was fixed on something over her shoulder, but as she turned she saw only the wall of the apartment building next door. Madison shivered.

Travis spoke, and his words would haunt Madison over the days to come. "I can tell you what I'm afraid of: I'm afraid she's wishing she were dead."

Chapter Five

Monday 11:07 PM

Madison sat at her desk and stared at the photo of Barrett. It was late for her, and she wanted to go to sleep. But Travis's last words had really gotten to her. *Wishing she were dead.* Madison believed there were fates worse than death. If Barrett were in that position, and it was Madison's job to find her, Madison would stop at nothing. It didn't help that Barrett reminded Madison of herself; she couldn't stop envisioning herself in the type of situation Barrett might be finding herself in. That was not productive. She had to separate her emotions from this job and be deliberate and methodical in her search for Barrett.

Before going to sleep she just wanted to do a quick background search on Barrett. While she couldn't find actual credit information because it wasn't public record, she could see what addresses Barrett had used for credit in the last seven years. She fired up her computer and put in the identifying information she'd gotten from Travis. In less than thirty seconds she had all of Barrett's addresses, any phone numbers used for credit purposes, and any companies she was associated with. Sometimes Madison could get vehicle information, but only if the person wasn't from California. Madison's state was one of the most stringent when it came to giving access to vehicle and driver information. Madison had other ways to get it, but Travis had said Barrett didn't have a car, so no point in searching for that.

Madison saw the address in Hillcrest that Travis had given her. She Google-mapped it and looked at the street view. It appeared to be a big ranch-style house, but Barrett's address had ½ in the number, so Madison figured Barrett had a small apartment in the back of this house. It was in a really nice section of San Diego called Banker's Hill, named in the nineteenth century for the affluent occupants of the homes there. Now it was a sleepy neighborhood between Hillcrest and downtown, with older homes, some of which had been restored and were now used as offices or bed and breakfasts. Madison would need to go to Barrett's house tomorrow, first thing.

Madison found that the phone number listed was the same one that Travis had given her for Barrett. She would like to get Barrett's cell phone bill, so that she could see the last phone calls that came in to and went out of Barrett's phone. Getting phone records was a tricky thing, which a lot of people didn't realize. Even the police needed a warrant to get phone records. That's why Madison had asked Travis if he had access to her account.

When Madison got to Barrett's house tomorrow, she would look for a computer; if she could get access to it, she might be able to use it to locate Barrett's cell phone, but only if Barrett had *Find My iPhone* enabled.

Next, Madison turned her attention to the "known associates of subject" section of the report. The only people listed appeared to be Barrett's neighbors on the street where she lived. Sometimes this report from Madison's database would have valuable information about parents, siblings, and spouses. Barrett appeared to be more of a loner than Madison, and there were essentially no known associates listed for her.

Barrett had a minimal Facebook, or at least what was visible to non-friends. The profile photo was the same one that Travis had provided to Madison, and the cover photo was of the tower in Balboa Park. Barrett had posted a photo of her father for the last Father's Day, with the caption "RIP." Madison looked at the photo closely. He had a warm smile. Madison knew what it was like to miss your father.

Madison stared at Barrett's profile photo. There was a fire in her eye. Hope. Life hadn't kicked her to the curb as many times as it had Madison. She hoped that wherever Barrett was right now, she still had that fire in her eye. Madison needed to find her before it went out.

Tomorrow she would start bright and early, set up her white-board with all of the information and clues she had so far, and find Barrett. But now it was midnight and there was nothing else to be done. She needed to wind down so she could fall asleep.

Madison walked out onto her landing, took a deep breath, and raised her arms up over her head, slowly bending down until she touched the deck. Standing again, she checked the alley for any unusual cars, just out of habit. Nothing out of the ordinary to be seen. Which meant she was left with her thoughts. Her wind chimes tinkled with the ocean breeze. She put the hood on her flak jacket up over her head and leaned on the railing. The thing she'd been avoiding thinking about all day was now the only thing she could think of.

She had always sworn that boobs didn't matter to her; she survived on her wits and perhaps her humor, and her looks were the last thing she needed to survive. She'd taken to calling them *foobs*, for fake boobs, because it was funny, but also because it was important to her to make the distinction. She didn't have boobs; they had been taken. She'd had a small mourning at the time, and then she had gotten on with her life. What she had didn't look real when she was naked, but they looked great in clothes, and she didn't even have to wear a bra. She didn't take them seriously. But she hadn't considered what life would be like without them. The fact remained that boobs made you feel like a girl. If they had to take the implants out in order to treat a recurrence, she would be essentially concave with scars across her chest and no nipples. Of course she should be worried about whether the cancer had advanced and whether she'd need chemotherapy and whether she'd survive it . . . but all she could think about was what if she had to lose her foobs and she no longer felt like a girl? How much can a person take before it's too much? How far would you go to ensure your own survival, before life wasn't fun anymore?

She decided in this moment to take it one day at a time; first, apply her motto from the last time she had cancer: she would hope that *if it were there*, they would find it. So many people had said to her, "Well, I just pray they don't find cancer," to which she would reply, "I hope they *do* find it—if it's there." The last thing she wanted was some hidden cancer growing out of control in her body. Go ahead and pray I don't have cancer, but if I have it, *pray they find it.*

A black Ford Fusion had driven through the alley from the east and appeared just below and behind her, on the north side of her apartment. It paused, which was what caught her attention. Madison lived at the intersection of two alleys: one running north–south and one running east–west. The Fusion was coming from La Jolla Boulevard and heading west toward the T intersection of alleys. The occupant or occupants couldn't see her yet, because she was standing on her landing on the west side, facing the ocean. When she heard the car stop she peeked around the corner. She'd never seen that car before. She memorized the license plate. If you want to live in a safe neighborhood, get a PI as a neighbor, Madison always thought. She didn't miss much. She couldn't see the driver: they had window tinting on all windows except the windshield, but it caused the interior of the car to be so dark at night that she couldn't make out the driver. They were pausing right below her apartment, which was also right where she parked her car. The Ford started to move down the alley toward her, and she backed up into her doorway to block their view of her. The car paused again below her landing and then turned left and went down the other alley to exit on Bonair. Madison jumped to the railing to see where it was going: they turned left, back the way they'd come.

Weird, she thought.

But a lot of Madison's life was being suspicious of things she saw, and most things never turned into anything.

She turned and went back inside, locking the door and setting the nighttime alarm, which would alert her to any infiltration through a window or door; however, only Spiderman would make it through one of her windows.

Once she'd changed and gotten into bed, she lay staring at the exposed beam ceiling and listening to the waves. Dave hadn't texted, and neither had she. It was probably fine; she'd text him tomorrow. They'd had an on-again, off-again relationship for years. There was something magical about them together that Madison couldn't get away from, despite the fact that her temperament didn't lend itself to a traditional relationship. She was independent, and she liked her alone time. Lately they'd fallen in to a comfortable routine: they saw each other when they wanted to, but Madison still got to have the big bed to herself when she needed solitude. Neither one of them was the kind of person who discussed their feelings or their relationship; they just lived it. Madison wasn't seeing anyone else, and she was pretty sure Dave wasn't either. Their unconventional relationship was working for them, and Madison figured that was all that mattered. The question was, how would he feel if she didn't have boobs anymore?

She rolled onto her side and closed her eyes. Her bed was her favorite place. She felt safe there. Where was Barrett right now? Lying in a bed? Tied up in a box? Dumped outside in the cold? She didn't know if Barrett was alive or dead, but either way Madison was going to find her.

"I'm coming, Barrett. I'm coming. Hang on."

Chapter Six

Tuesday 7:01 AM

Ping ping ping. Ping ping ping ping.

Madison had forgotten to turn off her phone before she went to sleep. A text was going off and it became part of her dream: she was trying to save Barrett, who was sliding off the edge of a cliff. Madison had a grip on her hand and was staring into her face, willing both of them to have the strength to hold on. Barrett looked determined. Slowly, though, her face began to register true fear as Madison felt their grip slipping. Suddenly Barrett's face became Madison's face, and it was Madison who began to fall. A weird alarm started to go off. Just before she hit the ground Madison jerked awake and realized it was her phone. She grabbed it off the nightstand.

Do you want to get a weather report every morning? Type Y for yes and N for no.

She must have used her phone number for something, and they'd sold it to a stupid app. Madison typed *N*, threw her phone back on the nightstand, and rolled over in her bed. She normally got up this early, but it had been a long week in Idaho, and she'd gone to bed really late. She crawled out of bed and padded to the kitchen to start the coffee.

While the coffee brewed, she got the whiteboard on wheels out of her closet in the living room. The dry erase markers were still sitting on the tray from her last investigation. She selected the black marker and wrote *Barrett Anna Brown* across the top. The marker was dry and didn't write well, which was annoying. She would need to go to the store later. Underneath the name she made columns, with the first column being *Timeline.* She wrote down everything she knew from her conversation with Travis. In the next column she wrote *Clues.* She didn't have any of those yet, and that would be the column she would start to fill.

The coffee maker squealed, and she grabbed a cup. She looked out her living room window over the garden. She didn't think she could live anywhere else. It was a classic Southern California fall day: bright and sunny, dry and crisp, with temperatures in the seventies. There wasn't a cloud in the sky. She loved fall more than any other season, mostly because it felt like the start of something new. It inspired hope in her, and hope was the one thing she couldn't live without. No matter what had happened to her in her life, if she had hope, she could carry on.

Just then her neighbor Ryan walked out of his side door partially wearing his wetsuit—he had the bottom part on, but the top part was pulled down, revealing his bare surfer's chest and shoulders. Because surfers spent a lot of their time paddling out against waves, they had extra strong upper bodies. Madison had no romantic interest in Ryan, but surfer torsos made her weak in the knees; if a guy could be a "boob or a butt" guy, then she could be a chest and shoulders girl. Equal opportunity. He looked like he was walking over to Madison's stairway, but she knew he kept his surfboard in a shed underneath her apartment. Sure enough, he immediately came back into view carrying his surfboard. He didn't turn to look up at her window, which was a relief. Things had been a little awkward since he became involved in her last investigation. She was glad that it appeared they could just move on from that and be polite when they ran into each other, and nothing else.

She went back to the whiteboard and wrote *To do*. Underneath she wrote *Go to Barrett's house*. Then she wrote *Go to her work, call Robyn for help with credit card info, figure out how to get cell phone bills and see who she was talking to last.* That would be a start. So the first thing she needed to do was go to Barrett's house and look around. She also wanted to call her friend Robyn, a private investigator in St. Louis, who had a knack for getting information that wasn't technically part of public records. It was an ethical gray area . . . actually, Madison had to admit, it wasn't a gray area. It was illegal for her to have bank information or credit information on a subject. Sometimes she did it anyway. She tried to do a don't-ask, don't-tell method with Robyn, to shield her a little bit from criminal charges should it come to that. But she had been using Robyn for years without an issue.

She put a bagel in the toaster and called Robyn.

"Robyn Contreras."

"Madison Kelly."

"What the hell, I bet you need something because that's the only time I hear from you."

"Of course I need something. I use you for your PI skills. Otherwise I wouldn't talk to you."

"Well, that I believe." Robyn laughed. "Seriously how are you. How's the surfer?"

"He's the same. Still gorgeous, still wants to see me."

"Well, why wouldn't he? You're a catch!"

Madison stuck her nose down by the toaster to check on the bagel. Not done. "Listen, I'm working on a missing girl and I need your help to run some searches on her bank and credit card info."

"Okay. Can you text me the info? I'm driving. When do you need it?"

"Well, she's missing and might be in some kind of danger, so take your time."

"You're hilarious. I wasn't gonna charge you for a rush job, but now I am."

Madison grabbed the bagel out of the toaster and immediately dropped it because it was too hot to hold. "You can charge me for a rush job, that's okay. My client has money. Get me the data as soon as you can. And of course, as usual, only use *legal* means."

Robyn laughed. "Oh, okay, I'll use only legal means of getting nonpublic record information about credit cards and banks. Gotcha."

Madison spread some cream cheese on the bagel and wrapped it in a paper towel.

"You are the best, gotta run."

They disconnected the call and Madison went quickly to her desk to text Robyn the information she would need. She had met Robyn several years before when she'd needed help on a case in St. Louis: one of her insurance claimants had skipped town and Madison needed to do surveillance on her in Missouri. Madison's PI license didn't transfer to Missouri, and so she needed a local PI under whose PI license she could work. She'd intentionally looked for a female name on a list of PIs licensed in Missouri. She had picked Robyn because she liked the spelling of her first name; sometimes that's all gut instinct was: the spelling of a name. As it turned out, she had chosen well. Robyn was an excellent investigator and they had become fast friends.

Madison went to her bedroom area to change her clothes. She generally had a uniform depending on the weather, and in Southern California there wasn't that much difference in the weather between seasons. October in San Diego could either be boiling hot or freezing cold, and sometimes both in the same day. She put on her yoga pants, an English Beat concert T-shirt, and she threw on her Doc Martens. Grabbing the bagel and her Ralph Lauren flak jacket, she picked up her purse, set the alarm, and was out the door. Madison was never a girl that dawdled when it was time to leave the house.

Barrett lived about twenty minutes from Madison. Madison decided to take Nautilus, right next to her house, which went up and over Mt. Soledad and down into Pacific Beach, where she could quickly join the 5 freeway. She jumped in her car, started it, and headed up the hill.

The views from Mt. Soledad, which was really a hill, were spectacular. Madison could see the ocean on one side and all of San Diego on the other. She managed to finish her bagel without dropping it on her clothes, which she decided to take as a good omen for the day. As she came down into Pacific Beach her phone rang. She saw who was calling on the car's dashboard, and hit the button on her steering wheel to answer it with Bluetooth.

"Madison Kelly."

"So, what? You don't write, you don't call?"

"I only call you if I need something, Tom. You know that." Thomas Clark, decorated homicide detective, long-term friend and foe, who had wanted a relationship when Madison hadn't wanted one. Everyone was happy in the end: Tom stayed with his wife, and he and Madison had vowed to remain friends. But the witty repartee was part of their charm.

"So I guess that means you don't have any work? Since you need my help to get your assignments completed, I'd expect to hear from you if you got a new one."

Madison got on the 5 freeway toward downtown San Diego. "Actually, I have a big assignment right now. But I don't need your help."

Madison didn't want to tell Tom about Barrett. She wasn't sure why. Tom could be helpful, but he could be controlling as well. She didn't want him to try to take over the investigation, and she didn't want to hear a lecture about how she had to be careful not to interfere with the police's investigation. Madison would never do anything to interfere with a police investigation, and if they were worried that she would get in their way, or perhaps steal their glory by finding Barrett before they did, that was their problem. If she got to the point that she needed Tom's help, she would brief him. Until then, her life and career were on a need-to-know basis.

"A new case? Really. Insurance?"

Madison hadn't done an insurance investigation in many months, maybe even a year. She was exclusively working on missing persons and cold cases. She hadn't gotten another murder case since the last one, but that was just the way it had worked out. Hopefully this case didn't turn into a murder case.

"No, not insurance. Missing jewels." Barrett was like a jewel, so it wasn't a complete lie.

"You're not telling me the truth, but okay. You don't want to tell me. You wanna have lunch?"

"Sure. Tell your wife to pick the restaurant."

"Fuck you. I gotta go."

Madison couldn't tell if he was angry or playing along. Such was the timbre of their normal conversation. "I'm kidding, yes we can have lunch. But I'm kind of busy with this case."

"Things are going well with my wife. I'm not going to do anything to mess that up. We're colleagues, right? Well, I have lunch with colleagues. You don't need to always be implying shit."

This conversation had taken a turn. Weren't women the ones who were supposed to get their feelings hurt? "Yes, Tom, we are colleagues. Yes, we can have lunch. I was just kidding."

Madison realized she had forgotten her thumb drive, which she wanted to use to download files from Barrett's computer, in case she had a desktop that Madison could get into. Also, she needed dry erase markers for her whiteboard. She would go to the Ace Hardware in Hillcrest on the way to Barrett's house. It was a great store that had everything you could need, and it was a fun place to shop with lots of cute tchotchkes to buy. She made a last-minute lane change to the 8 freeway east in order to get to where she needed to go.

That's when she saw the black Ford Fusion make the same sudden lane change behind her.

This was a surveillance 101 mistake—don't make quick moves behind the subject, because the subject will notice the movement in their rearview mirror.

She was being followed. This had happened before, but it had been a while. Who would be following her?

"Hey Tom? I need to go. There's an accident ahead and I need to concentrate." After her transition to the 8 freeway, Madison changed lanes and the driver of the surveillance vehicle, possibly regaining his composure, waited a few moments before making the same change to fall in behind her.

"No, there isn't. You're trying to get off the phone." Tom didn't believe her; she was usually such a good liar, and now both Tom and Dave had seen right through her. She was slipping.

"Oh my God, I'm not. We'll have lunch this week. Text me later." Madison hit the button on the steering wheel to disconnect the call.

She was approaching the interchange for the 163 freeway, which she needed to take south for just one exit. Since she wasn't doing anything particularly exciting today, she figured she would just let the person follow her. The Fusion had dropped back a bit, and there were a couple of cars between them. If he hadn't made that fast move, Madison didn't think she would have noticed him. Well, in fact, she hadn't noticed him. Who knows how long he'd been following her.

So someone wanted to know what she was up to. It didn't mean that there was a threat on her life. It just meant that someone was documenting her activities for some reason. Even though it was part of her own job, it definitely felt creepy to have someone following her, especially when she didn't know why. She didn't think the sex trafficker in Idaho was part of a bigger ring that would be angry at her for recovering Alicia, so that wasn't it. She'd been working on that case for the last couple of months, so there wasn't anything else hot going on. And she'd only been working on Barrett's case since that morning, hardly enough time to get on some bad guy's radar. This was a puzzle.

She took the exit on University Avenue into Hillcrest and turned left. The hardware store was up ahead on the right. There was a parking space right in front, and she pulled in and turned off the car. She could see the Fusion in her side-view mirror jump into a left turn lane. Across from the hardware store was the entrance to a mall, and the Fusion was trying to keep her in sight by pulling into the mall. It's what Madison would have done as well. She noted the license plate; this was the same Ford Fusion that had been in her alley last night. What Madison didn't know was how many vehicles were involved in the surveillance. A lot of investigators working for insurance companies did surveillance with only one person; but other investigators and law enforcement were appalled at the idea of doing surveillance with fewer than four people on the team. Madison saw the Ford Fusion turn left into the mall and disappear. Was there another car, or two other cars, that were now watching her?

It was a busy day during the week in Hillcrest, close to downtown. Known for its restaurants and nightlife, Hillcrest was also known for its active LGBTQ community. There were tons of cars on the street, cars parking, cars pulling away from the curb, people walking; it was a haze of activity and hard to pick out a vehicle that might be interested in her. The surveillance team, if it was a team, was doing a good job. There was nothing for her to do now but continue with her day and see what transpired.

She got out of the car and walked into the hardware store. She loved places where she could find cute items, doodads, and curiosities. Signs, mugs, and dishtowels with funny sayings on them, fragrant candles, incense, and every kind of gadget you could ever need for your home or office. She loved just window-shopping in places like this, but she didn't have time; Barrett was missing, and every minute that went by could be a moment of torture for her. It really cast a pall on everything Madison did. She walked directly to the section of the store containing office supplies, and grabbed a cheap memory stick and some dry erase markers.

As she was making her way to the cash register she saw a section on security cameras. There were nanny cams and baby cams and other more expensive hardware. This gave her an idea: she could put a camera in Barrett's apartment, and just see what might happen. She might see nothing, but she might see someone coming to search Barrett's apartment if she was being held for valuables or passwords to bank accounts. Madison didn't even know if Barrett had money; based on her small apartment, she didn't think so. But Madison had heard of women being held until they gave up their bank password info just to steal a few hundred dollars. She picked up a mid-priced model of a nanny cam that looked like a clock and took it with her other items to the cash register.

She completed her purchase and went back to her vehicle. As she walked out of the store she looked around casually, trying to see someone sitting in a car watching her or a vehicle slowing as it went by her. She knew from experience that a person could be parked a block away and be looking at her through binoculars, signaling someone else who was parked around the corner, out of her view, to get ready to follow her. It made the hair on the back of her neck stand up.

She opened the door to her SUV and lifted her leg to get in. She didn't lift it high enough and it hit the side of the vehicle, causing her to fall sideways into the seat. She fell on the bag with the camera box inside, smashing her foob. The surgeries had cut the nerves to her chest thereby making her numb, so it didn't hurt. But when something like this happened, the lack of pain made her concerned that she'd injured herself and couldn't tell. She righted herself in her seat and wondered if the surveillance team had seen her mishap. Embarrassing. She shut the door so that she was in the darkness caused by her tinted windows, and looked inside her shirt to make sure she hadn't done any damage. Just a minor scrape on her chest, no blood drawn. It might leave a bruise though.

She twisted in the seat and looked behind her and across at the mall parking lot. She still didn't see anything out of the ordinary. These guys were good. If she made them aware of her knowledge of the surveillance, they would just rent a new car, switch out the Ford Fusion, and it would be harder for her to spot the new surveillance vehicles. The fact was, she wasn't going anywhere that she wouldn't want someone to know about. She had been hired to find Barrett, and she was going to Barrett's apartment. They were welcome to come along.

Chapter Seven

Tuesday 9:12 AM

Madison pulled up in front of Barrett's house and parked. She sat for a minute in the quiet neighborhood. It was on a corner of a T intersection, but the intersecting street ended after only a block. It was near the Spruce Street Suspension Bridge, built in 1912 to provide pedestrian passage across a deep canyon, so that pedestrians in the developing neighborhood could walk to Fourth and Fifth Avenues to wait for the streetcar to take them downtown for shopping and business. Madison had walked across it once, and that was good enough for her; it was a long way down.

There were no pedestrians on the street near her, and no vehicles had followed her into the neighborhood. She was getting more and more impressed with the surveillance detail; it was ill-advised to follow your subject into a quiet neighborhood where you and the subject would be the only vehicles present. This team knew that. They were probably set up just outside the neighborhood, at various points where she might exit, so that they could resume the tail when she left. However, she expected at least one vehicle to drive by shortly, to see the purpose of her visit. She sat in her car to wait for them. With her tinted windows, if she sat very still, they wouldn't be sure if she was in the car or not. In order to see her inside the SUV, they'd have to stop their car, get out, walk up and put their forehead to her window, and cover their eyes to block out ambient light; she doubted they would do that. So she waited.

It didn't take long. Exactly three minutes after she had parked, a silver Ford Escape came down the street, in the same direction from which she had arrived. It was driving sedately, which was fine because it was a quiet neighborhood with perhaps a fifteen or twenty-five mile per hour speed limit. She watched it in her rearview mirror and then her side-view mirror as it got closer. Sitting in the driver's seat was a single man, white, mid-forties, with a baseball cap on. There was no one else in the vehicle. He was trying to look bored, but he was glancing left and right, a little too fast for someone who was actually bored. Madison kept her head against the seat, closer to the darker tinting at the back of her car, and remained completely still. As he got up next to her he tried to see in, but she knew he couldn't. The car passed, and she noted the license plate.

The car turned at the T intersection toward the exit to the neighborhood and was gone. Madison took out her phone, opened *Notepad*, and wrote down the license plate number of the Escape and the Fusion. She would look them up later, but she had a hunch she would discover the cars belonged to a rental car company that rented Ford vehicles.

Well, things just got a little more interesting.

Madison opened the car door and got out. As she was pressing the buttons on the handle to lock the car, an airplane flew low over her head. She was standing on the flight path for landing planes at San Diego International Airport. The sound was deafening, but exciting. She looked up and watched; the underbelly of the plane seemed so close she could touch it. Madison didn't like flying because she didn't like being enclosed in small spaces, but she loved the idea of airplanes and trains. She liked to imagine who the passengers were and where they were going: starting a new life? Visiting family? Running away? Leaving a loved one for a long journey, or coming home to someone who would cry tears of joy? It was dreamy.

Madison crossed the street and walked down the path leading to the side of the house. She could see a little gate to a garden and beyond that a stoop that must belong to the door of the back apartment. She jiggled the gate to see if any dogs came running, but none did. She entered the garden and walked along the paving stones to the stoop. There was a cute yellow beach cruiser bike chained to the rusted iron railing that outlined the entrance to the apartment. The door frame was wooden, and the numbers *145½* were painted on it with reflective white paint. Madison took out the key, put it in the lock, and opened the door to Barrett's apartment.

The first thing that hit her was the smell. Madison had started to walk in, but she froze on the spot. *Dear God,* she thought. *Did I just find Barrett?*

The apartment was small. Madison could see almost everything from the doorway. Either Barrett was a slob, or her apartment had been tossed by someone looking for something. There was a small living area with a couch and a coffee table, a chest of drawers against the wall, and a small twin bed against the opposite wall. There was a tiny efficiency kitchen straight ahead and to the left, and apparently a bathroom straight ahead, but the door was closed. Madison knew she had to walk ten steps and open that bathroom door. She took a deep breath, held it, and walked to the door. She used the sleeve of her jacket to open it. She didn't even need to step inside. There was nothing there, except a shower stall, a toilet, and a tiny sink. Madison exhaled and paused to get her racing heart under control. Barrett wasn't here. So what was the smell?

She turned back to the main room. The couch cushions were thrown onto the floor. There were cute knickknacks and candles and books that had apparently been on the coffee table but had been dumped on the floor, with the books disheveled and sitting on their pages, as if they had been gone through as well. Madison turned and went into the tiny kitchen; the kitchen drawers and cabinets were all open, and boxes of rice and pasta had been dumped onto the floor, apparently to see if Barrett was hiding something in the boxes. The refrigerator had been left open, and suddenly Madison knew the source of the smell. All of the food in the refrigerator had rotted. Madison peeked inside and saw meat and lettuce, all of which were growing things. There was an air popcorn popper sitting on the counter, with a jar of popcorn next to it.

Turning back to the living area, she observed that the contents of the bureau had all been dumped into the middle of the living room.

Madison wondered why Travis hadn't told her this, or even cleaned it. She didn't think the police would make this much of a mess looking for clues as to where Barrett was. Had the police taken photos already? She hadn't thought to ask Travis that, but she figured he would've told her if there were a problem with her coming inside the apartment. This was confusing. She took out her phone and called Travis. She got his voicemail.

"Hey Travis, this is Madison Kelly. I'm at Barrett's house and the place has been ransacked. Did you know that? Did this happen after you came here to check on her? Or before? Call me back." She wondered if he was the kind of person to check his voicemail, or if she should text him. She decided to leave it at a voicemail for the moment, and if she didn't hear from him she would text him.

The mess indicated to Madison that someone had taken Barrett because they wanted something that she had, and they came here to try to get it. Madison hoped that Barrett was being kept alive until they found the thing they were looking for. And she hoped they hadn't found it here.

Madison couldn't stand disorder. She couldn't think. The police had five days on her, so if they had wanted photos of the apartment in this state, they could have taken them. Madison took photos of everything for her own records, and then set about restoring the apartment to its former state. She found garbage bags and emptied the refrigerator, putting the dirty food from the floor in the kitchen into a garbage bag, and then she used the broom to sweep what she couldn't pick up. She put the contents of the drawers back and the drawers in the bureau. The couch was easy to restore, and then she set the knickknacks and books back on the coffee table.

Ping ping ping.

Hopefully that was Travis responding to her voicemail message. Madison placed the last book on the coffee table, Heda Kovaly's *Under a Cruel Star*, and grabbed her phone.

Would you like to get weather reports every morning? Reply Y for yes, N for no.

Honestly, these people were annoying. Who had she given her number to recently? She was usually careful about that: if a website asked for her phone number, she entered a fake one. They could email her if they wanted to reach her. So she was surprised that her phone number had been somehow sold to a third-party app.

N. STOP! Madison texted.

She then hit "Report" on her spam app to enter the phone number as a known spammer. Hopefully her spam app would block it the next time.

She picked up the two garbage bags she'd filled and walked out the door. She'd seen some garbage cans back toward the alley when she'd first gotten there. As she exited, she glimpsed the back door of the house opening. An older woman came out from what appeared to be the kitchen of the main house. She was over eighty years old, but she was dressed to the nines: yellow slacks with a cream and yellow blouse, jeweled flip-flops with perfectly manicured toenails, pearls, and her hair and makeup done, with coral lipstick finishing off the look. The woman's hair was a pale blonde and had been set in rollers that morning, so that it had soft waves that framed her face. Madison was slightly ashamed; this lady made Madison's yoga pants and unbrushed long hair look like she had just rolled out of bed and onto the street—which was actually close to the truth. Clearly she came from a time when people got dressed up to go into town.

"Young lady, my name is Betty LaDoux. I own this home, and I've lived here since my husband bought it in 1957, when we got married. I have several questions for you. First of all who are you?"

Madison steadied her voice. "Madison Kelly. I'm a licensed private investigator, and I've been hired to look into Barrett's disappearance. I'm just here to see if I can find any clues to help locate her."

The woman had narrowed her eyes and tilted her head as Madison spoke. "How did you get in?"

Madison felt like she was in trouble with the teacher. "Her boyfriend gave me a key."

"Okay. Next question: What do you mean by 'Barrett's disappearance'? I've been out of town for two weeks, visiting my daughter in upstate New York. Barrett was supposed to watch the house for me. I just got home last night, and I'm on my way to an appointment. I was going to knock on her door on my way out. So I don't understand what you're talking about."

This is not how Madison had thought this day was going to go, that she was going to be delivering bad news to the landlady. But maybe she could get some information about Barrett. "Can we go inside and sit down for a minute? I'll explain everything."

The woman looked at a tiny gold watch on her wrist and shook her head. She had gold bauble earrings on; they were the old-fashioned clip-on kind, and one of them flew off when she shook her head. Madison reached down to grab it and handed it to her.

"Thank you, dear." She put the earring back on. "I have a doctor's appointment, and I can't miss it. Can you give me your card?"

Madison said sure, and jumped inside to get one out of her purse. As she brought it back out the woman was speaking. "Barrett is the best tenant I've ever had. She is sweet, she helps me with things if asked, but we keep very separate lives. I'm a busy person and I don't want a tenant who tries to be part of my life. I think Barrett felt the same way about a landlord. So I don't think there's a lot I can tell you about her personal life. Do you think some harm has come to her?"

Madison figured this woman would see through any prevaricating. "I hope not, but I'm not sure. It doesn't make sense that she would just vanish. Also, her apartment had been ransacked."

Mrs. LaDoux nodded. "So someone was looking for something."

Madison was impressed with how quickly she caught on. "Yes, that's what it would appear."

"I don't like the way this sounds at all. Have the police been notified?"

"Yes, her boyfriend did that."

The woman looked at her watch again. "Good. I'm sorry, but I really have to go. I want to ask you more questions. I will call you later."

They parted, and Madison went back inside Barrett's apartment. Now that order had been restored, Madison could think. She was itching to get into Barrett's computer, but she needed to be methodical. First, she took the nanny cam out of the box. It looked like a retro clock, the kind that had hands going around a dial of numbers, set into a small wood-like base. She found a place for it on a floating shelf on the wall above the small bed, next to a scented candle.

She suddenly realized she needed Wi-Fi to make this nanny cam work, and she felt like an idiot. She downloaded the nanny cam app to her phone using her cell service, and followed the instructions to set up the camera and look for the Wi-Fi. She was in luck: apparently Barrett was using the Wi-Fi from the main house, and there was no password on it. Madison got the camera working, tested it, and set it to record on the motion detector setting. It would start recording on the included SD card only when the camera detected motion. An added perk was that an alarm would go off on Madison's phone when there was movement in Barrett's apartment.

Madison stood in the middle of the room and looked around. It was a nice space. She could imagine herself living here. Actually, she didn't have to imagine it, considering it was similar in size to her own apartment. Now that it was cleaned up, it was really cute.

Barrett had a small television with a DVD player hooked up to it. Next to it was a boxed set of *Friends*, every episode on DVD. It was Madison's favorite TV show. Whenever she was feeling overwhelmed or blue, she just had to watch an episode in order to feel better. She wondered if Barrett was the same way. There was a plant in a painted ceramic pot sitting on the coffee table. It needed to be watered, but it was doing surprisingly well considering Barrett hadn't been there for a week. Barrett obviously took care of it, and it just needed its weekly watering. Madison carried it into the bathroom and set it in the sink. She filled the sink with water so that the plant could drink from the bottom.

Madison realized nothing was on the floor in the bathroom, so maybe the searchers hadn't gone through the cabinets there. She opened a drawer and saw that the searchers had indeed been through them, unless Barrett was unusually messy. The first drawer had a box of Q-tips that had been dumped upside down in the drawer. There was a brush, some ChapStick, and some cortisone cream. In the next drawer down there was a makeup bag whose contents had been dumped into the drawer: foundation, bronzer, eyeshadow, and a tinier makeup bag that probably had eyeliner and lipstick in it. The tinier bag was really cute with red, yellow, and orange flowers on it in a circular pattern. Madison, being drawn to girly things, picked it up and unzipped it. Reaching inside, she pulled out an eyeliner and a tiny tape recorder.

"Well, well, well."

The searchers hadn't gone far enough when they dumped out the makeup bag.

Madison took the tape recorder into the living room and sat on the couch. She looked at it carefully. It was digital, and the last thing she wanted to do was accidentally erase what was on it. Fortunately, Madison had one like it. These days, if you wanted to record something you could just use your iPhone, but Madison didn't like to; she liked to keep her iPhone free when recording statements and use an actual tape recorder. There were two recordings on the device. She hit "Play" on the first one.

Restaurant and bar sounds, background chatter, glasses clinking, dishware clattering. And then a female voice. "How long have you worked here?"

The answer was from an older man with a deep voice. "About ten years."

"And how many pride parades have you worked, would you say?"

"Oh, I've worked all of them in the last ten years. It's busy and crazy but the tips are great."

Madison hit "Stop." This was obviously an interview for the newspaper regarding the gay pride festival held in Hillcrest every year. Madison liked Barrett's voice. It was young, but she sounded intelligent.

Madison selected the next recording and hit "Play."

"I just record because sometimes I forget what people say and I don't want to spend all my time writing while you're talking."

"I understand." This time it was a woman speaking.

"Do you mind if I call you Judy?"

"No, that's fine."

"Let me say, first, that I am sorry to hear about the death of your brother, Greg."

"Thank you."

"Tell me a little bit about Greg."

Madison hit "Stop." This sounded like another interview for a newspaper article, maybe an obituary of some kind. A dead end. Nevertheless, Madison would keep the tape recorder in case it became important later.

Madison looked around the room. It was time to get onto Barrett's computer. She wanted to see if she could get into the files, maybe her emails, and most importantly see if she could locate her iPhone. The computer was a desktop, sitting on a small table in the corner. There was a folding metal chair up against the table, and Madison pulled it out and sat down. Sitting next to the keyboard was a cell phone bill, unopened. Madison grabbed it and threw it next to her purse; that could prove handy later. The computer did not appear to have been messed with, so whatever the searchers were looking for wasn't something that was found inside a computer. Madison moved the mouse to turn on the screen, and it lit up and asked for her password.

Shit.

Well, it was to be expected. Most people had passwords on their computer, even if Mrs. LaDoux didn't put a password on her Wi-Fi. If it was a four-digit code there were ten thousand possible combinations of numbers. If it was a six-digit code the possibilities of course increased, and if it was a password with a combination of symbols and uppercase/lowercase, at that point the possibilities were endless. So was Madison going to attempt to guess it?

How security conscious was Barrett? Madison typed the word *password* into the box, but it gave the error message that her password was incorrect. If Madison tried too many times, she would be locked out. Next she tried *1234*.

Your password is incorrect.

Madison entered: *123456*

Your password is incorrect.

Madison thought for a minute. Then she entered: *1234!*

The computer chimed and the screen changed to: *Welcome Barrett!*

"Boom!" Madison said. Apparently, Barrett was not that security conscious. Did that mean she hadn't hidden whatever they were looking for very well, so they had found it in her apartment and Barrett was dead?

Madison couldn't think like that. She would locate Barrett either way. Madison had to just keep moving.

Madison clicked on the Outlook icon in the taskbar. It opened and offered her the choice of selecting email. Madison did so. No password required.

Thank God.

Madison looked through the emails. Most of them were spam, advertisements for things, notifications of concerts and events, etc. Nothing that could explain where Barrett had gone. Madison looked through the trash to see if she had deleted anything useful. Again, it was just advertisements and mailing list types of emails. Madison changed the settings so that any emails coming into Barrett's account would be forwarded to Madison's email address. A copy of the email would stay in Barrett's account, just in case Barrett was alive somewhere and had access and was checking her email.

Finishing with the email, Madison looked through the files on the computer and found some past articles Barrett had written. The most recent article was about a restaurant opening in Hillcrest. Nothing that fascinating.

Madison next checked to see whether Barrett had activated *Find my iPhone* on her computer. Barrett didn't have a Mac, the computer was a PC, so Madison would have to go to Barrett's iCloud account and hope she could once again guess the password there. Madison needed a lot of luck today. Google Chrome was Barrett's internet browser of choice since there was a button for it in the task bar. Madison opened Google Chrome to begin.

She went to www.icloud.com/find and the login screen appeared. Madison paused before she put the cursor in the box that asked for the Apple ID. An old boss of Madison's had said to her one time: "Being a good investigator is fifty percent skill and fifty percent luck. And Madison, you have good luck." At the time, Madison hadn't agreed with her. Her life had been filled with loss, and she'd felt that each day was an effort to overcome misery. Eventually Madison had decided to make it be true even if it wasn't. Sometimes, if she needed something to go her way, she would say it out loud.

"I have good luck," Madison said.

She put the cursor in the box and clicked the left button on the mouse. Google Chrome offered her the saved Apple ID: BarrettB2264@gmail.com. Madison selected it and the ID populated in the box; another box appeared for the password. Madison put the cursor in the box for the password and clicked the left mouse button. Google Chrome autofilled the password, but Madison couldn't see what it was—it was obscured with stars. Nevertheless, it would get Madison into the site. Just like Madison, Barrett had set up Google Chrome to save at least some of her passwords for her.

A compass appeared on the screen and started to circle, and it said *Locating* at the top. The computer was looking for the last known location of Barrett's iPhone. Madison waited. Could it be this easy? Was she about to find Barrett?

A map appeared on the screen, and Madison got so excited that she couldn't understand what she was seeing at first. Then she realized it was a map of San Diego and there was a gray dot in the middle of Balboa Park. A gray dot indicating where Barrett's phone was located. The tag read *one week ago*. Madison knew from experience that the gray dot meant the phone was turned off, or the battery had died. *One week ago* meant that was the last time the phone had been on, in that location. In other words, Barrett's phone had been in the middle of Balboa Park, and one week ago it was turned off or the battery had died.

Whether the phone was moved after it had shut off, Madison didn't know.

In any event, she now had Barrett's last known location, and it corresponded with the date that Travis had last spoken with her. Madison was just a few blocks from there. She took a photo of the map on the screen, grabbed her purse, and headed out the door.

Chapter Eight

Tuesday 9:46 AM

As Madison drove into Balboa Park down El Prado, she looked in the rearview mirror for the twentieth time. She hadn't seen any cars with suspicious-looking men in them since she had left Barrett's apartment a couple of miles away. Even if they were in a four- or six-man surveillance team, once she had been made aware of the surveillance, she wouldn't miss someone following her on quiet streets. They would be single men in nondescript vehicles. No old junk car that might not start when a PI needed it most, no pickup truck that guzzled gas. Only a fictional detective like Magnum PI drove a bright red half-million-dollar sports car that stood out like a sore thumb. Once you knew what to look for, PI vehicles were easy to spot. She had taken small side streets all the way to the park, and there was no one behind her for much of that time, and when there had been a lone vehicle, it was clearly not a surveillance vehicle.

Now that she was on a small street leading in to the park, there were even fewer cars sharing this route. Immediately behind her was a car with a middle-aged woman and a teenage girl; they were not tailing her. She felt sure that she had shaken the surveillance for the time being—or else they had just lost interest in what she was doing today.

The phone rang as Madison parked next to the fountain in the center of Balboa Park. The restaurant, El Prado, hadn't opened for lunch yet, and so she tucked her car next to the empty valet stand.

She hit the button on the steering wheel to answer the phone. "Madison Kelly."

"Hi Madison, it's Travis. You called me?"

Madison didn't know how much she wanted to tell Travis right now. He would have so many questions to which she had no answers. She did wonder about the state of Barrett's apartment, however.

"Yes, I went to Barrett's house this morning and it was trashed. Did you know that?"

There was a pause while Travis put his hand over the phone to speak to someone else. He came back to her quickly. "Sorry, yes, I should've told you that. I have just been so beside myself I'm afraid you're going to have to excuse me. Apparently, I'm going to forget details. Yes, the apartment was like that when I went there, and it was part of the reason I got so worried."

That would have made Madison very worried indeed. So worried that she wouldn't have forgotten to tell the person hired to investigate the disappearance. People were weird.

"Okay, well I just wanted to make sure, because it was really trashed and I didn't know if that had happened after you saw it."

A valet guy came out of the restaurant and waved at Madison. She rolled down the passenger window. "I'm only going to be a minute, I'll be gone before the restaurant opens."

The guy shrugged and then shook his head as he walked away. She didn't like to make people's jobs harder for them, but she really was going to be gone before he needed to park any cars.

Travis's voice came through her speakers. "Are you talking to me?"

"Sorry, I'm just somewhere trying to park. Anyway, I didn't know if the apartment had been trashed before or after you were there."

"Yes, it was before."

Madison thought for a second. "And tell me when you went to her apartment to look for her?"

"Let's see . . . I talked to her last on Wednesday night . . . I called her on Thursday and didn't hear from her, but I didn't get panicked until Thursday night. So, I called hospitals on Thursday night and then Friday morning I called her work and they said she hadn't been in for two days, and that's when I went to her apartment and saw that it was trashed."

Okay, that timeline made sense to Madison. That means whoever took her on Wednesday night, or maybe Thursday morning, had all of Thursday and Thursday night to search her apartment for whatever they were looking for.

"Thanks, Travis. I need to run now. I will keep you posted."

"Do you have any update? Do you have any new information or clues on where she might be?"

Madison examined her surroundings, the site where Barrett's phone was last located. The fountain, the restaurant, the botanical garden and lily pond, a smattering of people taking the day off to walk in the park on a crisp fall day without a cloud in the sky. "No, not yet. I will let you know as soon as I have any information that might be helpful."

They disconnected after she promised to call him back later that day. Madison sat in the car for a minute. She didn't see any vehicles that might contain an investigator following her. She grabbed her phone and got out, locking her purse inside the car. She looked at the photo she had taken of the map from the *Locate my iPhone* website. It was fairly exact as to where it said her phone was located a week ago: near the Plaza de Panama fountain, in front of the San Diego Museum of Art, and right in the center of the Plaza. Madison walked across the traffic circle to the fountain and stood for a moment, thinking.

If Madison wanted to meet someone at Balboa Park, this was at the top of the list of places she would suggest. It was a huge landmark for anyone from this area, and only a short distance from Barrett's house. There was a rental company scooter parked next to the fountain. It was exactly the kind of thing Barrett might've rented to get over to this spot. It had been a week, but Madison knew that these scooters had lost their popularity, not to mention she didn't think there were tons of single people walking through the park who would suddenly have the urge for a scooter. So it might've been here the whole time. Madison took a photo of it.

She looked back at the map of Barrett's iPhone location. As best she could tell, she was standing at the exact spot where the phone was last powered on. She looked down in the fountain but just saw a bunch of pennies that people had thrown into the fountain, ten thousand wishes for wealth, happiness, and love. Madison circled the fountain, keeping her head down and her eyes scanning. The yellow and blue Mexican tile that covered the fountain glinted in the bright October sun. Maybe she should throw a penny into the fountain, wishing that she would find Barrett.

And then she saw it. It was face down, so the light blue iPhone cover blended perfectly with the bottom of the fountain. It was closer to the center, and she would need to wade in to the fountain to get it.

There were only a few people strolling through the park in the middle of the week. No one seemed to be paying attention to what she was doing. She set her phone on the ledge of the fountain, and reached down to take her shoes off. She set them next to her phone on the ledge. Then she pulled her yoga pants up over her knees. She took her jacket off, because the sleeves were long and would get wet. She sat on the edge of the fountain and swung her legs around, putting her feet in the water. She waited; no one was paying attention. She stood up and walked over to where the phone was. She reached down, grabbed it, and turned to go back to the edge of the fountain.

"Hey! You there! You're not allowed to be in the fountain!" He was a small man wearing groundskeeper-type clothes, a beige and khaki uniform, and carrying a sharp stick, the kind that is used to pick up trash. He had driven over silently in an official golf cart and had jumped out to confront Madison. He looked proud of himself.

"Oh, really? I didn't realize." Madison finished walking to the edge of the fountain, sat down, and swung her legs to get out. "Sorry."

The man walked away shaking his head. He thought she was some dumb woman that wanted to go swimming in the fountain. Well, let him think that. He got back in the driver's seat and did his best to peel out in a golf cart.

Madison set the phone on the edge of the fountain. She couldn't be sure it was Barrett's, but all things pointed in that direction. Madison's favorite fictional detective, Nero Wolfe, used to say, *In a world of cause and effect, all coincidences are suspect.* She was looking for an iPhone that had last been powered on at that fountain, a phone that was now powered off, and here was an iPhone sitting in the fountain.

As she put herself back together, she thought about what this phone might be able to tell her. Probably nothing. Madison had dropped her phone in the toilet one time, and despite running and putting it into a jar of rice it had never spoken to her again. She couldn't imagine that a phone sitting in water for a week would ever turn on again. She had a friend, Arlo, who was a magician with computers, in fact she had heard he turned down work for the NSA, and he might be able to do something with it; but she doubted it. It couldn't hurt to try, and she would take it to him and see what he could do.

The fountain was in the middle of a huge plaza surrounded by buildings: a museum, a restaurant, and the main road leading in to the park. Madison turned in a circle, evaluating the location. There were many different species of trees, thanks to Kate Sessions planting one hundred trees a year beginning in 1892, along with all her other horticulture and floriculture efforts in the park. The foliage in the park knew that it was autumn, and the fall colors were on full display with leaves of gold and rust both on the branches and crunching under Madison's feet. In sunny Southern California, it was nice to have a place where one could see the seasons change.

Madison sighed. The good news was that this was no place to hide a body. While it wasn't the most populated area, it wasn't a deserted street; it was a busy part of the park at all hours of the day and night. The point that Madison was trying to make to herself was that Barrett couldn't have been murdered in this spot. She could possibly have been dragged into a car quickly, but even that would have been rough with the number of people around. Even late at night there were people at the restaurant, coming and going from the theater in the park. Maybe at four in the morning it would be deserted. But perhaps Barrett had never come to this park—just her phone had.

The possibility existed that Barrett had agreed to meet someone here, had traveled here on foot, in a car service, or on a scooter, and had never made it home. But that was just a theory based on nothing more than speculation at this point.

Madison couldn't figure this out with the data available. She needed to get the phone to Arlo to see if it could be salvaged. In the meantime, Madison wanted to go to Barrett's work and see if she could learn more about Barrett, and see if maybe she was working on something that might have had something to do with her disappearance.

As Madison crossed the Plaza to return to her vehicle, she saw the silver Ford Escape that had been at Barrett's house with her. She stopped and stared. The driver was glancing left and right as he drove down El Prado, and then he spotted her car which was to his right. If he had looked to his left he would've seen Madison standing staring at him. She jumped behind a large information kiosk that had a map of the park on it.

She peeked and saw he had turned onto the traffic circle where Madison's car was parked, and then slowed as he came up next to it. He pulled in front of it at the curb, the only place for him to stop, but the valet guy waved his arms and yelled at him. The Ford Escape continued forward, turning left on El Prado to return the way it had come. He would probably be waiting for her at the outlet to that street. As soon as he was out of sight Madison ran across the road to her car, jumped in, and used the traffic circle to make a U-turn and drive in the other direction, farther into the depths of the park. He would be expecting her to take the shortest route out of the park, which would be the way he had just driven. Therefore, she wouldn't do that. She would drive to the other side of the park, exiting on Park Boulevard.

Now that she hadn't found Barrett at the location of her phone, she could examine her feelings about it. Obviously, after a week, if Barrett had been at the location of her phone she wouldn't be alive. So in that regard, Madison was relieved. She had promised to find Barrett and bring her home either way, but she so wanted Barrett to be alive. So, in actuality, this "failure" was a relief.

She was only a couple of miles from Barrett's work. Hopefully, the information she gathered there would bring her closer to finding Barrett alive.

As she exited the park and pulled onto Park Boulevard, something was needling the back of her mind: *How had that investigator known where to find her, when no one had followed her into the park?*

Chapter Nine

Tuesday 10:16 AM

The newspaper office was in a converted California Craftsman bungalow on Fourth Ave in Hillcrest. Madison loved old houses, and she guessed that this classic piece of California architecture had been built in about 1905. She knew it would have the artistic touches that Craftsman homes were known for, such as built-in bookcases, wainscoting, and a wide front porch beneath an extension of the main roof, which she could see as she walked up the path. The front door was massive, some heavy wood like oak, with an enormous piece of beveled glass in the center. It was Madison's dream home. Across the top was a handmade wooden sign that said "Hillcrest Holler."

"Cute name," Madison said. She stood for a moment on the porch. She had seen no one following her from the exit to the park to her parking space in front of the newspaper office. She didn't see any surveillance vehicles on the street in front of the office now. She turned and opened the door.

It was as she had expected: lots of beautiful wood, exposed rafters on the ceiling, and built-in bookcases on either side of what used to be the living room, which you would pass through on the way to the dining room and kitchen. On the right side of the living room was an original wood-burning fireplace with a beautiful mantle, and a cluster of chairs with newspapers and magazines stacked on them was placed in front of it.

A man in his late twenties was sitting at a reception desk. He stood as Madison entered and walked around the desk to greet her. He had dark skin, dark eyes, and his long braids were swirled into a loose knot on the top of his head, with the sides of his hair buzzed close to his skin. He was wearing a button-down striped shirt buttoned to the neck, with skinny jeans and Italian loafers. A tight tweed jacket finished off the look.

This guy has some serious style, Madison thought.

"Can I help you?" His smile was big.

"Yes, my name is Madison Kelly and I'm investigating the disappearance of Barrett Brown. Do you have a few minutes to speak with me?"

When Madison said Barrett's name the man seemed to freeze in place. There was an awkward pause before he seemed to start breathing again. "Investigating? For who?"

Interesting question, Madison thought. Was this an awkward way of asking her if she worked for the police? Why was he acting so weird?

"I was hired by an interested party to find her. I assume you still haven't heard from her, in the last week or so?"

The man walked past Madison to shut the door that she had left open. He looked out on the street before turning back to her and speaking. "I have not spoken to her or seen her in a week, that's true."

This wasn't going as Madison had anticipated. "May I know your name?"

The man smiled again, which worked toward relaxing them both. He had charm to go with his clothing style. "I'm sorry, I'm sorry. I'm just . . . this has been difficult, and I've never experienced anything like this before. I'm not quite sure how to act or who it is appropriate for me to speak to. My name is Cornell Jones, and I'm the editor of this fine periodical." He walked over and cleared some newspapers off a cluster of chairs in the corner. "Won't you sit down?"

Madison sat down next to the fireplace. She saw some leftover ash and wished there was a fire going. It was quite chilly for October in San Diego.

"Have the police been here to question you?"

"They have not." He sat down across from her in one of the chairs. "That's probably why I acted strangely when you got here. I think I had been waiting for the police to come and ask questions and they haven't, and then you come and you are not the police . . . anyway I think I'm just trying to catch up here. Who is it that you work for?"

"Her boyfriend hired me to find her."

"I see." Cornell furrowed his brow and looked into the fireplace.

"Does he not seem like the type to hire a P.I.?"

"No, no, I just . . . I didn't know much about her personal life. I'm sorry, that was probably an inappropriate question anyway, asking who hired you."

Past tense? "I didn't know much . . ."?

"No, that's fine."

Cornell smiled again, and Madison could see he used his smile to smooth awkward social situations. It worked. "Can you tell me what Barrett's job is here?"

This seemed to be firmer ground for him, and he jumped in with confidence. "Sure. She is tasked with keeping track of current events in town and writing about them. For example, Pride Week is a big time for us and she would cover everything from the parade down to a heartfelt article about someone coming out to their parents during that week."

"Did she work on any type of investigative reporting?"

Cornell paused. "Well, she wasn't supposed to."

Madison laughed. "But she did?"

The phone rang on the desk, and Cornell jumped up to get it. "Hillcrest Holler, this is Cornell, may I help you?"

Madison scanned the room while Cornell spoke on the phone to someone apparently interested in a subscription. The hardwood floors were a little dusty in the corners, but they were hard to keep clean. She would love to have a tour of this house, but it wasn't the time. Cornell returned.

"I'm sorry, it's just me here. What were you saying?"

"Is it just you and Barrett who work here?"

"I have a couple of freelancers who send stories for consideration." Cornell pulled an invisible piece of lint off his jacket. "But on the staff list it's just Barrett and me."

"So, before the phone rang, you were telling me about the kinds of stories Barrett wrote."

"Is this really going to help find her? I mean, we are like a dinky newspaper for a subsection of a subsection of a subsection of readers. How can her work here have anything to do with her disappearance? Wasn't she just grabbed off the street or something?"

Grabbed off the street. That seemed sort of a callous way to discuss what has happened to your employee. Not to mention it was a possibility that Madison had considered.

"What makes you say that?"

Cornell stared at her. "Say what? That we are a dinky newspaper?"

That was intentional obtuseness. Madison's hackles went up. Problem was, it could be nothing more than what he said earlier: he'd never dealt with a missing person before and he didn't know how to act. Just because he had an employee didn't mean they were close. Madison tried not to read into people's attempts to hide things during an investigation. We all have things we want to hide. Literally every single person has something they would rather not have other people know about. It didn't mean they were responsible for a girl's disappearance.

"No, the part about 'grabbed from the street.' That part. What makes you think she was grabbed from the street?"

Cornell put his head in his hands.

What is going on with this guy?

He looked back up at Madison. "I'm sorry, that was an insensitive thing to say."

"So why say it?"

"Honestly?" Cornell's jaw tightened, and his earlier nervousness dropped away. "Because, I'm a Black man who works with a White girl who's gone missing. Guess who's going to be the first suspect?"

Okay, suddenly it all made sense to Madison. She hated that she lived in a world where he had to feel like that.

"Let me tell you this: I came in here today with no preconceived idea about this place or anybody who worked here. Nothing has changed since I saw you. I'm sure there are people who would feel like you should be the first suspect, but all I noticed was how great you dress."

Cornell laughed and puffed out his chest. "I do have that going for me."

"Yes, you do. And I am not suspecting you of anything right now. That might change in the future, but it won't be based on your skin color. Okay?"

Cornell had completely relaxed. He was like a different person from the one she started talking to. "Yes, okay. So what is it you want to know? What kind of reporting she did?"

"Yes, I think it could be that something she was working on led to her disappearance. I can't know, but I'd like to examine that possibility."

Cornell scooted to the edge of his seat. He got more animated, using his hands while he talked. "Like I said, she's supposed to just work on lighthearted fare, things that our readership might be interested in doing or seeing in the neighborhood. However, Barrett wants to be an investigative reporter. She spends a lot of time down at the courthouse and the County Administration Center looking for things to investigate."

Madison was looking at his braids. They were really cool, but they were also tugging at a memory. She needed to keep going and question him while she had him there; she'd have to figure what was nagging at her later.

"What kinds of things does Barrett find at the County Administration Center?"

Madison had visited that building on numerous occasions; it's where the county recorder was located, so that meant property titles and deeds were filed there, births and deaths were recorded, and just generally where you'd find records of the major events in people's lives.

"Not much," Cornell said. "She was always looking for the next big story from liens placed on property, births, deaths, and down at the courthouse she'd look for criminal and civil suits that had been filed recently for anything interesting."

Madison knew that big news organizations in New York and Los Angeles, like TMZ, had messengers who sat at the courthouse and just looked at every single filing that was done, hoping for a celebrity filing a divorce or a lawsuit of some kind. Barrett must've been taking her lead from that.

"Okay, that is helpful. Let me ask you something else: her apartment is cute, it's not lavish, but it's cute and the fact is, this area is expensive. How much does she make with you?"

"We don't pay much here. I think she has some money from when her parents died. A trust that pays her each month, maybe? She mentioned it one time, but I wasn't paying attention."

"I see. And does she have a computer other than a desktop computer at home, that you know of? A laptop that she kept here?"

Cornell stood up and started to stack the magazines that had been on their chairs, tidying up the reception area.

"No, we can't provide that kind of technology, we don't have the budget for it. And I think she'd been saving up for a MacBook Pro, but as of now she would type her stories at home or on my computer here."

"Do you know anything about friends or her boyfriend?"

"We didn't socialize outside of the office. She had her own life and I had mine. I'm just her employer."

"Really? Not even drinks after work?"

Cornell shook his head and the ends of his braids jangled where they were coming out of the loose knot. "No, really. We kept it professional. I didn't see her outside of work."

"And when was the last time that you talked to her?"

Cornell stopped what he was doing to think. "Last Wednesday. She was going to the County Administration Center, I know that. But she didn't come into the office because she didn't have a story to type or anything. It's been kind of slow around here."

"And you talked to her? What did you guys talk about?"

"Nothing in particular. She just checked in in the morning and said she was going downtown and she would talk to me later. But I didn't hear from her later."

"And by 'downtown' that meant the County Administration Center?"

"Well, that and the courthouse. But I think she mentioned the County Administration Center."

Madison stood up. "I appreciate you talking to me. I'm going to give you my card, and will you call me if you hear from her or if anything else occurs to you?"

Cornell walked with her to the door. "No problem. And I appreciate your understanding. Let me give you my number in case you have any other questions." They exchanged business cards. Madison looked down and saw that his cell phone number was listed. That could be helpful if she thought of anything to ask him after business hours.

Madison walked out the door, not sure she had learned anything useful, but with something nagging at her. She got into her car and sat for a moment staring straight ahead down Fourth Avenue.

The way she conducted investigations was to pull on every string she saw until it either led to nothing or it led to something. Currently, she was having trouble seeing a string to pull. Cornell had seemed suspicious at first, but once he explained what was going on, her concerns were allayed. Barrett's house had been trashed as if someone were looking for something. Madison would have thought it would be passwords to her bank account, especially for that trust fund payment, but they had left her computer alone. So it made Madison think they were looking for a *thing*, not a number or a bank record. Her best bet was to continue down this line of figuring out what Barrett might have been working on. Trying to find the latest big story can certainly cause you to interact with someone who doesn't want their big story told. Since she had so little to go on right now, she decided to just go with that. She was close to downtown and the County Administration Center, and since that was the last place that Barrett was known to have been, Madison would begin there.

She started the car and drove down Fourth Avenue. Madison opened the sunroof and put a knit cap on her head and turned the heat on her feet. The air was crisp and cool on her face and head, and toasty and cozy inside her car. She opened the music on her iPhone and set it to shuffle. There were some maple trees in this neighborhood and the leaves were falling, leaves as big as your hand. One of them flew into the sunroof and Madison caught it and set it on the passenger seat. She suddenly had a flash of being with her mother at six years old; it was art day, a day once a week set aside just for the two of them. They were dipping huge maple leaves into paint and making art on construction paper. Her mother's gentle hand guiding Madison's tiny one, dipping the leaf in the paint dish and then quickly onto the paper. What colors had they used? Madison couldn't remember.

She wouldn't spend too much time at the County Admin Center, because it felt like a long shot right now. But her only other choice was to make flyers and put them up and sit at her house and wait for someone to call and tell her they'd found Barrett. The police were also working on this, and they could investigate other angles, such as someone on the street grabbing her randomly.

Were the police working on this? Why hadn't they interviewed Cornell? She was starting to think she needed to talk to Tom about this.

She checked the review mirror and didn't see anyone following her.

And then it hit her. She yanked the car over to the curb, causing the person behind her to swerve, and without turning off the car grabbed the photo of Barrett out of her pocket. The photo Travis had given her, the one that was her Facebook profile photo, where Barrett is in a restaurant in Mexico. A bunch of people looking this way and that, Barrett laughing and reaching for the camera. And right behind her, facing the other direction, black braids piled in a loose top knot, sides of the head shaved, and a muscular black shoulder leaning against Barrett's, his face out of view of the camera. Cornell. Cornell who doesn't see Barrett outside of the office was with her in Mexico.

Madison had decided she would do a background check on Cornell when she got home, and in the meantime she would continue to the County Admin Center since she was almost there. But this case had just gotten a number-one suspect. Was this a jealousy thing? Had Cornell and Barrett been seeing each other, and she tried to end it and he killed her?

As she turned right on Ash Street, her phone rang. She hit the button on the steering wheel to answer it.

"Madison Kelly."

"Hi Madison, this is Megan from Dr. Schultz's office."

The San Diego Bay came into view. Madison could see that the wind had caused a rough sea, with white caps on churning dark water. Surfers called this condition "Victory at Sea," after the 1940s movie starring Bette Davis. It was impossible to surf choppy waves.

"Hi Megan."

"We can get you in to see the doctor the day after tomorrow at one PM, if that works?"

"Yes, that works." Madison paused. "Can I ask you, Megan, if my cancer has come back does that mean the implants have to come out?"

There was silence at the end of the line. Madison knew better than to ask the staff of a doctor's office anything having to do with medical conditions or treatment; they were not supposed to say anything. But she couldn't help herself.

"Let's just get you in to see the doctor and she will answer all your questions."

Madison was frustrated that she had to wait two days to get an answer to her question. She was not naturally a patient person. "Okay. See you Thursday."

Madison pushed the button on the steering wheel to end the call. She found a parking space directly in front of the County Administration Center building on Pacific Avenue.

Madison loved this building and didn't mind when she had to come down here. Now that everything was accessible on the internet, investigators didn't need to travel to these various sites to gather information; they could just look it up on a website. On the occasions when she needed to come down here, she loved remembering the history of the building. It was designed in the Beaux-Arts/Spanish Revival style and completed in 1938, and had been part of President Roosevelt's New Deal. It sat directly across from San Diego Bay. As Madison got out of the car, two seagulls landed on the sidewalk next to her and stood staring at her.

"Sorry guys, I don't have anything for you."

Madison walked down the path that split the massive green lawn and stopped at the entrance of the building. She turned and glanced at the street, but she didn't see any surveillance vehicles. She entered the building and walked down the hallway to the county recorder's office.

Madison pulled the door open and removed her reflector aviator sunglasses, clipping them to the front of her T-shirt. There were a few people milling about, and she walked up to the counter. She was relieved to see Rosie, a clerk who had acted as a source when Madison had been working a real estate fraud case. Madison hadn't bribed Rosie for that information; rather, she had gotten information, and then demonstrated how grateful she was by giving Rosie a present. It was a fine line, but Madison had no problem walking it.

"Well, well, well, they always come back."

Rosie was heavyset with brown hair that had turned grayer since Madison had seen her last. Her hair was pulled back in a severe bun, the better to show off her elaborate earrings that looked like a Mondrian painting. A security pass hung around her neck on a lanyard, to which she had added colorful pins with fun sayings and jeweled clips and little animals. On a separate chain was a ring of about twenty keys that jingled when she walked. She was like a cat with a bell on its collar.

"You knew I'd be back, hmm? It's not you, it's your corn tamales."

Rosie threw her head back and howled with laughter, which then turned into a few seconds of coughing.

"Well, you're not getting any. I make tamales for my friends, not for people who disappear on me for two years."

Madison glanced around the room. There were a few people at computers searching for deeds and other recorded documents, as well as a couple of clerks working behind the desk.

"I am your friend. I just figured you didn't like me anymore, since you stopped calling."

"Ha!" Rosie pounded the counter for emphasis, and a customer at a microfiche machine nearby looked up, annoyed. "Nice try. You were supposed to call me."

"Really? Oh dear. Well, as you can see, there was some confusion."

"Be quiet you know you're lying," Rosie said. She slapped the counter again. "Okay so what brings you down here? Are you going to ask me for another favor? I don't mind as long as you are as grateful as last time." Rosie made an elaborate wink and nudged Madison.

"I don't know what you're talking about. But I am wondering if you've ever seen this girl."

Madison slid the photo of Barrett across the counter. Rosie lifted her reading glasses, which were on yet another chain, up to her face and looked at the photo more closely. She tapped Barrett's face with a long pointed red fingernail. "I seen this girl. She came here a lot. I remember because she looked just like you. She your daughter?" Rosie cackled at her joke, which started another fit of coughing.

"Quit smoking. And I'm not old enough to be her mother, but thanks for that."

"Ha!" Another slap on the counter. "Okay yeah, she looks like your sister. Sure, I remember her. I seen her a lot."

Madison knew that Rosie didn't miss a thing. She had counted on her recognizing Barrett. "Do you remember the last time she was here?"

"What, you think I have a photographic memory? I can give you an idea, but I don't know the exact day. Prolly like a week ago."

Madison knew that was right, since Cornell had told her Barrett had come here last Wednesday.

"Do you know what she was doing here the last time? Was she looking at anything in particular?"

Rosie looked across the office to a middle-aged man with dark hair sitting behind a desk. He too had a security badge. She leaned in more closely and lowered her voice.

"This girl is always talking to Eddie. You want me to ask him?"

Madison followed Rosie's gaze and sized up Eddie. Feeling their attention on him, he turned to look at them. He suddenly appeared nervous; he glanced back and forth between Rosie and Madison, and then looked back at his desk.

What are you looking guilty about? Madison wondered.

"Who is he? What kind of guy?" she asked Rosie.

Rosie stared at him. He was now shuffling papers on his desk and had started to whistle tunelessly. Madison hated people who whistled like that. She'd rather someone whistle the entire Boston Pops version of *Boléro* than whistle aimlessly. She didn't like the sound, but she was more annoyed at the poor attempt to mask nervousness.

Rosie turned back to Madison and gave her a knowing smile.

"Eddie Vincente. Clerk of Vital Records. I don't like him. I don't trust him. I work with him since fifteen years, and there is just something about him. He came into a lot of money recently and bought a fancy car, and now he thinks he better than the rest of us."

Madison would not want to be on Rosie's bad side. She was jovial and fun, but she had an underlying strength that felt like a steel blade, and Madison would not want it between her ribs.

Madison tapped the photo. "She's missing. I know she was here last Wednesday, and I'm trying to figure out what she was working on."

Rosie walked away from Madison without saying anything. She walked to the other end of the counter and grabbed a logbook. She returned and slammed it on the counter, causing the woman nearby to make a scoffing sound without looking up from her computer. Rosie opened the book.

"Let's see if she requested copies of something." Rosie ran her red fingernail down the entries in the logbook until she got to the week before. "What's her name?"

Madison could read upside down, and she saw Barrett's name. "Right there. That's her name."

Rosie looked at the information in the logbook and then went to her computer. She tapped the keys with her long red fingernails. "Hang on."

Madison could hear a printer in another room power on and start printing. Rosie walked away abruptly and then returned with six pieces of paper. She held them to her chest. "How grateful you gonna be?"

"Very grateful, Rosie."

Rosie handed her the six pieces of paper. They were death certificates.

Madison was blinded by the bright sunshine as she exited the dark administration building. She paused to put on her sunglasses. She was fifty dollars poorer, but it was worth it. She didn't pay that much every time, but to keep Rosie on the line, she had to reward her once in a while. The death certificates were folded and placed in her purse; her plan was to race home and study them carefully to see if she could figure out why Barrett had requested copies of these particular death certificates. As she walked back down the path on the way to her car, she saw the black Ford Fusion pass in front of her.

How do you keep finding me?

This was starting to make Madison nervous. It was bad enough that she was being followed, but how did they keep locating her after they had clearly lost the tail?

Madison got to her SUV and intentionally dropped her keys on the ground. When she bent down to get them she got on all fours and looked underneath her car. There was nothing unusual there. She thought they might have put a GPS tracker on her car, but she knew what one looked like, and there was nothing there. She stood up again and wiped the dirt off her knees. She got in the car and sat for a minute.

Who was following her, and how did they keep finding her? She didn't have time for this. She needed to find Barrett, and this surveillance thing was a distraction.

She started the car and set off for home. She had a lot to do there. She wanted to look into that cell phone bill from Barrett's house. She could attempt a phone gag on the phone company to try and get Barrett's last phone calls. Investigators called it a "gag," but really it was just calling and tricking someone into giving you information. All the investigator had to do was figure out who they needed to be to get the information they wanted from the person on the other end of the line. In this case, Madison would need to be Barrett.

As Madison jumped on the 5 freeway north, she realized the death certificates were the biggest string she had found in her quest for Barrett. It was vital that she figure out why these six death certificates were so interesting to Barrett. And then something else occurred to her.

The copies of the death certificates had not been at Barrett's house. So where were they?

Chapter Ten

Tuesday 12:02 PM

Since the people following Madison knew where she lived, she didn't bother trying to lose the tail on the way home. She drove past the beach to check the parking lot. Dave's Jeep wasn't there; in fact, there were just a few cars of tourists in an otherwise empty lot. The conditions at Windansea were still *Victory at Sea*, so there were no surfers in the water. Madison paused to look at the ocean, the wind blowing the tops off the choppy waves to create white caps.

The silver Ford Escape had to wait behind her while she paused to look at the water; he must have been dying, since PIs tried to avoid sitting right behind their subject, and Madison's decision to stop in the middle of the road couldn't have been anticipated. He had been trading off with the black Ford Fusion the whole way home. This led Madison to believe that there were only two cars on the surveillance team. She resumed driving, turning left on Bonair and then left into the alley; as expected, the Ford Escape continued up the street, likely getting set up to follow her if she left home again. She would have done the same thing: since this surveillance team didn't know that she had already spotted them, they wouldn't want to risk exposing themselves by following her down the alley that led right to her parking space. Madison got out of the car, locked it, and walked into the garden.

Dave was sitting on her steps.

"Hey," she said.

"Hey." He must have walked from his place, which is why she hadn't seen his Jeep. But his hello was somber. Madison felt a weight in her stomach.

"I came by . . . I figured I'd wait a bit . . ."

Dave trailed off. Madison stopped beneath him on the stairs. She wasn't used to him being unsettled like this. He was the most confident person she knew.

"Do we need to talk?"

Dave's head was down, and he looked up at her through his long blond hair. "Yeah, I guess so. That would be good."

"Okay, come on." She walked past him, and he stood and followed her up the stairs. She used her key to open the door, and as the alarm started beeping she went to the panel and turned it off. Then she froze. Her alarm system had a feature where it notified her if someone had come to her door; there was a motion detector on her landing. It could be nothing, a salesperson. But they didn't get many random people at their doors, tucked in the back as they were. She went to her computer and pulled up the app for the alarm system.

"What's going on?" Dave asked.

"Somebody was at my front door. I just want to see who it was."

She selected the video that had begun recording when the motion sensor was triggered, and she hit "Play."

"Hey, sorry to interrupt." Dave and Madison both whipped their heads around to the open door. Ryan, her downstairs neighbor, was standing there.

Madison hit "Stop" on the video and stood up.

"Oh, hey Ryan, you know Dave, right?"

Ryan was six feet tall. He was a surfer like Dave, but she didn't think he was in the Windansea Surf Club; he wasn't a good enough surfer, frankly, but that wasn't a knock on him—you had to be a really high-caliber surfer to be accepted into the club. Madison had gone on an ill-fated date with Ryan in the middle of her last investigation, and they hadn't spoken much since.

"Yeah, so listen," Ryan said. He seemed nervous, switching his weight from his left foot to his right. But Dave had that effect on other guys. He was wearing board shorts and a surf contest T-shirt, which was exactly what Dave was wearing. The surfer uniform. "So, yeah, just being a good neighbor and all that. There was a guy up here on your landing a couple of hours ago."

Madison went back to the desk and sat down. "Was it this guy?" She hit "Play" on the video.

Ryan came over and leaned down to see the computer screen. "Yeah, totally, that was him."

"Thanks, Ryan. I appreciate it." Madison stood. Ryan looked back and forth between Madison and Dave. Dave looked back and forth between Madison and Ryan.

Awkward much? Madison thought.

"No problem, just trying to be a good neighbor." Ryan walked to the door and out without saying anything else.

"Who is he?" Dave said. He was trying to sound casual, but his words were weighted; he didn't achieve the throw-away remark that he'd been going for.

Never in her life had she imagined Dave Rich would be jealous. He was the unattainable surfer, and for the longest time she thought the reason they had never fully explored a committed relationship was because of his predilection for beautiful blondes. It was only recently she had realized that she herself was the one with the commitment problem. Nevertheless, Dave being jealous was not something she was used to.

"Just my neighbor, Dave." Madison went back to the computer screen and tried to figure out who was at her door. It was a man in his thirties, and she was sure she had never seen him before. He had dark clothes on, and his shoulders were huge; he had no neck. She couldn't rule out that he was one of the people who had been following her. In the video he knocked on the door, looked around, and then tried the doorknob. He took another glance at his surroundings, and then he got a small billfold out of his pocket. He fiddled with the billfold. It was hard to see from the camera angle what it contained.

"Just a neighbor? Then why was it so awkward?"

Madison hit "Stop" and turned and looked at Dave. "Is this what we do now? You want me to ask you about girls I've seen you with at the Pannikin?" Madison named the local coffee house that had been a fixture in La Jolla since 1969. It's where Dave spent most of his time when he wasn't in the water. His family was old money, and Dave didn't have to work. Madison's family was old money too, it was just so old it was all gone.

Dave's jaw muscles started working and his face got red. Madison didn't know why she was arguing with him. She knew exactly what was going on: she had made him feel jealous by lying about why she didn't want him to come over the night before. All she had to do was explain what that was really about, and he would relax. She didn't need him getting angry at Ryan: Dave had two black belts, and he could knock a man to the ground before the guy saw the fist coming toward his face. Dave's childhood had been violent, and Madison thought he had probably learned martial arts to protect himself from his mother. Madison couldn't hide the fact that physical strength in a man was appealing to her; she could never achieve the upper body strength of a man, and she relished it. Dave's kindness just made him all the more irresistible. She didn't want things to be weird between them, but something about his tone in demanding to know who her friends were got her goat.

It appeared Dave was not going to answer her about girls and the Pannikin, so she turned back to the computer. She hit "Play" and continued watching. Now the man was fiddling with the doorknob. She guessed that the billfold contained a lock pick kit. Good luck picking the lock on her doorknob. Her new door hardware and alarm system had just paid for itself. After a couple of minutes the man stood up and casually walked back down the stairs.

The time/date stamp on the video was almost exactly two hours before. So this meant while the Escape and Fusion were watching her and then following her from the Admin Building, someone else was trying to get into her apartment. This was an elaborate investigation into her, professionally done. Why did she warrant a carefully organized, professional investigation? In a way it was almost reassuring: she had previously been the victim of a stalker, someone who intended her great bodily harm. This felt more professional and less stalker-like, despite them trying to get into her place. Breaking into her apartment was a crime, but she knew investigators who did not shy away from breaking in and gathering information when they needed it for an investigation. She would never do it, because she was worried about karma. Plus, breaking the law risked losing her PI license, in addition to going to jail. But she knew investigators who weren't concerned about it. They often got really good information for their clients.

"Are we going to talk, or are you going to stare at the computer screen?"

My God, Madison thought. She did not want to deal with this. She wanted to find Barrett. She wanted to know who was following her all over San Diego. Her doctor's appointment was Thursday, and as her mother used to say, *Tomorrow will take care of itself.* She had enough problems today; she didn't need to borrow problems from tomorrow.

However, if she were honest with herself, she would have to admit the truth: she didn't want to talk to Dave about this because she didn't want to confront the fact that her cancer might be back. Telling Dave made it real. Which meant she'd probably better get it over with.

"Sit down, Dave."

Dave sat in the wingback chair that a long line of strong women had had in their living rooms. Madison's third great-grandmother had left Ireland during the Irish potato famine, when her whole family and everyone she knew was dying of starvation; she took a six-week ocean voyage at fifteen years old to make it to the New World. Her daughter would become a teacher and take a train from New York, where her entire family lived, to the Wild West of Idaho with her railroad agent husband. Madison lived on the West Coast because of that brave woman's journey, and the brave women that followed. Madison's mother had been a teacher too, but she hadn't made it to her fifty-fourth birthday. All of those brave women had died of breast cancer.

Madison stood and took her shirt off. She didn't have to wear a bra, because her pectoral muscles held the implants in place; in fact, they held the implants in place so tightly that she had constant upper back pain as her pectoral muscles yanked her shoulders forward due to the pressure of the implants underneath them. Madison had done a lot of research before agreeing to reconstruction with implants; she now felt that research was missing data: the medical community had failed to do studies with women who had lifted weights. Madison's pectoral muscles had never relaxed as the doctors had told her they would. They remained tight and uncomfortable. And she had lost strength because her pectoral muscles were sliced through during two different reconstruction surgeries.

"Hey!" Dave laughed. "That's not where I thought this was headed, but I don't mind."

He reached out to pull her onto his lap, but she backed up out of his reach. He was so strong that if he had gotten his hand on her arm she would've been face to face with him before she'd had a chance to explain. Many people underestimated Dave's strength because of his lithe appearance; in reality, he was like Bamm-Bamm from *The Flintstones*.

"Look." Madison pointed to the two red growths along her mastectomy scar on her right foob.

Dave squinted, causing deep furrows in the tanned skin around his eyes. His bright blue eyes had been damaged from spending every day in the sun since he was a child, and it was already affecting his vision.

"What is that?"

"I don't know. I'm going to the doctor on Thursday."

Dave stopped squinting abruptly. He looked up into Madison's face.

Madison continued. "We shouldn't worry yet. We don't know what it is."

"But what do you think it is?"

"I don't know." She sat down in her desk chair and swiveled to face him. "And I don't want to speculate. Obviously, I'm going to the doctor because I'm concerned. And the implants would probably have to go. But we don't know that now. We just have to wait and go through the process. Like before."

Dave looked at her with such love and compassion that she felt her throat tightening with the grief and fear of loss that she'd been suppressing.

Sometimes if you start crying you'll never stop.

Madison filled the silence. "I guess we're gonna find out if you really are a leg man and not a boob man." She laughed, but a tear escaped and she left it there to roll down her face, suddenly confused about whether brushing it away would make her grief more obvious.

Dave stood up and walked over to her. He bent down, and she felt the weathered skin of his hand as he placed it gently on her cheek.

"You will always be the most beautiful girl I have ever seen in my life."

Madison put her face in her hands and sobbed.

Dave stood next to her, silent. He put a hand on her shoulder. He knew how she hated to cry.

As her tears subsided, they were both quiet for a moment. Finally, Dave spoke.

"So if I made a move on you right now, would that be taking advantage of you?"

Madison laughed. She stood up and put her arms around his neck. He wrapped her up and rested his head on top of hers. They stood like that for a long time.

Chapter Eleven

Tuesday 12:33 PM

Madison brought a rice cake with some sliced turkey and a glass of water over to her desk and sat down. She stared at the death certificates again. Something about these certificates had made Barrett want to get copies of them on the last day she was seen alive. What made them special?

As much as Madison had wanted Dave to stay, now that they were back to their old selves she had no time to waste, especially on crying. She had sent him on his way and set about figuring out what about these death certificates was remarkable. She needed to find Barrett, and everything else could wait.

As she ate her lunch she studied them. The first thing she noticed was that they represented the deaths of three couples: six people had died, but each had been married and their spouse had died with them. One couple died in a car accident; one couple died in a light plane accident; and one couple died by drowning during a harbor cruise. The dual deaths were almost exactly one month apart. All of them had died that year, beginning in the summer; one couple died, and then a month later another couple, and a month after that the third couple.

The next thing Madison observed was the signature on the certificate for the "local registrar" was a stamp, rather than someone having signed the death certificate. The stamped signature was that of a doctor, probably the local health officer whose responsibility it was to make sure the death certificate was completed properly. Obviously, the public health officer for a county as big as San Diego was not necessarily going to read every single death certificate that came across her desk. She had clerks for that. The clerk had initialed next to the stamped name, so there would be a record of which clerk had approved the death certificate. The initials on each of the six death certificates were the same: *EV.*

What do you want to bet EV *stands for Eddie Vincente?* Madison thought.

Madison picked up the phone. She searched through her contacts for Rosie's phone number and called.

"Twice in one day? You're not getting any tamales."

"I will get tamales out of you before this is over, just you wait."

Rosie laughed. "What do you want?"

"On the death certificates, next to the signature of the local registrar, are the initials *EV.* On all of them. Is that because Eddie initialed these death certificates?"

There was a pause at the other end of the line. "Yes, that would be him," Rosie said. She was suddenly serious. "Did he do something?"

"I don't know yet. But don't let him know that I'm asking about him."

"Are you kidding me? I taught you everything you know. I can keep a secret better than you."

"I'm sure you can. I'm not good at keeping secrets. I may have more questions for you."

"That's fine. Listen, Maddie, all jokes aside I need you to tell me if you find out he did something, like something illegal or fishy even, okay?"

There was that steel again, reminding Madison she would not want to be on Rosie's bad side. "You got it."

"I don't like this guy. I work with him for so long. Can you get rid of him for me?"

Madison wasn't sure exactly what "get rid of him" meant to Rosie. "Do you mean fired? Or something else?"

"Whatever it takes."

Madison figured she was joking. Well, she hoped she was. "Will I get tamales?"

"Shut up and tell me what you find." Rosie hung up.

Madison went back to looking at the death certificates. So Eddie had signed all six death certificates, or at least initialed them. He was basically approving them, saying that the information supplied by the funeral director who completed them was accepted, it was complete, no further investigation of the death would be required. Which meant that if no autopsy had been conducted, then none would be required. Eddie's initials said: "All good here."

Not one of the six bodies had been autopsied.

Madison could see a situation where an autopsy wouldn't be required in an accidental death; maybe if the family refused to allow it for religious reasons, or if the body was too decomposed. But it seemed strange that six deaths in a row, all from accidents, had not been autopsied. And it was Eddie's signature approving the lack of an autopsy on all of the deaths.

The doctors listed as certifying that the person was dead were all different. Six different doctors, but for each couple the doctors worked at the same hospital, likely where the bodies were taken from the accident scene. An emergency department doctor would've been required to declare the death and state the time that it had occurred, even if the people had expired at the scene.

Madison realized that the reporting party on all six death certificates was the same: "Crystal Ladessa, attorney." Madison recognized the address listed for Crystal as a cluster of offices next to liquor store on the corner of Pearl and La Jolla Boulevard in La Jolla. She googled the address and saw that it belonged to an attorney named Joseph L. Viceroy. She jumped to his website and saw that Crystal was his assistant, not an attorney.

Madison knew, unfortunately from her experience with her parents, that the reporting party on a death certificate was normally a family member. Typically, the family member was sitting with the funeral director arranging the funeral, or cremation, or whatever the deceased person's wishes had been, and the family member would provide the information that the funeral director needed to complete the death certificate. The funeral director then filled out the death certificate, listed the family member as the reporting party, and filed it with the county. So, why would an attorney be the reporting party on all six of these death certificates? Not criminal or illegal, just . . . weird.

She googled Joseph L. Viceroy's name and his Yelp reviews came up. There weren't that many reviews, and those that were there were not favorable; they included allegations that he had stolen money from client settlements. She jumped to the State Bar website, and saw that he had previous discipline but was still allowed to practice law. They didn't give the specifics of the discipline; Madison would have to drive to the State Bar to view the files for that, but she figured it would correspond to the reviews alleging theft of client money. Madison knew how hard it was to get an attorney disbarred; she couldn't believe what attorneys could get away with before finally being removed from the profession. To be fair, the State Bar could have him under investigation right now, and there would be no announcement of that fact.

She did a quick background check on Viceroy, just looking for his address and property records, and she found that he owned a house in Del Mar, a ritzy suburb of San Diego. She did a Google-map search of his address and saw that it was a huge home, two stories, in an expensive part of Del Mar. The real estate websites estimated the cost at three million dollars. When the Google Street View camera had gone past the house, there was a Mercedes G Wagon in the driveway. For a small-town attorney, this guy had a lot of money. It didn't fit.

Something about the names of one of the couples was stirring a memory. She took those two certificates away from the others and set them on the table next to each other. She stared at them, trying to remember if she had seen their names before. Greg and Isabel Thomas. Greg and Isabel. The names weren't uncommon, but something was nagging at Madison. Greg. Greg. Someone named Greg who had died. *Sorry to hear about the death of . . .*

"Oh my God!"

Madison grabbed her purse and pulled out the tape recorder she had taken from Barrett's apartment. She hit "Play" on the second file.

"I just record because sometimes I forget what people say and I don't want to spend all my time writing while you're talking."

"I understand."

"Do you mind if I call you Judy?"

"No, that's fine."

"Let me say, first, that I am sorry to hear about the death of your brother, Greg."

"Thank you."

"Tell me a little bit about Greg."

Madison hit "Stop." Her hands were tingling. Barrett had decided there was something about these deaths that needed investigating, and she had found Greg's sister, Judy. Madison took a deep breath and let it out, hit "Play" again, and listened.

Barrett's investigative style was decent for someone just starting out, but it left a bit to be desired. All she managed to get out of Judy was information about Greg's childhood, his work, and their relationship. Judy was sad about the deaths, but there was nothing about the deaths that seemed suspicious. It was only about a fifteen-minute interview. But it showed that Madison was on the right track: Barrett was investigating something to do with these death certificates and these deaths. Madison would need to find Judy and interview her as well, to see if she could get more out of her and to see if anything had been discussed while the tape recorder was off.

Madison stood up and stretched. When she was deep into investigating she could sit and not move for hours, and she would regret it later. She walked over to the window and looked out. The midday sun was shining on her little garden, which the landlord had clearly modeled after English gardens. A hummingbird tapped against the glass, looking for the feeder that had fallen in a storm years ago.

She refilled her water glass and returned to the desk, suddenly remembering that she wanted to do a background check on Cornell. She did not know what to think about him. He was absolutely right that he would be the first suspect, probably even before the boyfriend. Wishing life wasn't a certain way didn't make it not that way. If he had told Madison he had vacationed with Barrett, or even seen her outside of work, Madison wouldn't automatically have suspected him; however, he would've gone on the list. Not because he was Black, just because he had a relationship with a missing girl. But Madison knew there were other people who would suspect him just because he was Black. So, he was right to be concerned about revealing any type of relationship with Barrett. But was that the only reason he was hiding it?

She got out his card: Cornell Jones. She ran his name through her database and quickly got his particulars. He lived in a small apartment in Pacific Beach. He had family on the East Coast, and no criminal record that she could find. His Facebook and Instagram were set to private, his Twitter had only a few tweets from a year ago, and his LinkedIn showed that he worked at the newspaper. He just seemed like a normal guy. A normal guy with a lot of style. A normal guy who lied about knowing Barrett outside of work.

Madison went to the whiteboard and added his name to the list of suspects, listing out the reason why. She put Viceroy's name there as well, along with the information that he had a lot of money for a small-time attorney. She then added all the information about the death certificates and listed Judy as a witness to be interviewed.

She wasn't going to confront Cornell just yet. She had the advantage right now, knowing he had lied, while leaving him to think he had fooled her. She would just continue to investigate and see where the investigation led her. Pull on a string until it either led to a dead end, or led to Barrett.

Her phone rang, and she saw on the caller ID that it was Travis.

"Madison Kelly."

"Hi Madison, this is Travis. I'm sorry to bug you, I know we just spoke not long ago, I'm just wondering if you've figured anything out?"

Madison should probably tell him about the cell phone being found, the death certificates, and her progress in general.

She liked to keep things close to the vest, but he was the client and he was worried about his girlfriend.

"Why don't you meet me at the Pannikin in La Jolla in an hour." She could take her computer with her and do some of her searches while waiting for him.

"I can do that! Thank you so much."

She wanted to get to Barrett's cell phone records before she left to meet Travis. To do that, she had to call the cell phone company and pretend to be Barrett.

Normally she wouldn't do this, because it was illegal to pretend to be someone in order to get their private information. But she figured if she found Barrett alive, she would be forgiven. And if she found Barrett dead it wouldn't matter.

Madison logged into her email and checked the forwarded mail from Barrett's account. Nothing of interest. She noted the email address: barrettb2246@gmail.com. Madison realized that she hadn't even started a file for Barrett. Even though everything was kept on her computer, sometimes it was helpful to have hard-copy things in a file so that she could stare at them when she was trying to get a bright idea. She went to the closet and got a file folder out, brought it over and wrote Barrett's name on the edge with a maroon magic marker. She put a two-hole punch into the top of the cell phone bill and slipped it over the metal bars. She wrote Barrett's email address on the inside flap. She then compiled Barrett's identifying information from the info Travis had given her, as well as her database report, and she wrote all the important details underneath the email address. Now everything she needed for this phone call to the cell phone company would all be in one place so she wouldn't stumble when asked for information on the phone.

Even though she was experienced at these kinds of pretext phone calls, she got nervous and shaky every time. The worst thing that could happen would be the representative refusing to give her information. But being a goody two-shoes was a hard habit to break. She envisioned the rep saying, "I'm calling the police and reporting you!" She shook her head to get rid of that vision, and took a deep breath to settle her voice. She entered *67 to block her phone number from being revealed on caller ID, and then dialed the customer service number listed on the phone bill. She pressed the buttons to get to a live person.

"Acacia Wireless, this is Elaine, we keep you in touch, how may I help you?"

The representative had a delicious Jamaican accent that Madison could listen to all day long.

"Yes, hello. I hope you can help me, Elaine. My name is Barrett Brown, and I'm hoping that you can email me the outgoing and incoming calls since my last statement."

"I'm happy to help you, can we start with your phone number, the last four of your social, and your billing address?"

"Absolutely," Madison said. She read her the information she'd just compiled on the inside flap of the file.

"I'm happy to get the information you requested, but did you know that you can access that information on our website?"

Madison figured this was going to happen, and she was ready. "I know, you guys have a great website and I really appreciate all of the things you offer. I don't know why my friends want to stick with the big carriers when they could be saving money and speaking to human beings on the phone instead of computers and robots."

"Well that is nice of you to say, Ms. Brown."

"Call me Barrett."

"Thank you, Barrett, I will. So are you having trouble accessing our website?"

"Actually, I'm out of town, away from my computer. And I don't care what people say I refuse to use a computer at a library or at an internet café or something, because people always steal your information from there."

"That's true, I can understand your concern."

Madison stood up and started pacing. "I was wondering if you could email the information to me? I can give you my email address."

"I have your email address here, is it barrettb2246@gmail.com?"

"That's right." Thank God she had access to Barrett's email. It made her seem legitimate to the representative, since they had her email address on file already.

There was a pause on the other end of the line. Madison was tempted to fill the silence with further explanation, but that was the death knell for most investigators, and people in general: they didn't know when to shut up. Madison's father had taught her that in some situations, *The next person who talks, loses.* Madison was silent.

"I'm happy to help," Elaine said. There was a pause and Madison could hear the clicking of the keyboard. "All right, that has been sent, do you want to just check that you received it?"

Madison sat back down at her desk and refreshed her inbox. It would take a minute longer since the email was being forwarded from Barrett's account to Madison's, but not that much longer. Suddenly the number *1* showed up in the inbox, and it said she had an email from Elaine at Acacia. Madison quickly opened the email and downloaded the attachment, selecting it from the bottom of her browser once it had downloaded, and opening it. All of Barrett's incoming and outgoing calls for the last three weeks were displayed before her on her computer screen.

"Elaine, you are an angel. Is there a survey I can fill out for you?"

"Why yes, I would appreciate that. I will transfer you to the three-question survey at the end of this call."

"Thank you, Elaine, you have a great day."

Madison's heart was racing she was so excited. She pushed the buttons to complete the survey, telling the company how great Elaine was. She got up from the desk and stretched her arms up over her head. Although she had paced while on the phone with Elaine, she had been tensing her shoulders and back. She went out onto the landing and looked at the ocean. It was a stunning day: not a cloud in the sky, warm with a cool breeze, and the waves looked like they were calming down as the wind died down. She stretched her arms up overhead again, lowering herself until she touched the landing. She tried to clear her mind of all things Barrett, cancer, and Dave. Even thirty seconds of her version of meditation could last her hours.

She stood up and went back into the house, shutting the door and locking it. She sat at the desk and looked at the last phone number that had called Barrett on Wednesday night, which was also the last time Travis had spoken with her. The call came in at 9:01 PM. The number was a San Diego phone number.

She compared the number to those listed on Cornell's business card, including his cell. Not a match.

Madison's investigator database was not that great for cell phone numbers. She didn't know why. She could find out just about anything else about a person: where they lived in the last ten years, people they've associated with, family members, etc. Cell phone numbers? Not so much. Sometimes even Google was better than her database.

However, she decided to start there. She pulled up the website, logged in, and entered the cell phone number into the search box. It provided her a few names, but the dates associated with those names were all a couple of years before. She printed out the search results and put a two-hole punch on the top of the papers. She wrote *last number to call her?* across the top, and slipped it over the two metal bars at the top of the file folder.

Next, she entered the last number to call Barrett into the Google search bar. She scanned through the search results on the first page. There were websites that listed out a million phone numbers just to get you to click on the website. She was experienced enough to ignore those. However, there were no names associated with this phone number on Google.

That left only one way to figure out whose number this was: call it.

Madison had on numerous occasions gotten someone to identify themselves using a variety of phone gags to do so. It was just a matter of deciding who she needed to be to get the person to reveal information about themselves. Offering someone a credit card was usually successful, but not if they were wealthy with a great credit rating; then they considered her a spam call. If they were middle to lower income and needed credit, they jumped at it and told her anything she asked. It was the most successful way she had found to get information from someone at the other end of a phone line, so she was going to give it a shot.

She used the *Flame* app on her phone to create a throwaway phone number. It would give her a way to call someone from a fake phone number: the fake phone number would show up on the person's caller ID, and they could even call it back and the *Flame* app would route the call to Madison's cell phone, never revealing her actual phone number. Madison couldn't believe it was legal, but she had gotten it from the app store.

Using the *Flame* app, she called the number.

It rang five times, then went to a robotic voice telling her that the person's voicemail had not been set up yet. She disconnected without leaving a message.

"Dammit."

She would just have to try later. She added it to the whiteboard with a big circle around it. Finding out the person who may have been the last to speak to Barrett, at least on the telephone, was her biggest lead yet.

She needed to get out of her apartment. As much as she liked it, when she was working on an investigation, sitting at her desk made her feel like she was accomplishing nothing. And yet, so much that an investigator did in the twenty-first century happened at their desk in front of a computer screen. Records that a PI used to have to drive to get—to the Admin Building, to the courthouses, to the library for reverse telephone directories—were all done by computer now. For a girl who liked to be outside, it could get tedious. She had an itch to do surveillance on someone, to go look at things, to just drive until she found Barrett.

She needed to meet Travis soon, but she'd better look up the license plates of the vehicles that had been following her. She didn't think it would lead to much, but sometimes part of investigating was just crossing *T*'s and dotting *I*'s. She went to the third-party website that provided access to DMV records, something she'd had to practically give blood to get, and logged in. She ran the license plates. Sure enough, they were registered to a huge rental car agency. Madison had tried in the past to get renter information from a rental car agency, and she had failed miserably each time. They would only give out that information to law enforcement with a warrant, and every time she had tried to use a phone gag on them, it hadn't worked. The fact was, if she were the renter, she'd know her name and address and wouldn't need to call the rental car agency to ask them. "Hi, I rented a car from you and I don't know my name" did not work. And anything more official required a warrant.

Madison decided to take her laptop with her to the Pannikin and finish all of the computer work that she needed to do while waiting for Travis.

She grabbed her backpack, put Barrett's file and her laptop into it, picked up her purse, set the alarm, and was out the door. She locked the deadbolt, and then paused to look closely at it. She could see little scratch marks around the keyhole, but frankly those could have been there; she didn't usually study the lock on her way in and out of the house.

She walked down the stairs, glancing at Ryan's door as she walked through the garden to her car parked just off the alley. She didn't see him. It was nice of him to tell her that someone had been messing with her door, especially since he'd had no idea that she had a camera to record it. Maybe they could end up friends.

As she drove across La Jolla Boulevard on Nautilus Street her phone rang. She hit the button on the steering wheel to answer.

"Madison Kelly."

"Yes, dear, this is Betty LaDoux."

"Hello Mrs. LaDoux."

"I've been thinking about Barrett, and I'm so worried. Are you any closer to finding her?"

Madison turned at the high school. "Not really, I'm sorry to say. But I'm dedicatedly working on this, and I'm not going to stop until I find her. Have you thought of anything that might help me?"

"I really haven't. We just lead such separate lives."

"Has she ever disappeared before? Where you didn't see her for a week?"

"No, not at all. She went on a trip one time, where was it . . . Mexico? And she told me that she'd be gone for a week. Although we lead separate lives, we check in with each other. You have to as a woman, you know."

The photo Madison had of Barrett was from that vacation. So Barrett wasn't the kind of person who took off for some solitude.

Madison drove past the Pannikin. There were no parking spaces anywhere on the street, which was common in the middle of the day in La Jolla. She turned on Pearl to drive behind the Pannikin into the residential neighborhood. Sometimes there was parking available on the small side streets there.

"That is true. Women need to stick together. So there's nothing you can think of that might help me?"

"I really can't think of anything. But I will certainly keep your number and let you know if I hear anything or obviously if I see her."

Madison found a parking space in front of an apartment building on the street behind the Pannikin. "Thank you for calling."

They disconnected. Madison decided to do her computer work in the car, rather than lug her backpack two blocks to the Pannikin patio. The item that needed the most attention was the cell phone records: what other numbers had called Barrett, and what numbers she had called, in the weeks leading up to her disappearance. Madison got the paperwork out of her backpack, opened her computer, and got set up in her car. It helped to have a big SUV when you sat in your car a lot. She was more comfortable there than sitting in a restaurant with people crowding her.

She was all but invisible in her surveillance vehicle, so she could sit in her little cocoon and work.

She methodically went through the phone numbers on the records, making notes on a notepad each time she identified a phone number after searching Google for it. Barrett liked sushi, she liked Chinese food, and Madison had her first impressions confirmed: Barrett didn't have a lot of friends. At least friends who called her on the phone. Or that she called. These days everything was done by text, and there would be no record here of a text coming in or going out. While a lot of phone companies kept text messages on a server for three months, the police would have to get a warrant for that.

Some of the phone numbers that called Barrett were listed as *unidentified*, which Madison knew indicated the caller had blocked their caller ID or for some reason didn't have it. The other incoming numbers she was able to identify, and they weren't that interesting. Barrett called her work a lot. There was a cell phone number that she called and received calls from frequently, and Madison recognized the number. She reached into her wallet and got out Cornell's business card. Yes, the number was for Cornell's cell phone. Not terribly unusual; they obviously needed to speak to each other about work and it sounded like Barrett didn't go into the office every day, so they would need to stay in touch. But she put it in her mental file, along with the information that Cornell had been in Mexico with Barrett, despite telling Madison that he didn't socialize with Barrett outside of work.

Cornell. Madison kept coming back to that. Was he creating a self-fulfilling prophecy, whereby he was so afraid of being considered a suspect in her disappearance, that he was making himself a suspect?

As she finished up the cell phone calls for the last three weeks, Madison realized there was something missing.

Something huge. She looked through the numbers again, for the entire three weeks available. Travis's phone number was not there.

Madison stared out the windshield. There was a school up ahead, and it must've been at recess because all the kids were playing in the yard. The clamor traveled on the wind and sounded like people screaming.

Did Barrett have another cell phone? Some people had two phones, one for work and one for pleasure. Did Madison only have Barrett's work phone number? But Travis was the one who had given her this number. Had he not given her Barrett's personal phone number for some reason? This made no sense. She was due to meet him shortly. She looked at the calls again to be sure; no phone calls to or from Travis. It was strange.

All she could do was ask him. It was a string to pull, just not from an area where she'd thought she'd find one. Madison felt suddenly like she had too many strings to pull; like she was walking through a graveyard of strings. There was Cornell, and then the accident victims, and the phone number that had called Barrett. Her head was swimming. But all she could do was keep putting one foot in front of the other. Like the song from that Claymation movie from the seventies that got rerun each year near Christmas: Kris Kringle and the Warlock who only had a few kernels of magic corn left: *"Just put one foot in front of the other, and soon you'll be walking out the door . . ."* Funny how childhood movies could shape your thinking for life.

Before she walked over to meet Travis she wanted to quickly look into the victims of the accidents on the death certificates. She took out the first one and googled the name: Rebecca Brady. There was a news report about the car accident that had killed Rebecca and her husband, Jason:

Authorities say a single-car accident on state Route 18 that resulted in the deaths of 27-year-old Jason Brady and his 25-year-old wife Rebecca was the result of excessive speed and poor road conditions. It was raining heavily at the time, unusual for this time of year, and the couple's Honda CRV plunged over the side of the road and flipped several times before coming to rest a hundred yards below. A spokesperson for the Sheriff's Department reports that neither drugs nor alcohol was a factor in this accident.

Madison knew that road; it was the route she took in the winter to go skiing on Big Bear Mountain. Madison was an experienced driver—her job had her in the car more than anywhere else—but even she got nervous on that winding mountain road with the sheer cliff dropping off right next to the highway. She refused to drive if there was any snow on the ground, and heavy rain was probably worse. This accident had occurred in the summer, but rain would've made the roadway slick, and coupled with excessive speed, the car would have hydroplaned straight off the embankment. What a terrible way to die.

Picking up the next couple's death certificates, Madison saw they belonged to Greg and Isabel Thomas. Their death certificates stated they had died in a light plane accident. She googled their names and again found a news report:

The FAA has completed its investigation into the light plane accident that killed 25-year-old Greg Thomas and his 23-year-old wife Isabel. The investigators believe Mr. Thomas, who had won a contest for tuition to a flight school, something his family said he'd always dreamed of, became disoriented while flying his wife on a solo flight, causing him to crash into the ocean. Funeral services were held last week.

Out of the corner of her eye, in her side-view mirror, Madison saw a tall, dark-haired man get out of a shiny Mercedes that had stopped in the street behind her. She turned her eyes fully to the mirror and realized it was Travis. Why was he getting out of a car a block away from the Pannikin? She looked more closely and realized there was a woman driving the car. Travis walked over to the driver's side and kissed the woman. There were two kids in the backseat.

Chapter Twelve

Tuesday 2:05 PM

"What in the actual fuck?" Madison punctuated her words by throwing her purse on Travis's table on the patio of the Pannikin. "What kind of game are you playing? Did you take her?"

The people on the patio suddenly went silent. The traffic noise from the busy intersection at Pearl and Girard was the only background music to Madison's voice. Travis's mouth dropped open. Madison was so angry she didn't care about the scene she was making.

"Start talking motherfucker. My next move is to call the police."

"Please sit down." Travis's voice was quiet, a poor attempt to sound soothing. "I can explain."

"First of all, don't talk to me like I'm a mental patient. Second of all, don't tell me to calm down. I am exactly as calm as the situation warrants. You have lied to me from the first moment we spoke, you have continued to lie to me, and there is a girl missing. You are not going to get out of this by doing the guy thing of gaslighting and turning it around on me. You have fucked with a private investigator. I am not your average girl."

Madison was still standing in front of him. The broken turquoise tile on the table in front of him reflected a bright sun into her eyes; she had been so livid she hadn't put on her sunglasses when she left her car to follow him to the Pannikin. She had waited three minutes to give him a head start, and then walked from her parking space to meet him. She was now vaguely aware that someone had walked up the path behind her and was standing, waiting. The tables on the patio were full, and the staff at the counter inside the cottage-like coffee house were pouring coffee and taking orders for breakfast and lunch food.

Madison turned to the person behind her on the path. It was an older woman with pearls and an Hermès handbag.

"I'm sorry . . . I just . . . can I get by you?" the woman said timidly. Angry-Madison was intimidating.

Madison realized that the people at the tables were waiting to see how she reacted. "Of course," Madison said. She stepped out of the pathway. "I'm sorry."

Madison sat down across from Travis. Most of the tables had begun talking again, but the table next to them was silent. Madison turned to them and spoke.

"Okay you guys, the show is over." The women at the table quickly looked away.

Madison stared at Travis. "Start talking."

"Thank you. I realize this looks bad. But it is not as bad as you think." Travis's left knee started bouncing.

"Oh, I am so relieved that it is not as bad as I think. What do I think?"

"Look. Okay. Yes, I have been having an affair with Barrett. No, I have not taken her. Why would I hire you to find her if I had taken her?"

He had a point there. Madison wasn't world famous, but the thing she was known for was finding two people when no one else could. She would hardly be your first choice if you didn't want the person found.

"Yes, that was my wife you apparently just saw me with. No, she does not know about Barrett. I obviously don't want her to know."

"Did Barrett know you were married?"

Madison felt the table next to her lean slightly in their direction.

"Do you mind?" she said to them. It was a group of three women in their mid-thirties, clearly there for coffee and gossip. Madison had fulfilled the latter for them, for sure. She turned back to Travis

"Continue. Did Barrett know that you were married?"

"Yes, she did."

Madison was surprised, but she didn't know why. It's not like she knew Barrett. But she somehow felt that she had begun to understand her and identify with her. She felt like Barrett was similar to her. Madison would never sleep with a married man. It wasn't even a statement about her morality; Madison just didn't like getting hurt. Being someone's second fiddle was a surefire way to get hurt. Not to mention it was insulting: "I like you; I just don't like you enough to make you a major part of my life." Why was Barrett willing to put up with that? Maybe because, like Madison, Barrett was fiercely independent and didn't need a normal relationship with a guy? Maybe it worked out for her that Travis couldn't spend the night, couldn't always see her, wasn't always there. Barrett liked being alone, just like Madison. But it was not how Madison would've handled it. Madison was disappointed in Barrett.

"Is this why there is no record of you calling her cell phone or her calling your cell phone in the three weeks leading up to her disappearance?"

Travis's face hardened. "I'm starting to get angry now. Are you looking for Barrett or are you investigating me? I realize I should have told you that I was married, but *I'm* trying to find a missing person. I didn't think my personal issues were relevant. I'm paying you to find someone who's in trouble. And *you're* trying to figure out how many times I called her?"

Madison felt ashamed for a second. Why *did* she care about Travis's calls to and from Barrett? Well, she didn't, not really. It's just that her livelihood depended on her ability to notice things that shouldn't be there, or notice things that should be there and weren't. A lack of phone calls from a boyfriend to a girlfriend on a cell phone bill: something that should be there and wasn't. She noticed it. And those types of things bugged her until she had an explanation for them that made sense. It was why she was a good investigator. But it didn't necessarily mean that the missing things meant something nefarious; usually they didn't. There were explanations. Like in this case, a man cheating on his wife.

Nevertheless, Travis was still turning this around on Madison, which she hated; she wasn't the one who had been lying. She figured his cheating explained the lack of phone calls, but she needed to hear it. She leaned in.

"Answer my question."

Travis's arrogance turned into defensiveness, and he got a slight whine in his voice. "How can you think I would do something to her? Why would I hire you if that were the case?" People were starting to look in their direction again.

Madison just stared at him, saying nothing. *The next person who talks loses.*

"Jesus." He ran his hands through his hair, which Madison hated to admit was appealing. "I can't call her from my cell phone because my wife checks the cell phone bill, just like you're doing with Barrett's. I have a burner phone I use to call Barrett, and the caller ID is blocked. She doesn't call me because there's no point; I only have that phone turned on when I call her."

It made sense. There had been blocked numbers on the cell phone bill, and that explained those as well; one less thing for Madison to track down. Travis was continuing.

"Don't you realize that if it weren't for me, no one would be looking for her? Her job would just think she'd quit. Her landlord would think she'd moved on. I'm the only person she sees regularly. I'm the only person who cares if she is missing."

That hit Madison in the gut. That was her life.

Dave would look for me.

Travis put his hands through his hair again. "Have you gotten any other leads? Other than looking into me?"

Madison sighed. She was exhausted from the anger. "Yes, I have. I found her phone at the fountain in Balboa Park. And I found a phone number that called her Wednesday night."

"You found her phone? Can that help us find her? What was on it?"

"Unfortunately, it was at the bottom of the fountain. I'm going to see what I can do with it, but I'm not sure anything can be done." She never mentioned Arlo to people, even casually. He preferred it that way, and she didn't blame him. It was better if the general public thought that he had a small business fixing computers in Pacific Beach. No one needed to know that he was a computer mastermind.

"And what about the call she got Wednesday night? Can that help us find her?" Travis's knee was still bouncing up and down and it was getting on Madison's nerves.

"I haven't figured out whose number it is yet. Still working on it. I also found out that she may have been working on a story for her newspaper, but I'm not sure if that will amount to anything."

Travis stopped bouncing his knee. "That's it? A dead phone, an unknown caller, and a newspaper story?"

When he put it like that, it did sound pretty dismal. But she'd only been working on this case since this morning. The police had had it for a whole week—and they hadn't even gotten to Barrett's work to interview Cornell.

"I've been working on this case for about seven hours. Have you heard anything from the police? Are you calling and asking them for updates? Any info they give you could help me."

"Yes, I've called them. They say they're working on it, and they have no new updates. That's all they ever say to me."

Madison knew the police wouldn't share their leads on a missing person with the boyfriend. It didn't mean they weren't working on it.

"Well, instead of working on the case, I'm sitting here talking to you, so yeah, in seven hours I've only managed to find her phone, her last known location, discovered the story she was working on, and gotten her cell phone records."

"Yeah, and investigate me."

Madison sighed. Cute guys usually ended up annoying her. It reminded her of the many times she'd tell a guy what she did for a living, and he'd say with mock concern, "Oh, an investigator? Oh my! Oh, goodness! I hope you're not investigating me!" That remark did two things: it trivialized her work, but also Madison saw a hint of truth behind the mockery. She made these guys nervous because they were hiding something. Most people are. The fact that she'd hardly announce her profession if she were actually investigating them was lost on these guys.

"I'm not investigating you, calm down. I go where the investigation takes me."

"Okay, well you have exactly one week for this investigation to take you to Barrett, or I'm hiring someone else."

She wanted to find Barrett. A week was not a long time. Frankly, she would run out of the retainer and need money by then anyway. She knew she could find Barrett better than another investigator. She wanted to find her. She knew her.

Madison felt like Barrett was waiting for her.

"Fine. A week." Madison stood up. "I need to get to work."

"Yes, you do," Travis said. "And spend less time worrying about me."

"Yes, I'm looking for Renée?"

"This is Renée, who is speaking?"

Madison had returned to her car parked behind the Pannikin. Even though she was only two miles from home, she hadn't wanted to sit in her apartment. She wanted to *do* something. She had decided to find a relative of one of the victims of the accident. Barrett had requested copies of these death certificates on the day she went missing. These death certificates had to have something to do with her disappearance.

Madison sat up suddenly as she remembered an important detail.

Where are the copies of the death certificates that Barrett got from the Recorder's Office?

Madison hadn't found them when she put Barrett's apartment back together. She had realized this on her way home from Barrett's apartment, but then Dave had been waiting for her and she'd forgotten to put it on the whiteboard. That's why Madison hated getting emotional: it interfered with her analytical process. So were the death certificates what Barrett's kidnappers had been looking for? Did that mean they'd found what they were looking for and had no more need to keep Barrett alive?

"Hello? Are you there?"

Madison had gotten so lost in thought that she'd forgotten she was on the phone.

"Yes, I'm sorry. My name is Madison Kelly and I'm a private investigator. I'm looking for a missing person. And the car accident involving your sister Rebecca and her husband Jason has come up sort of tangentially."

"Mommy is on the phone. I will help you when I get off the phone. How is my sister's accident relevant to your investigation?"

Madison figured the first part of the sentence was not meant for her, so she ignored it. "Frankly, I'm not sure that it is. I am grasping at straws at the moment. I'm sure this is a painful subject, and I hope you will indulge me for just a few minutes."

"You said someone is missing?"

"Yes, a girl is missing. And just before she went missing she was looking into three different accidents involving three different couples, and one of the couples was your sister and brother-in-law. I'm trying to see if the girl's disappearance has anything to do with the investigation she was doing."

"Don't pull your sister's hair!"

Even though Madison knew that Renée wasn't speaking to her, it was startling. She decided to just start asking questions before Renée lost her patience with her children and with Madison. "Did you have any suspicions about the accident?"

"I mean, not really. There was an investigation, and they said the car hydroplaned off the side of the road. They say the car was going too fast."

Madison racked her brain to think what could be the common denominator between these three accidents, other than the fact that they were a month apart and involved young couples.

"Do you know if your sister knew Greg and Isabel Thomas, or Rex and Tammy Hacks?"

"No, those names don't sound familiar to me."

"Did your sister have any children?"

"No, they didn't. I was the fertile one in the family. I'm not sure how this is going to help you, and it is painful to discuss. Do you want to go on time-out?"

"Do I . . .?"

"No, that wasn't for you. It's just that this is painful to discuss."

"I'm sure it is, I'm going to hurry. Was there anything about the accident that was suspicious?"

There was a pause while Renée thought, and then the sound of glass breaking in the background, which she didn't remark on. "I mean . . . not really. It was raining and their car slid off the road. The car burned up, so there was no way to check the engine to see if anything had been messed with. My sister and her husband were freaks about safety and speed, so I thought it was weird they would die in a car accident related to speed. But other than that, no. Give it back to your brother!"

"Okay. I'll just ask a few more intrusive questions and then let you go. Did they have money? Was there a large estate?"

"No, no, they were a young couple just starting out. At any rate, I wouldn't have gotten anything since there was a trust, and I wasn't the beneficiary of the trust upon their deaths."

"Oh, I'm sorry. Who was, if you don't mind my asking? Other family?"

"Wait. I mean, that sounded bad. I don't want you to think that I . . . it's not that I expected any money. But when someone dies you do sort of look for material things to indicate how they felt about you. If they left you even the small amount of money in their checking account. My sister and I were close. At the funeral I talked to Jason's parents, and they were just as surprised that there was a trust and no one in the family was the third beneficiary in case they should both die. It was some charity."

"A charity?"

"Yes," Renée said. "Their living trust benefited each other if one died before the other, but if they both died it benefited a charity. A cancer charity. They were pretty active with charities and cancer work."

It didn't sound like much. Not really a suspicious death, no money to fight over. What was unusual about these deaths?

"I noticed on the death certificates that someone named Crystal was listed as the reporting party. Do you know who that is?"

"Oh, yes. Crystal. She's a sweet girl. She works at Jason's attorney's office, and she contacted us right away and offered to take care of everything. It was really nice of them. They were helpful through the whole thing."

"And do you recall the name of the attorney she worked for?" Madison knew, she just wanted to check what Renée knew.

"Yeah, I have it somewhere. You are not getting a birthday party!"

Madison was glad she didn't live in this woman's house. She suddenly wanted to get off the phone. "It's okay if you don't recall the name."

"It was like Victory or something."

"Viceroy?"

"Yes, that's right. Viceroy. I never met him, but Crystal was really sweet. I'm sorry, I must go now. If you punch your sister one more time you're both going on time-out and I'm moving away!"

"I'll let you go. I really appreciate you talking to me. One last thing: Have you heard of someone named Barrett Brown?"

"No, I haven't."

"Okay, thank you for talking to me."

They disconnected and Madison sat and thought for a minute. Now that she had remembered those death certificate copies were not in Barrett's apartment, she felt strongly that Barrett's disappearance had something to do with the article she had been working on about these deaths. What had Barrett uncovered? Madison realized she was not just looking for a missing person, she was walking in that missing person's footsteps, discovering what she had discovered in the days leading up to her disappearance.

Madison had used the obituary for Jason and Rebecca Brady to find the sister, Renée. Obituary notices in the newspaper gave a lot of family information. Madison had already tried to find contact information for Judy, the sister of Greg Thomas, whom Barrett had interviewed. Madison had used her investigator database to get Judy's particulars, and from that she'd looked for a phone number. But she hadn't been able to find one. She had, however, found Judy's Facebook. That was probably how Barrett had reached Judy as well. Madison had sent Judy a friend request and a Facebook message at the same time. Madison knew that if she wasn't friends with Judy on Facebook, the message would go into a different folder and she might not see it. However, she would see the friend request and that might cause her to look for a message.

Madison next tried to find an obituary for Rex and Tammy Hacks, but couldn't find anything. The death certificates indicated death by drowning for both, and San Diego Harbor as the location. She found a paragraph in an online paper near the time of the deaths:

Police say they don't suspect foul play in the deaths of a couple who drowned over the weekend after a night on the

Sunset Nights Dinner Cruise. The couple had been drinking, and police have concluded that they fell overboard. Their bodies were found later that night.

Madison didn't want to call another grieving family right now. She would see what information she got after Judy called her back, and decide then. She couldn't see what made these deaths suspicious, other than the similarities on the death certificates. She stared at the apartment building she was parked in front of, a block behind the Pannikin. It was part of the new construction that she hated.

It's not that I hate progress, I just don't want anything to change. Madison chuckled at her illogic.

She should probably go home and use her desk. But she wanted to have a look at attorney Joseph L. Viceroy's office, he who had a girl named Crystal report all six deaths to the funeral directors. It was on her way home anyway.

She made a U-turn, turned left on Pearl, and stopped at the light at the corner of Pearl and Girard, where the Pannikin was. She glanced to her left and saw Dave's Jeep parked in front of the Pannikin. That was a common occurrence. She didn't have time to stop and say hi.

Joseph L. Viceroy had the top floor of offices in a small corner building less than a mile from the Pannikin. The wall facing the street was all glass windows. Madison parked across the street in the corner of the gas station and used her field glass to look in the window across the way. She saw a young girl with stringy hair sitting at a reception desk. The girl had a harried expression on her face, and Madison could feel her stress through the field glass all the way across the street. She was answering the phone and dealing with someone standing at her desk at the same time.

A pudgy bald man came out of an office in the back and spoke to her while throwing his arms in the air. The girl shrank back as if she was going to get hit.

What is going on in that place?

Madison assumed the pudgy bald man was attorney Viceroy. He was wearing a rumpled suit with a tie that had been loosened. He turned and went back to his office with his arms still flailing. He didn't look like a wealthy man, but she knew he was, based on the cost of his house and car.

Madison felt someone looking at her. When you live your life by having a fine-tuned awareness of the environment, you sense when someone is staring at you. She lowered the field glass and looked at her surroundings. The black Ford Fusion was to her right, in the parking lot for a frozen yogurt store across Pearl.

Now she had to decide if she wanted them to know what she was doing, whoever they were. She decided she didn't want them to know.

She pulled out of the gas station and headed south on La Jolla Boulevard toward her apartment. She drove slowly so that the Ford Fusion could catch up. He did so within just a few blocks. She turned right down the alley that led to her apartment. As she knew he would, the Fusion continued without turning behind her; he figured she was going home, and he wouldn't risk the surveillance by following her straight to her parking space, the time when most people start looking in their rearview mirror to see if someone is following them home. However, instead of parking, she turned right at the T intersection of alleys by her apartment, exited the alley at Nautilus, and turned right to head straight back to La Jolla Boulevard where she'd come from. He would be positioning himself on Bonair or nearby, so that he could pick her up when she left her apartment again; but she wouldn't be there.

She drove back to Viceroy's office and parked on Pearl, about a block past the offices. Although La Jolla was small, her tailers would have to spend a long time driving around every block to find her car. She would be done here before they found her.

As she pushed open the door to Viceroy's office, she could see that not much had changed in the twenty minutes she had been gone: the girl, whom she assumed was Crystal, was still stressed and answering phone calls. From the back of the office Madison heard someone yelling:

"Crystal! Goddammit get me those files! And find out where the messenger is!"

Madison stood in front of Crystal's desk.

"Joseph L. Viceroy's office may I help you?" Crystal said into the telephone.

Crystal put her finger up at Madison as if to say, "One moment."

Madison waited patiently. She looked out the window at the cars traversing the busy intersection. She didn't see the Fusion or the Escape.

Crystal hung up the phone and looked at Madison. "May I help you?"

Madison thought fast. What kind of attorney was he? Estates and Trusts. Madison didn't understand either one.

"Yes, I'd like to discuss estate planning for my husband and me."

"Do you have children?" Crystal asked it rotely, as if it were part of a script. She was sorting through a stack of files on her desk, not looking at Madison.

"No, we do not."

Crystal stopped what she was doing, with her hand midair. "Can you wait?"

"Sure."

Crystal got up and walked to the back where the offices were. She returned almost immediately.

"This way please."

Madison followed Crystal to the back. From behind, Crystal looked even younger than she did from the front; it appeared she had slept on wet hair and had forgotten to brush the back of her head that morning, and she was stick thin, almost malnourished looking. She had given herself blonde streaks at some point in the past, but they had almost grown out. The top of her head was mousy brown.

Crystal paused to let Madison walk through an office doorway. Joseph L. Viceroy stood up from behind a large desk as Madison entered.

"Welcome! Welcome. Please, sit down."

He moved quickly, almost frantically, and picked up some books and newspapers that were on a stained brown leather armchair across the desk from his executive chair. Madison moved over and sat in the chair.

Viceroy walked with tiny steps, almost a prance, and his arms danced about as he spoke. "How can I help you on this fine day? Well, first, may I ask who referred you?"

Madison composed her answer carefully, in case this was an important question.

"I don't know, actually it was my husband who told me to stop by today. He heard about you from someone, I'm not sure who."

"I see, I see. All right, so my assistant mentioned that you're interested in a trust?"

Madison had not told Crystal that she was interested in a trust.

"Yes, that's right."

Viceroy spread his arms out wide. "Well, that is certainly our specialty. I help couples prepare for their future every day.

By setting up a living trust you are protecting yourself from an invasion of privacy should one or both of you die, while also saving on estate taxes, making sure your assets stay in the family, and avoiding probate altogether in many cases. It is the first really grown-up thing a couple does, and I'm happy to help them with it."

To Madison, the office appeared to have expensive furnishings, but no one had bothered to take care of them. It was subtle; someone with a less trained eye wouldn't even notice. There was a faint film of dust on the windowsill and on the fake plant in the corner, and the wall-to-wall carpeting had some stains if you looked closely. But there was also an expensive Persian rug on top of it, and the cost of that was probably what most people noticed. An antique globe sitting on a solid maple stand, which Madison recognized as costing probably fifteen hundred dollars, sat unused and unadmired in the corner, gathering its own film of dust. Madison saw the effect as an effort to demonstrate opulence, but the occupant had no actual attachment to, or affinity for, the objects. They were for show, but to Madison what they showed was a lack of care.

"That's what I heard. But is it too soon for us to do this? We don't have any assets to speak of."

Isn't that what Renée had said about her sister and brother-in-law? They had a trust but no money?

"That's not a problem!" Viceroy took a monogrammed handkerchief out of his pants pocket and patted his brow, which had developed beads of sweat. The handkerchief went back in his pants pocket. It was a practiced move; this man sweated a lot. "Many of my clients start out when they have very little money. But then it is all ready for you when you start to make money. It's important to think toward your future. If you don't plan for it, it's not going to happen, is it? If you build it, they will come!"

"I see."

Madison *could* see: she could see how a young man would find this talk attractive. Act like you have a lot of money, and you will get a lot of money. A young man would see Viceroy as successful and offering advice on how to be successful yourself: "Man to man, this is how to protect your family and build wealth; just follow my lead here, kid."

"Also, have you thought about a contingent beneficiary? Someone who benefits from the assets in the trust should you both die? It is so unlikely to occur that you really don't need to even think about it, but it's nice to have all the *T*'s crossed and the *I*'s dotted. A lot of my clients select a charity to be the beneficiary should both the husband and wife die, and we have several to choose from, depending on where your interests lie."

There was the mention of the charity. Renée had said the beneficiary of the trust was a charity. "We do like to do charity work."

"Exactly! What kind of charity do you usually support?"

Madison couldn't remember the name of the one that had been the beneficiary on Renée's sister's trust. Something to do with cancer. She couldn't think of it.

"We generally support cancer charities."

"There you go! You could name a cancer charity as the entity to receive the assets in your trust, should you both die with no children."

"But I have a brother. I would want him to be the beneficiary if we both died."

Viceroy opened his arms. "Whatever you like! I am here to set the foundation for you to make your dreams come true. We can make whoever you like the contingent beneficiary. It's just important that you have one."

"It's sort of gruesome to discuss death this much."

Viceroy took out the handkerchief again and stamped it around his face. "That's true, that's true. It's difficult to discuss. But then when the time comes, you'll be very happy that you dealt with it now."

"I think you helped some friends of mine, and unfortunately they died. Jason and Rebecca Brady?"

Madison had gone too far. Viceroy's mouth shut into a thin line. His hands stopped moving.

"I'm sorry, I can't discuss other clients. That would violate attorney–client privilege."

"Oh, I wasn't asking you to discuss their financials, I just knew them, and I assume they were happy that they had set up a trust through you."

Viceroy had pressed the button on his phone and Crystal appeared behind her. Viceroy spoke to her. "Mrs. . . . uh . . . Mrs. . . . she needs an appointment to set up a trust, let's set something up for next week."

Viceroy got up from his desk and scurried to Madison's side, putting out his hand. "I'm sorry we can't set this up today, but I have another client. Crystal will arrange an appointment for you. And thank you for coming in."

Madison gave him her hand, and he squeezed her fingers in that male to female patronizing way, instead of just shaking it. His hand was damp. Then he walked out of the office.

Madison got up from the chair and followed Crystal into the other room. She knew she didn't have much time left in this office, since the mention of the dead couple had raised Viceroy's suspicions. She stopped in the hallway and blocked Crystal's progression. Madison took out the photo of Barrett and held it up in front of Crystal.

"Do you know this girl? Have you ever seen her?"

Madison had heard descriptions of the blood draining from someone's face. She found that trite sayings were often trite because they described things that happened a lot. Crystal's face had gone white.

"I don't . . . I haven't . . . I'm not . . . No." As Crystal spoke her hands fluttered around her face, like the wings of a bird that had been disturbed on a perch.

Madison stared at Crystal, which increased Crystal's discomfort.

"I haven't seen her. I'm very busy." Crystal tried to get by Madison, but Madison wasn't moving.

"Crystal!" came from the back room. "I need those files! And where's the messenger?"

Madison spoke softly but firmly. "How long have you worked here?"

Crystal's brow furrowed. She squirmed to the side and got past Madison, who didn't want to actually put hands on her. Madison followed her, and they made it back to the lobby.

Crystal spoke. There was real fear in her voice. "You're going to get me fired."

Madison felt she couldn't push Crystal anymore. There was something going on in this place, Crystal knew what it was, and if Madison played her cards right she could get Crystal to help her.

"I'm going to give you my card. Will you please call me?"

Madison held out her card and Crystal stared at it like it was a snake.

"I . . . can't."

Madison set the card down on the desk.

The phone rang and Crystal walked behind her desk and sat to answer it. Madison stood there, not quite sure what to do next. Crystal's and Viceroy's reactions had told Madison that she was on the right path. Something about these death certificates, Viceroy, the accidents, the charities, all had to do with Barrett's disappearance. It's the only thing that made sense right now. Why else would Crystal get so upset at Barrett's photo?

A messenger came in behind Madison, and she stepped aside to allow him access to the desk. Crystal reached her hand out for the package and the clipboard to sign her name. While still talking to someone on the telephone, Crystal opened the small package and turned it upside down. A thumb drive fell out of the package onto the desk.

"Crystal! The goddamn files! I'm on the phone I need them!"

Crystal disconnected the call, jumped up, and ran to a large filing cabinet located across the room. She started searching through it, pulling files out and loading her other arm up with them.

Madison did something she had never done in her life. She reached down and took the thumb drive and put it in her purse. She then reached into the zippered pocket inside her purse and got the empty thumb drive she had picked up earlier at Ace Hardware, and she put it on the desk. It wasn't the same color or the same brand, but she was counting on Crystal being so harried that she wouldn't notice, at least until someone tried to get the data off the thumb drive and it was empty. If someone had asked Madison right then what she was doing, she couldn't have told them. She was desperate to find Barrett and there could be information on that thumb drive that explained some things. If there wasn't, she could bring it back later and say she had accidentally picked it up. There was something about this office that had to do with Barrett's disappearance, and she was going to figure out what it was.

"Excuse me!"

Madison stiffened. Someone had seen her. She had never stolen anything in her life, she would never before have risked her PI license by stealing something, and the first time she had done it someone had seen her. Possible explanations were flooding her brain, threatening to freeze all thought processes. She turned and saw that a woman had walked in behind her; the woman was yelling at Crystal, not Madison.

"I have not been able to reach Mr. Viceroy. I paid you a retainer! I expect to be able to reach my attorney!"

"I'm sorry ma'am, if you'll please have a seat I will be right with you."

Viceroy resumed screaming from the back room. "Crystal! The goddamn files! And did the messenger get here?"

"Yes sir!" Crystal returned to her desk with a bunch of files in her arms, and she grabbed the thumb drive that Madison had placed there. As soon as they stuck that thumb drive into a computer, they would see it was empty. Of course, Viceroy would probably just blame either poor Crystal or the person who had sent the item by messenger.

"Young lady! I am not going to sit here and wait much longer!" The woman continued to berate Crystal.

Crystal stopped in the middle of the room. Madison wasn't sure if she was going to start crying or what. Crystal didn't seem to know either. It was like when you give a computer too many commands and it freezes.

"I'm only seventeen!" Crystal said to the room.

The woman and Madison looked at each other. Crystal found her feet again and walked to the back office. That was Madison's cue to leave. She turned and walked out the glass door and down the steps. She didn't run to her car, because she didn't want to draw attention to herself, but she certainly walked briskly.

Her phone beeped and she took it out of her pocket to look at it. It was a response from Judy, the sister of Greg Thomas, who had died in a light plane accident with his wife Isabel. Judy, the woman Barrett had interviewed.

I'm happy to speak with you. Please call me at this number.

Madison didn't want her to have a chance to change her mind, so she dialed the number as she was walking back to her car.

She identified herself when Judy answered. "Wow, that was fast. Yes, I'm happy to talk to you. You said you're investigating a missing person? Who is missing?"

Madison made it to her car, and opened the door to get in. "It's a bit of a long story, and I can certainly explain it to you. I can go into detail later, but briefly I think you spoke with her: Barrett Brown? She was working for a newspaper?"

"Oh, yes, she was a nice girl. Is she in danger?"

"I'm not sure. And I'm not sure if what she was working on was related to her disappearance. Do you mind if I ask you some questions about your brother's death?"

Madison got into her car and kept an eye out for the Fusion and Escape. They were probably still parked near her apartment, waiting for her to leave from the alley. Pretty soon they would do a drive-by of her parking space and realize she had slipped out somehow.

"Sure. I can answer any questions you might have."

"First let me ask you, do you know these other couples, or do you think your brother and his wife did?" Madison read out the other names, but Judy said that she didn't recognize them.

"I'm sorry to be so intrusive, but did your brother and his wife have much money in their estate?"

"No, they were just starting out. I mean, not that I would have gotten any, they had a trust set up apparently, and I don't know who the beneficiary of the trust was, but it wasn't me."

Boom. This thing had to do with trusts. Madison understood so little about them. She was worried she wouldn't be able to figure it all out when it had to do with an area that she was so unfamiliar with. She might need to get help from someone. Haley. She would call her friend Haley, who was a genius attorney and would understand all about this stuff.

"Do you have any idea who set up this trust for them?" Madison expected her to say Viceroy. It made sense since Crystal had been the reporting party on all three couple's death certificates.

"I don't, I'm sorry."

"Wasn't your family curious? Like, your mother and father? Didn't they wonder who the beneficiary of this trust was?"

"Honestly, no. My mother died when we were teenagers, and my father was so broken about losing his only son that he really just withdrew into himself."

Losing a child must be the absolute worst thing that could ever happen to a person. Madison couldn't imagine the pain. But she could imagine that the last thing you'd be interested in was who the beneficiary was of a trust with no money in it.

"Thank you so much for your time, and I'm sorry for your loss."

"Thank you. Would you mind letting me know if you discover anything?"

"I don't mind at all. By the way, it said in the newspaper article that your brother had won the flight school lessons or something?"

"Yes, it was very weird. He had always been interested in flying, and he mentioned it to anyone who would listen. And by some strange happenstance he got notified that he had won flight lessons. It was on his first solo flight with his wife that the accident happened."

"That's terrible, I'm so sorry. Was there anything strange about the accident? Did the officials suspect foul play?"

"No, not at all. It was just a new pilot error. It was the same thing that happened to JFK Junior: spatial awareness or disorientation or something; he suddenly lost the ability to tell the difference between the ocean and the sky at night, and he went down into the ocean thinking he was going up into the sky. With my brother it was daytime, but they think it was clouds or haze that caused the confusion."

Oh my God how awful, Madison thought. She was familiar with JFK Jr.'s death, and it had been so tragic. His wife Carolyn and her sister Lauren also died in the crash when John got confused at night and plunged them into the ocean.

"I'm so sorry. And yes I will certainly let you know if I discover anything."

They disconnected.

Madison sat in her car thinking about the call, but her mind went to the thumb drive she had stolen. She took it out of her purse and stared at it. Something so tiny, something done so impulsively, could cause her to lose her PI license. What was she thinking? Well, she was thinking she wanted to find Barrett. She had always prided herself on being a PI who didn't break the rules, who never broke the law, who colored in between the lines. Now she was the kind of PI who stole things because she had a good reason to. Finding a missing and endangered person was a good justification for breaking the law, but it was still just a justification.

Well it was done now. Hopefully it would turn out to be worth it. They couldn't prove she took it, and frankly she could drop it outside Viceroy's door late at night, and it would seem like maybe the messenger had dropped it. That's what she would do. And in the meantime she would hope that this small piece of technology had some information on it that would help her understand what was going on, and where Barrett was.

There was only one way to find out: see what was on it. She picked up her laptop, but then put it back down. Most people used PC computers, not Mac like her laptop. She might only have one chance to see the information on this thumb drive, and sticking it in the wrong kind of computer might mess with it. She wanted to put it into her desktop computer and see if she could open the files that it contained. She was only five minutes from home.

She started the car and drove back to La Jolla Boulevard. She didn't see anyone behind her. Her phone rang and she saw on the screen on the console that it was Haley. Madison's life was like that sometimes: getting a call from someone she had just been thinking about. She wondered if it was because she felt them thinking about her as they got ready to call her, or if she was managing to summon them with her thoughts. Too weird to contemplate; Madison did not think she was actually psychic, but she did notice weird coincidences like that.

Madison hit the button on the steering wheel to answer the phone.

"Long time no talk to!"

"Why don't you ever call me? I always have to call you. I am a confident woman, but you can make me feel insecure."

Madison laughed. She had known Haley for several years, and it was easy to get the wrong idea about her. Haley looked and talked like a modern version of Marilyn Monroe, but in actuality, Haley was smarter than Madison. Many people had realized too late that they had underestimated Haley's intelligence just because she was pretty. She knew how to work that to her advantage as a high-powered attorney for a downtown law firm.

"I could never make you feel insecure," Madison said.

"Yes, you could. I'm shivering and shaking in my boots. Let's have lunch."

"I'm in the middle of a really important case. I'm trying to find a missing girl. As a matter of fact, you might be able to help me. Do you know anything about trusts?"

"Sure. I know lots of things."

"Of course you do. There are three couples who died in tragic accidents one month apart, and there are a few things connecting them. The first is this attorney, Joseph L. Viceroy, whose office was the reporting party on the death certificates for all six people."

"That is unusual. Not unheard of, but it is unusual. Were they wealthy?"

"That's the thing, at least two of the couples were not wealthy."

"Okay, that's weird."

Madison drove the couple of blocks around her apartment before heading home, to see if she could find the surveillance vehicles. She didn't see them.

"It gets weirder: with at least two of the families, they had living trusts set up, but the beneficiaries of the trust, in the event that both husband and wife died, were not other family members."

"Again, not terribly unusual, but sort of weird when the estate is not a wealthy one. Was this attorney Viceroy the contingent beneficiary of the trusts or something?"

Madison hadn't thought of that. But why would these couples make an attorney the beneficiary of their estate, an estate that had no money in it?

"I don't think so, but honestly I don't know. One of them had a charity, a cancer charity, as the beneficiary if both husband and wife died. But I'm hoping you can find it all out for me. What is the deal with having trusts for people with no money, and having a contingency beneficiary that isn't a family member for people with no money? I don't imagine this is a public record, so I know I'm not getting it with just my PI license."

Madison drove past the beach. Dave's Jeep was not in the lot. Madison figured it would be soon because he usually liked to surf in the late afternoon.

"No, it is not public record."

"Exactly. And I don't know for sure if this has anything to do with my missing girl. She was working on it the day she went missing, I know that, for a story for her newspaper. And the people at Viceroy's office are all acting weird, and the girl that works there almost fainted when I showed her the photo of the missing girl. I'm just going where the investigation takes me right now. So, if you could help it would be great."

"I might be able to find something out for you. You want to text me the details? Is this the cost of the lunch?"

"I will buy lunch if you can get me this info. I mean, the fact that I could find a missing girl, don't let that figure into it at all. Just get a lunch out of it."

Haley laughed "Each shit. I will find out what I can."

Madison's phone beeped to indicate there was someone on the other line. She disconnected with Haley and answered the phone.

"Madison Kelly."

"Hey it's Robyn."

Madison pulled into her parking space and parked. "Hey Robyn. I hope you have information for me, I could use a break right now." Getting Barrett's financial information was going to tell Madison something about what had been happening since Barrett went missing. Madison grabbed a notepad out of her backpack, and a pen, and got ready to take down the information.

Just then Madison got a text and she grabbed the phone to look at it.

Do you want to get daily weather reports? Press Y for yes and N for no.

"What the hell?"

"What?" Robyn asked.

"Sorry, not you. I keep getting these texts asking me if I want weather reports. And I keep pressing *N* for no, and they keep sending it to me again. I hate spam texting it is so annoying."

"That's not a spam text."

Madison paused while she tried to figure out what Robyn was saying. Of course it was spam. Was there another word for getting a text that you hadn't requested? Was Madison not up on texting lingo or something?

"What do you mean it's not spam? Of course it's spam, it's a text I don't want."

"That is an investigator sending you a portal to a GPS locator."

It was occasions like this that Madison felt she was behind the times. She had no idea what Robyn was talking about. On the other hand, that's why she had people like Robyn and Haley in her life: to take up the slack for things she didn't know. She couldn't know everything.

"I literally don't know what the words in that sentence mean. What are you saying?"

"When you hit either *Y* or *N*, doesn't matter which, it sends your location to whoever sent you that text. Someone is trying to locate you. You are sending them your GPS coordinates when you answer that text. Even if you say no, you don't want weather reports, just by responding you are sending them your location."

Holy shit.

Chapter Thirteen

Tuesday 4:04 PM

Madison slipped the thumb drive into the USB outlet on her computer. She had taken a quick look as she went up the stairs and unlocked the door to her apartment, but she hadn't seen any unusual vehicles. Now that Madison knew what this weather report text meant, she realized that every time the surveillance team had lost her, they had sent her a text in order to get her location. This most recent time, they'd figured out she'd ditched them when she went to Viceroy's office. They had probably driven through La Jolla trying to find her, and when they couldn't find her they had sent her the text, not realizing she was arriving home at that moment. Thanks to Robyn, Madison hadn't replied to the text about the weather report. Nevertheless, her car was in her parking space and they would see it if they drove by again.

The question of who was following her was just going to have to wait. They weren't doing anything threatening, and Madison would be the first person to admit that they weren't doing anything illegal—although the weather report text was questionable. Madison needed to find Barrett. She couldn't waste time on them right now. She knew how to lose a tail if she needed to, and otherwise they could follow her to their hearts' content.

Madison had emailed Haley all of the info she would need to get to the bottom of the weird trusts, and now it was time to see what the memory stick would tell her. Her desktop computer recognized the thumb drive right away and opened Windows Explorer. So far, so good. But when she clicked on the thumb drive icon, it asked for her password.

Dammit.

She had stooped to a life of crime and it wasn't going to do her any good apparently. *Crap.* She would take it to Arlo when she took him Barrett's phone. Hopefully he could crack the password. He'd done harder things, so she had hope he could do this. She'd better take the items to him today.

Robyn had said she emailed Madison a report of everything she had learned about Barrett's financial activity. Madison logged in to her email and found the message from Robyn. She printed out all of the attachments, put a two-hole punch in the top, and put them in the file on Barrett.

On the night that Barrett went missing, she used her ATM card to rent a scooter at 9:10 PM. This would have been shortly after receiving the phone call from the unknown number at 9:01 PM. Madison remembered the scooter she'd seen by the fountain. That would fit with the theory that someone had called Barrett and she had gone to meet that someone at the fountain at Balboa Park. The scooter was still there.

The next financial activity was when Barrett withdrew one thousand dollars in cash from her checking account, leaving twenty-six cents in her account. The withdrawal was made from the First Republic Bank on Fourth Avenue at A street in downtown, at 9:46 PM. Madison knew this was maybe half a mile from where she had found Barrett's phone in Balboa Park.

Madison went to the whiteboard and updated it with the information she had just learned. She made a timeline with the theory forming in her mind: someone called Barrett at 9:01 PM and asked to meet her. At 9:10 PM Barrett rented a scooter somewhere between her house and Balboa Park. She then took her scooter to the meeting point at the fountain. Barrett's phone ended up in the fountain, either because she threw it there or someone else did. Barrett was then at the ATM machine at her bank, less than a mile away, at 9:46 PM, withdrawing one thousand dollars in cash.

What Madison didn't know was whether Barrett had withdrawn that money under her own free will, or whether someone had forced her to do it. The police could get the video footage from the ATM machine.

That got Madison thinking. Where were the police on this investigation? Why hadn't Madison run into them? Had they actually ignored Travis, because they thought Barrett was just a girl that was ghosting him? It was conceivable. It might be time for Madison to make sure the police knew that this was *not* a girl ghosting her boyfriend. Well, if it was, she had also quit her job at the same time without telling anyone, and left without telling her landlord, which made no sense. No, Barrett was missing, and it didn't seem like the police were doing anything.

Madison decided to tell Tom about her case and see if he could look into what the police were doing.

She picked up her phone and texted him.

Can you call me later? I need to go over something with you.

Madison stared at the whiteboard. That phone call was everything. She had to know who called Barrett at 9:01 PM. It was vital. Madison grabbed her phone and opened the *Flame* app. She used the same phone number she had created on the app earlier. She checked the number that had called Barrett at

9:01 PM Wednesday night on the cell phone printout she had gotten from the cell phone provider, and dialed the number from inside the *Flame* app.

This time someone answered.

It was a man. Madison could hear a keyboard clicking in the background, and soft voices.

"Hello?"

Madison jumped in with the first thing she thought of. She put on her cutest voice, making each sentence go up on the end as if it were a question.

"Oh my God there you are!"

"Who is this?"

"Is that what we're doing now? You want me to pretend to be a stranger? Where are you? I thought we were meeting up?"

The guy wasn't biting. "I think you have the wrong number."

Madison tried to sound cute and confused; she had to keep him on the phone until she could get his name.

"Oh really? I'm sorry. This isn't 619-555-2165?"

"Yes, it is. Who is this?"

"It sounds like you. I feel like you're playing games. Danny?"

The guy chuckled. "No, this isn't Danny. This is Eddie."

Boom.

"Oh, I'm sorry, I must have the wrong number." Madison disconnected the call.

Eddie Vincente, the clerk from the County Admin Center, the clerk who had signed all six death certificates and was always seen by Rosie talking to Barrett, had called Barrett the night she went missing. Right before she rented a scooter. Right before she took a thousand dollars in cash out of her bank.

Madison looked at the clock. The thing she wanted to do the most was follow Eddie home from work. Would he lead her to

Barrett? Was he the one who took Barrett? Or was it a coincidence that he'd called her that night? Why was he calling her? Sitting in her apartment coming up with scenarios was not going to get Madison anywhere. Madison could do surveillance on Eddie when he left work for the day, see where he led her, and make a judgment call on whether to speak to him or what to do next. She leapt into action.

She grabbed her surveillance duffel bag and started throwing things into it: a towel, a couple of protein bars, a couple of bottles of water, and Travel John disposable urinals because she couldn't pee into a bottle like a male private investigator. She threw in the latest Thomas Perry book, because it was important to always have a book with you.

She ran down the stairs after locking the door and setting the alarm and got into her car. And then she paused. This was an occasion when she did not want someone following her. She didn't know who these tailers were, but she did not need a choo-choo train of people tailing Eddie from work; they would probably all end up running into each other.

She started the car and drove down by the beach. Dave's Jeep was in the lot; he was probably in the water surfing. She drove south on Neptune Street, looking in her rearview mirror the whole way. She didn't see any of the known surveillance vehicles, but she couldn't be sure she had spotted them all and could recognize everyone at this point.

She turned left on the one-way street heading away from the beach. It was a small street, and there was only one car behind her as she made her way toward La Jolla Boulevard. Robyn had explained to her that the GPS coordinates the investigators received after she answered the text were only good for a one-time use. Since she had ignored the last text, they did not have her GPS location.

She got to La Jolla Boulevard and turned left, and the car that had been behind her followed her. It was a common route in La Jolla; it didn't necessarily mean they were tailing her, but she had to make sure. She drove north, going slowly, until she saw a break in the southbound traffic; she suddenly whipped a U-turn and changed her direction to head south on La Jolla Boulevard. The car that had been behind her paused for a moment but continued on. Any investigator following her would not want to repeat her sudden action, because it would expose the surveillance. She drove until she entered the town of Bird Rock, a quaint community just south of La Jolla, which technically shared the La Jolla ZIP Code. She turned off La Jolla Boulevard into the small residential side streets behind the main drag, and then she pulled over to the curb. Now she would wait to see if any cars came past her.

She checked the time: she had mere minutes to get to downtown before Eddie likely would leave work for the day. She was desperate to know what Eddie had to do with Barrett. Was he holding her against her will? Was this the type of thing where he had been obsessing about her and she was chained up in his basement and it had nothing to do with the story Barrett was working on? Madison's head was spinning.

She felt the coast was clear, and she started driving just as Tom returned her call. She pressed the button on the steering wheel to answer the phone.

"You have perfect timing."

Tom paused before speaking. "Really? Because I actually think what we have had is really poor timing for a really long time."

Madison blushed. It used to happen all the time when she was young, and she hated it so much because the whole room knew she was embarrassed; it was literally like waving a red flag.

It happened much less now that she was an adult and had worked on controlling her emotions. But Tom had caught her off-guard. Fortunately, he wasn't there to see her face turn beet red from neck to scalp. Tom was married, but he and Madison had had a long-term flirtation that had resulted in a drunken kiss and nothing else. Of course he had gotten slightly obsessed with her after that, but they had discussed it, and Madison had thought they were done with all that.

"Right. Not what I meant."

"Relax, I'm only kidding. What have you got going on?"

Madison kept her eye on the rearview mirror as she drove toward the County Administration Center. She didn't see any of the surveillance vehicles, or any vehicle for that matter that stayed with her for long. To be sure, she pulled over again, waiting for several cars to drive past her before pulling out into traffic again and continuing.

"I'm working on a case of a missing girl, and I feel like I should have run into the police investigation by now, but I haven't."

"What's the girl's name?"

"Barrett Brown. She is twenty-four, five foot seven inches tall, blonde hair and green eyes. Her boyfriend Travis reported her missing a week ago, after he couldn't reach her. She hasn't contacted her work or her landlady."

"That's an interesting name. I feel like I would remember that from briefings. It doesn't ring a bell."

Madison knew that not every case was known to every detective, but cases with missing blonde-haired green-eyed girls usually got mentioned at some point or another at the police station.

"I feel like I should be walking over ground that has already been trampled on by the police, but so far no. Her boss said the police haven't talked to him, and same with the landlady. I've collected some evidence, and I'm happy to share it with whichever detective is handling the case." Well, not happy, but she would.

"Okay, let me ask around and I'll get back to you. I'm on a case where I'm doing surveillance at night for the next three nights, so I may not be able to get back to you for a few days. Is that okay? Or you need this information right away?"

Madison was conflicted. On the one hand, she wondered what the hell the police were doing to find Barrett. On the other hand, she was afraid the police would interfere with her investigation and make her stop trying to find Barrett. She was at the moment doing all the things the police would do, except perhaps get the ATM video. She would like that ATM video. Especially if they had already gotten it and she could just look at it.

"Could you make some calls from your surveillance? Just casually, to see if anybody has heard of the case?"

"Who am I making calls to in the middle of the night?"

"Right. Right. Okay. Well, ask the guys on your surveillance. Maybe they've heard something."

"And I bet you don't want me to tell anyone that you're working on it."

"You know me too well. But I do want the police to be working on this. Whoever finds her, hooray, I don't care, I'm getting paid either way. I just want her found. But no, I don't want my contribution to be terminated because the police find out that I'm working on it."

"I understand. Let me see what I can do. I'll see if I can get the information without mentioning you."

He could be a really great guy. Sometimes she wished their timing had been better.

They disconnected and Madison pulled into a parking space on the street near the staff parking lot for the Admin building. She could watch the back door where she knew the staff came out, because Rosie had met her there with tamales in the past, and see which car Eddie got into.

She hadn't been there five minutes when she recognized staff leaving for home. She had made it just in the nick of time. She was sitting quietly with her windows rolled up. Humans were predators, and they reacted to movement; if Madison held still she wouldn't be seen. Fortunately it was late afternoon in the fall, and so it was crisp and cool. No need for the car to be running for the heat or air-conditioning.

And then Eddie walked out the back of the building. He was carrying a quilted lunch bag and a briefcase. Madison wondered what was inside the briefcase; what did a clerk need to bring to and from work? He walked toward the back of the parking lot and got into a brand-new Mercedes S class. That was an expensive car. How did a government clerk afford a brand-new Mercedes? Hadn't Rosie mentioned that he had come into money recently?

Interesting if true, Madison thought.

Eddie pulled out of the parking lot and drove in the direction of the freeway entrance. His car was an unusual electric blue; it made it easy to follow. He jumped on the 5 freeway south and quickly transitioned to the 94 east. After he made that transition the tail was fairly simple: Madison stayed to the right and let him move a couple of lanes over to the number one lane. The great thing about following people on the freeway was that in California, most of the exits were on the right-hand side of the freeway. So all Madison had to do was stay on the right, and when he was ready to exit the freeway he would change lanes and move directly in front of her. In this way, she could tail someone for miles without ever being directly behind them. She just kept her eye on him from the right side of the freeway.

As they got more into the rural section of San Diego County, he transitioned to the 125 freeway northbound. Within minutes he exited at Grossmont Boulevard, right in the center of La Mesa. Madison came up behind him at the red light at the end of the ramp. This was when it got tricky: people had a tendency to look in the review mirror as they got closer to their home, concerned if they saw a car behind them for any length of time. Madison wasn't sure if this was because everyone was suspicious, or if it was a big-city phenomenon of being afraid of robbers following them home, or what. But it was a fact of her life: people looked in their review mirror as they got closer to their home. As they sat at the red light Eddie began looking at Madison.

It was against the law in California to tint your windshield; technically speaking, it was against the law to tint the front passenger and driver windows as well, but Madison had done it. She had been pulled over a few times and got a ticket for having tinting on her front windows; she would just remove the tinting, take it for inspection, clear the ticket, and then put the tinting back on. At that moment Madison was facing due east, so the sun was behind her. There was no light shining through the windshield. She was hoping this worked to conceal her. Eddie had only seen her once, at the Admin Building with Rosie, but the one thing Madison had as a strike against her was that she was memorable: unusually tall for a woman, with hair color that caught the light and stood out. She turned her head and looked down at the passenger seat, pretending to look for something in her purse. When she glanced up the light was turning green and Eddie was moving through the intersection.

Madison took the opportunity of Eddie having to look directly ahead as he maneuvered through the intersection to grab a black knit cap from her surveillance bag; she drove with her knees while she tucked her hair completely up inside the hat. This would give the illusion of a woman with short dark hair, or even a man, given Madison's height. The next time Eddie looked in his rearview mirror, it would look like a different person driving; since Madison's SUV was non-descript and common, it would look like a new vehicle had moved in behind him, not the same car that had been behind him at the light a minute ago. Eddie turned right on Grossmont Boulevard and Madison followed him.

He quickly turned right on a road paralleling the freeway, and Madison slowed, allowing him to make the turn without her. His turn was so immediate after leaving the freeway that Madison was concerned for a moment that he had spotted her; nevertheless, she couldn't let him go because of the possibility he was leading her to Barrett. If he saw her, he saw her. But she wouldn't confirm it for him by following right behind and making every turn immediately after him.

There was no one behind her, so she just stopped in the middle of the street and waited as soon as he'd turned; this would give him a little bit of time and he wouldn't see her make the same turn right after him. She counted to ten and then gunned the V-6 engine on her Explorer and made the right turn. She saw him up ahead making a left. She hit the gas and shot up to sixty miles an hour. She made the left about twenty seconds after he had; she could just see him a few blocks ahead. She gunned the engine again and reduced their separation by a couple of blocks. She was able to see him turn left into a driveway. She pulled over for a moment so that she wouldn't be driving past the driveway immediately after he'd turned in.

Timing was everything when tailing someone. If you're too close they see you; if you're not close enough you lose them. There was an art to it, in addition to the techniques that she'd been taught by her mentors. A good investigator had a feeling for timing and lived off instinctive decisions. A bad investigator failed, and either lost the subject or was burned when the subject spotted them. A good investigator had good luck and everything went right. Madison had good instincts that served her well. When it felt right, she proceeded down the street and was able to see him walking from the driveway to the front door of a large house. He didn't even turn in her direction.

His was one of two houses on a small cul-de-sac off the main road. Madison got a glimpse of a large sprawling property before driving down the road past his house.

This was a rural part of La Mesa. Larger homes set far back from the street, lots of trees and greenery. Madison made a U-turn and pulled over onto the dirt beside the road. She would be able to see him pull out of his driveway from this location. She paused there to consider her options.

The way he had driven to this location, and the way he had immediately walked into the house, left Madison comfortable with assuming this was his home. Was Barrett inside? Madison suddenly felt so tired. It was exhausting to have someone's life riding on your shoulders. Having to make a decision about the correct thing to do, knowing if you made the wrong decision you could kill someone, was overwhelming.

Because Madison was a girl and nonthreatening, she could get information from people where the police and other PI's would be turned away; it made up for her memorable appearance. She used this benign presence to her advantage whenever possible. The police could have the information she obtained by questioning people; it was just more likely that she would get her questions answered.

She studied the neighborhood. She could always knock on Eddie's door using some pretext, but once she had done that it would be hard to question neighbors. She got out of the car and walked over to the house two doors down from Eddie's. She knocked on the door.

A woman opened the door. She was much shorter than Madison and had dark hair and dark eyes. She was dressed in scrubs, the kind of clothes that nursing assistants and housekeepers wore.

"Hello. I'm sorry to bother you. Your next-door neighbor has applied for a job with the government, and I work for a third-party investigation firm hired to check into his background. He knows that we're doing this, and you would be helping him get a new job if you could answer a few questions."

"I am the nurse. The man who lives here is elderly and I take care of him. I'm not sure I know the neighbor."

"His name is Eddie Vincente, and he lives two doors down. He drives a nice blue Mercedes. Do you know him?"

The woman chuckled. "Oh yes, I know Eddie. He is very nice."

"What does he do besides work? Does he go bowling? Garden?"

"I'm not sure. I've seen him with golf clubs on a Saturday, so I think he likes to golf."

"When was the last time you saw him playing golf?"

"Last weekend."

Madison thought about what she could ask that would tell her if Eddie had Barrett. It was conceivable he would go for a carefree round of golf with a girl chained up in his basement, but Madison thought that was pretty confident; what if something happened while he was gone, and Barrett got away? On the other hand, the same argument could be said for someone who had to go to work every day. Why did she think Barrett being chained up was a possibility anyway? It was pretty extreme. But she had to consider everything.

"Does he keep regular office hours? Do you see him up late at night?"

"Oh, no, he's not. I work the night shift one weekend a month, and last weekend he was going to bed early he said. Then I saw him when I got off at six AM, and he was going to play golf."

"He lives in a nice house and has a fancy car. However, from his résumé it appears he doesn't work at a job that would pay him that much. Do you know how he affords such nice things?"

The woman looked toward Eddie's house. She looked like she was considering whether her answer would help him or hurt him.

"He told me his aunt died and left him money. He makes new additions on his house."

Interesting if true.

"How long ago did he start buying things and making additions on his house?"

"About a year ago."

Madison thought for a moment. "Have you ever been inside?"

"Oh yes, I clean for him for extra money."

"That must be a lot of work! It looks like a big house. Did he have you clean the whole thing?"

The woman smoothed her smock down and adjusted the collar. "Oh yes, he has a finished basement and two stories. It took me all day on my day off to clean it."

"Was he there when you cleaned?"

"No, he went to play golf. He gave me the keys. I can be trusted." She jutted her chin out slightly on the last statement.

"Oh I'm sure you can be! I was just wondering."

Barrett was hardly chained up somewhere on his property if this woman was given free reign over his house to clean it. That was a relief, at least.

Madison took Barrett's photo out of her pocket and showed it to the woman. "Have you seen this girl before?"

The woman took the photo and held it up close to her face. "No. I have never seen her." She handed the photo back to Madison. "Is he in trouble?"

"Not at all. It's just routine. I do this all day long. My job is boring. I think your job is probably more exciting."

The woman laughed. "I don't think so. I sit in a quiet room all day long and read my book."

"That sounds delightful. Is Eddie married?"

"No, he lives by himself. He asked me to go to dinner, but I am married."

"Well, thank you for your help."

Madison turned as the woman shut the door. She felt sure that Barrett wasn't being kept at Eddie's house. It didn't mean that Eddie wasn't involved in her disappearance. Madison decided to grab the bull by the horns. She walked the half block to Eddie's front door.

Just before she started up the stairs, she got a text:

Are you interested in getting the weather report each morning? Type Y for yes, N for no.

"Nice try, assholes." They must be wondering where she was. She deleted the text without answering.

She rapped her knuckles on the big oak door. Hopefully Eddie wasn't going to open it and say, *Why have you been following me?* Madison suddenly got afraid. Why had she come up to this door by herself? She turned to walk back down the steps.

The door opened.

"Yes?"

Madison turned back. "Eddie Vicente?"

"Yes. And you are?"

Madison still didn't know how she was going to play it. Sometimes she planned out her pretexts, and sometimes she didn't. Sometimes she just had to act on instinct.

She grabbed the photo of Barrett out of her pocket and shoved it in front of Eddie's face.

"Where is she?"

Chapter Fourteen

Tuesday 6:06 PM

Eddie started to shake. Madison had never seen anything like it. It was like a large set of teeth chattering.

"I don't know anything! I swear!"

Madison was sorely wishing she had waited for Tom, or whoever was handling this for the police. She was not equipped to take down a kidnapper. Well, she could keep talking and just report back to them what had happened.

"Yes you do. You've been seen with her."

"Seen? When?"

"At your work. You talk to her all the time."

As soon as Madison had started her explanation, he had visibly calmed. It was as if Madison had given him a shot of something.

"Oh. You're not…Okay I see. I'm sorry, I don't know who that is."

What had changed? Had he thought Madison was someone else?

"Yes, you do know who that is. You talk to her all the time at work. Then you gave her copies of death certificates, all of which you had signed as okay when they clearly needed autopsies. So where is she?"

Eddie looked out the door, past Madison to the street.

"I don't know who it is. And you need to stop asking questions."

That definitely sounded like a warning. "Why do I need to stop asking questions? What can happen?"

"I am not going to answer your questions. I don't know who you are, and I don't know what you're talking about."

Madison thought for a moment. When he'd opened the door and she'd showed him that photo and said where is she, he had thought she was someone else. Who had he thought she was? What had he said? *I don't know anything.*

She tried again. "Look. This girl is missing. I'm trying to help find her. If you have any information on where she might be, please tell me. Did you meet her at Balboa Park on Wednesday night?"

Eddie looked out on the street again, up and down. It was a quiet street, with no cars, so Madison wasn't sure why he kept looking.

He lowered his voice, so softly that Madison had to lean in to hear him.

"I tried to warn her, but I was too late. You need to *leave this alone.*"

He slammed the door in her face.

Madison had learned long ago that once someone has slammed the door in your face, there is no point in ringing the bell. They were done talking. She turned and walked down the stairs, and started walking up the street toward her car.

It felt like Eddie was scared of the same thing that had caused Barrett to go missing. Madison felt sure Eddie had not taken Barrett. But what was he afraid of? A person? A situation? And he said he had tried to warn Barrett. Is that why they'd met in Balboa Park at the fountain? He was warning her of something? But then he said he was too late. He'd tried to warn Barrett, but he was too late.

Madison got in the car, started it, and headed for home. She felt like the police wouldn't have gotten any more information out of Eddie, and in fact probably less, since he would just get an attorney and refuse to speak.

Could the police do anything with this information? Maybe. It was pretty tenuous. When Tom got back to her on who was handling the case, she could certainly share the information. Until then it would get added to the whiteboard. *Eddie tried to warn Barrett, but it was too late.* Also, *Eddie was scared.*

So what should she do next? Going to bed was a start; it wasn't that late, but she was tired. It had been a long day. Hard to believe this was her first full day investigating Barrett's disappearance. She wanted to take Barrett's cell phone as well as the thumb drive she had gotten from attorney Viceroy's office, the thing that had reduced her to a life of crime, over to Arlo. She had wanted to do that today, but the surveillance on Eddie had jumped in the way. She felt sure Arlo could get into the thumb drive, although she wasn't so sure he could get into a drowned cell phone. All she could do was ask. She would do that first thing tomorrow.

She wondered where her surveillance team was; it was kind of lonely out here without them. She chuckled to herself, and then she realized she must be getting punchy. She had successfully lost them, and she assumed they would be waiting for her at her home. What did they want with her? She still hadn't figured that out. It was like getting used to having parasites living on your skin.

Her upper back was hurting from muscle tension. She used one hand to steer and the other hand to rub her shoulders and what she could reach of her upper back muscles. She was reminded once again that although she would miss her foobs if the implants had to go, she would not miss the upper back pain. And the lack of strength. They were almost her kryptonite. The fact was, she had lost her breasts three years ago; if she lost the implants, it would just be the ending to a story that had been started with her mastectomy surgery. She didn't have breasts anymore, so she couldn't lose them again. It was true, but it didn't make her feel any better.

She drove the block around her apartment and spotted a newer model black Ford Fusion, but it had a different license plate from the one that had been tailing her. The car was too shiny for the neighborhood, where after a day the salt from the ocean and the sand from the beach dulled even the best paint job. She memorized the license plate. Whoever was following her clearly preferred Fords. So did Madison, so she couldn't argue with them on that.

She parked in her space, locked the car, and walked to the garden path. A figure stood from the bottom of her stairs, and at first she thought it was Dave.

It was Travis.

"Hey. What are you doing here?"

"How do you feel about irony? My wife saw me talking to you at the Pannikin and she kicked me out."

Madison threw her head back and laughed. It was the perfect end to the day.

"Sorry. I'm sorry to laugh. I'm sure that's not funny. But honestly, it's funny."

Travis looked at her with a wry smile. "Go ahead and laugh. I deserve it."

Madison finished laughing. And then chuckled one more time. She really was punchy.

There was a duffel bag sitting on the stairs next to him, and Madison eyed it suspiciously. "Okay, so why are you here though?"

"I know this is irregular, but I wanted an update, and I was going to call you, and then I thought I'll stop by, and anyway . . . here I am."

"How do you know where I live?"

"Google."

"Ha! Hoisted on my own petard. Nice. All right, but again, sorry to be dense, why are you here?"

Did this guy actually think she was going to let him stay in her studio apartment?

"I didn't have anywhere to go."

"Really? You could go stay at Barrett's apartment. You could go to a hotel. I have a studio apartment. I barely know you. You're not staying here."

This was bizarre. Madison thought perhaps he had overestimated his ability to charm the ladies if he thought she was going to let him stay in her apartment.

"No, no it's nothing like that. I guess I just felt a little . . . lost. Normally I would have gone to see Barrett, but I can't. I realize the situation is of my own making, I just . . . I miss her. And I'm worried about her. And I guess you are my only connection to her right now."

Madison sighed. This is the guy who'd given her an ultimatum that she had a week to find Barrett, and now he was here because she made him feel safe and cozy?

"Come upstairs and I'll make you some coffee and give you an update. But then you're leaving."

Travis picked up his duffel bag. "Understood."

Madison unlocked the door and deactivated the alarm.

"Will you wait here for one second?"

Travis nodded his assent and Madison went inside and shut the door. She took the whiteboard and put it back in the closet. She didn't want him second-guessing everything she was doing and demanding an explanation for everything on the whiteboard. She grabbed a towel off the back of her office chair where she had left it that morning and hung it in the bathroom. She returned and opened the front door.

"Come on in. I'll be back in one minute."

She went into her bedroom area to change into sweatpants and a sweatshirt. She jammed herself into the small bathroom in order to change in privacy, since her bedroom was only separated by a bookcase. It was chilly by the beach at night in October, so she turned on the wall furnace to get some heat in the apartment. She returned to the living area.

"This must be a great view in the morning."

Travis was standing at the living area window looking out in the direction of the ocean. Right now it was just darkness and a lone streetlamp over the backs of the big houses that ran along Neptune. It was silent, except for the waves crashing on the shore. Madison walked up behind Travis.

"Don't get any ideas. You won't be seeing it."

Travis laughed. "I wasn't suggesting anything. So do you have an update for me?"

Madison poured coffee into the coffee maker, and filled the back of it with water.

"The biggest clue I have right now is that she requested copies of six death certificates, and these death certificates were all signed by the same clerk at the Admin building."

Travis stared at her for a moment. "Is this helping us find her? What about the information on her cell phone? Didn't she call someone before she went missing? Or were you too busy looking into how many times she called me?" Travis started pacing. "How is figuring out what she was working on going to help us?"

Madison walked over and sat at her desk. "Would you please sit down?"

Travis came and sat in the wing chair. He ran his hands through his hair.

"I just don't understand how this is getting us closer to her."

"I have to go where the investigation takes me. I can't wave a magic wand and find her. I can't stand on my landing out there and scream out into the universe 'Where are you Barrett?' and wait for her to answer. I have to be methodical."

"I guess so, it's just so frustrating. Every minute that we're waiting, something could be happening to her."

The coffee maker sounded and Madison got up to get two mugs. She spoke from the kitchen.

"I realize that. You don't think I realize that? I am constantly thinking about what she could be going through. But putting pressure on myself like that doesn't help me find her any faster. I do believe she is missing because of something related to what she was working on. I have to retrace her steps so that I can see where she stepped off the grid."

Madison put two coffee mugs, a small container of half-and-half, and some sugar on a tray. A tray might be a little fancy for a late-night coffee visit, but old habits die hard. Her grandmother had trained her well. She set it on the corner of her dining table/desk and sat down in her office chair. Travis took one of the mugs and poured cream into it.

"Okay, I guess I understand. Continue."

"I followed the clerk from the Admin building to his house. I talked to his neighbor, and then I talked to him."

This had gotten Travis's attention. "What did he say? Does he have her? Is he keeping her there?"

Madison sipped her coffee. She didn't normally drink coffee at night, but her adrenal glands were shot and it probably wouldn't matter. "I don't think he has her there. He seemed afraid. But not afraid like you're holding a girl in your basement, more afraid of whatever caused Barrett to disappear."

"And what about the neighbors? Did you show them Barrett's photo?"

"Yes, I did. The neighbor I spoke to had not seen her and she seemed to be in regular contact with this guy."

Travis ran his hands through his hair again. "Now what?"

Madison decided not to tell him about her next steps with taking Arlo the thumb drive and phone. She didn't need him micromanaging her every move. She was the investigator.

"Now I keep working. Now you go back to being the client. And figuring out what to do with your wife, who does not deserve the treatment you've been giving her."

"Our marriage had been bad for a while, it had nothing to do with Barrett. My wife cheated on me first, and when I said I'd forgiven her, apparently I hadn't. It's just . . . have you ever met someone and had a connection, an unusual feeling that you've met the person before, just an unbelievable attraction for someone?"

Travis lifted his eyes up from the floor and met Madison's. It was so rare for her to feel this kind of pure animal attraction for someone, and so weird that he was talking about it as she was feeling it. Was he talking about Barrett right now? Or her?

Madison had to control her voice so it wouldn't shake. "Yes, I have felt that."

Travis leaned forward so that their faces were close together. Madison's breath caught in her throat. Travis put his hand up to touch her face, and she could feel the heat of it before it even made contact.

Madison used her feet to shoot her office chair backward and stood up.

"Okay! Time for you to go."

Travis stood as well. "I'm sorry. I don't know what it is. I haven't felt this kind of attraction for someone since Barrett. And that was unusual in itself."

The fact that Madison was feeling the same way made no difference to her. Not only was he a client, not only was he married, she was trying to find his missing girlfriend. This was absurd.

Madison picked up his duffel bag and handed it to him.

"Gotcha. Interesting story. So anyway, I'll call you tomorrow and give you another update."

Madison walked over to the door and opened it. "Sorry you couldn't stay longer."

Travis walked sheepishly to the threshold. "You must think terribly of me right now. I'm sorry. You're just the most—"

"Don't finish that sentence. We're not going to talk about this again. And you're not gonna try anything again. I'm not angry. I'm just serious."

Travis walked out the door and she shut it behind him. She walked over and turned off the furnace. She was sweating.

Chapter Fifteen

Wednesday 8:05 AM

Madison rolled over and looked at the clock. She'd had such trouble going to sleep, first of all because of the caffeine, second of all because of her thoughts about Travis. She was old enough to understand that lust had nothing to do with love: being attracted to someone didn't mean anything. But the attraction was startling. She hadn't been with a guy other than Dave since her mastectomy; what would another guy think about her foobs? And what if her implants had to come out? Dave had said she would still be beautiful, but what would another guy think? It must matter to them. If you took off your shirt and all you had was a flat chest with two scars running across it, that mustn't be appealing to a guy. *Yes, I'll sleep with you, oh by the way, I have no boobs.* It reminded her of the male plastic surgeon she'd consulted with before her mastectomy. When she'd told him she was considering just going flat, he was aghast and tried to talk her into getting implants: "They'll feel just like real breasts!"

"To *whom*?" Madison had said. They only felt real to a man who was grabbing at them. To Madison, they were numb blobs of chemicals pushing up against her pectoral muscles; they didn't feel real at all.

She rolled to a sitting position and contemplated standing. She also didn't know what to make of Travis's attempt to come onto her. Could it be nothing more than he was feeling the same attraction she felt, but he was a guy, so he automatically acted on his feelings? Was she normalizing male dominating behavior or something? Those thoughts were too deep first thing in the morning when she was exhausted. She got up, put her hair in a bun, and jumped in the shower.

The most important item on the day's agenda was to get the thumb drive she had stolen from Viceroy's office, along with Barrett's phone, over to Arlo. She decided to forego breakfast and get coffee on the way. She toweled off, put on yoga pants and a vintage Aerosmith concert T-shirt that she'd picked up at a thrift shop, and walked into the living area.

She looked out the window and saw a clear blue sky. That told her nothing when it came to temperature, so she opened the front door. The morning air was cool and crisp. Madison took a deep breath and put her hands up over her head, and then bent at the waist, lowering until her palms were touching the one-hundred-year-old wood on the landing. She normally worked out several days a week, but her life was on hold until she found Barrett. She stood and looked out over the ocean. Why did autumn feel so much like new beginnings? It made more sense that spring would feel that way, but to Madison the autumnal change in the air felt like hope for a new day. Her phone went off with a text, and she went back inside.

It was from Travis:

I'm embarrassed. I don't know if it's the stress, or the . . . nmd. no excuses. I'm just sorry and I hope you'll forgive me. We need to find Barrett, and I did something so inappropriate.

"Yeah, you did." Madison threw her phone in her purse.

She put on her Doc Martens and Ralph Lauren flak jacket, grabbed her purse, set the alarm, and walked out the door, locking it behind her.

She kept an eye out as she walked down the stairs and through the garden to her car. The surveillance team wouldn't park in her alley because there were no parking spaces, and they would stand out. That didn't mean they weren't on the street waiting for her to come out of the alley. Because of the two alleys that joined by her apartment, there were three exits she could take out to the street. She figured they knew that, and they would have people stationed at each exit. However, she had only seen two vehicles following her, and there were three exits. She sat in her car and thought about that for a minute. She would say nearly one hundred percent of the time she took either the alley out to Nautilus, or the alley out to Bonair. The alley that led north to La Jolla Boulevard was longer and had more potholes, which meant she had to go more slowly for a longer period of time, and then it let out onto a busy street where it was hard to make a left turn. So she rarely took it. She figured that the team had noticed this, and there was one person sitting on Bonair and one person sitting on Nautilus. So she took the alley to La Jolla Boulevard.

She normally would have gone to Busy Bee's Bagel Bakery for her coffee, on the corner of La Jolla Boulevard and Nautilus, but today that was too close for comfort. She made a right turn, heading toward Pacific Beach where Arlo had his office on the second floor across from the post office. She drove sedately on La Jolla Boulevard southbound, checking her rearview mirror. She absolutely could not be followed to Arlo's place. It was out of the question for anyone to know that Arlo was a source she used. Just to be sure, she made a left turn into a small neighborhood to see if anyone made the turn after her. She pulled over and waited. After about five minutes she decided no one was following her, and she took the tiny side streets to Ingraham and then followed it down into Pacific Beach. There was no one behind her the entire way.

She stopped at Java Earth Coffee, across from the laundromat where she used to do her laundry when she didn't have the communal machines at her place. Before she could get out of the car, her phone rang. It was Haley.

"Please tell me you have something for me. So far my life sucks," Madison said.

"I have something for you."

Madison sighed and put her head back on the headrest. "God bless you."

Haley laughed. "It's a lot of information. I think we should meet. Lunch?"

"Yes, anywhere you want anytime you want as soon as possible."

"Okay, well I just got to work so I don't think they would appreciate me going to lunch right now. How about at noon, and I can meet you at the Pannikin."

"I love you."

"Okay, calm down."

"No you don't understand. This is the most bizarre case. I am trying to find this guy's missing girlfriend, and last night in my apartment he tried to kiss me."

"That is . . . inappropriate."

"Right? What the hell? I mean, I'm not gonna lie to you. I have this unnerving attraction to him. But I wasn't going to act on it. I mean, just because you're attracted to someone doesn't mean you're in love with them. Right?"

"Right. But animal attraction can be pretty strong."

"I know, but I don't want to act on an attraction to a guy whose girlfriend is missing. Oh, and by the way? He's married."

"Have you considered him as a suspect for this missing girl? He sounds bizarre."

Had she considered Travis enough? "I mean, the boyfriend, especially the married boyfriend, would always be a suspect in a girl's disappearance. But he paid me five thousand dollars to find her. Why would he do that if he had done something to her?"

"Good point. I didn't think of that. Okay, so apparently you are irresistible."

"I am not, but thank you. I'm getting coffee right now, which might help my attitude. Well, actually, you have helped my attitude since you have something for me. Is it something that can help me find her?"

"I don't know, but it's going to explain a lot about what has been going on."

"I can't stand it, can you give me a hint?"

"No, I cannot. It's too long a story. I'll see you at noon."

They disconnected and Madison got out of the car to get her coffee. She was surprised at herself for sharing the Travis story with Haley. She wasn't a gossipy kind of girl; she played her cards close to the vest and didn't share a lot about her personal life with anyone. But she'd known Haley for a long time, and . . . well, it felt good to have a friend.

When she returned to the car with her coffee, she scanned for surveillance vehicles. It was a sleepy part of town, and there were no unusual cars in the neighborhood she was in. She drove a mile to Arlo's office. She didn't park in his parking lot, just in case the surveillance team was looking for her and happened to see her vehicle there.

She walked up the steps to the second-floor landing. She had forgotten that Arlo kept strange hours and might not be open in the morning. She was in luck, and the door opened when she turned the handle. A little chime jingled on the door. Arlo was sitting behind the counter, with classical music coming out of an advanced sound system in the walls, where you couldn't even see the speakers.

Arlo looked up briefly and smiled, and then returned to the motherboard he was tinkering with.

"Madison Kelly. What exciting thing have you brought me today?"

Arlo was about thirty, soft spoken, with pasty skin from never being outside. He had brown hair that was buzzed on the sides and long on the top, a dollop of product causing it to stand up. He had spacers in each of his ears, and both his arms were tattooed from shoulder to wrist. His beard was closely cropped and neat. He did not look like a guy who had turned down a job with the NSA.

"I do bring you exciting things, don't I?"

He put on safety glasses. "There is never a dull moment with you. So what do you have?"

"I have a cell phone that has been sitting in a body of water for a week."

"That does not sound exciting. That sounds impossible." Arlo squinted and bent closer to the desk as he soldered a tiny part of the motherboard.

"I thought nothing was impossible with you."

"Flattery will get you everywhere. What else have you got?"

Madison smiled. He had looked up at her only once since she came in. She pulled the thumb drive out of her purse and set it on the counter.

He looked up briefly and then went back to what he was doing. "What is that?"

"It's a thumb drive, it holds lots of computer information. Some people call it a memory stick. You put it in the USB outlet on your computer, and then you use the file Explorer to open the files contained on the memory stick."

Arlo stopped what he was doing and laughed. He was such a quiet guy that Madison really enjoyed when she could make him laugh. He took off his safety glasses and finally gave Madison his full attention.

"Thank you for that explanation. I might not have known otherwise. So am I not asking where you got this?"

"You are not."

"Oh, Maddie, why don't you visit me more?"

"Because I would fall in love with you and you wouldn't be able to return my love and it would end badly."

"You're probably right." He went back to his task. "Okay, what is on this memory drive and what do you want me to do with it?"

"What I want you to do is tell me what is on this memory drive. It is password protected."

"Oh, I see, something easy."

Madison knew that Arlo was kidding. This would not be easy. It might even be impossible. "I thought you were magic."

"I'm magic only on Tuesdays and Thursdays. You missed it."

Wednesday. It had been a week since Barrett had gone missing. A week. If Barrett was hanging on, keeping herself alive, how many more days could she hold out?

Madison shook her head to get the thought out. She had to keep moving forward. That's all she could do. Worrying about what was happening to Barrett would not make Madison find her any faster. In fact, it would cause her thought processes to freeze. She came back to the present.

"I'll pay extra for you to be magic on Wednesdays."

"Sounds good. When do you need this?"

"Later today?"

"You're hilarious. How about in a week?"

"How about there is a girl missing, I'm trying to find her, and the information on this thumb drive might help me find her."

Arlo stopped what he was doing and looked up at her. "Gotcha. Just give me a couple of days. If I have it sooner, I'll let you know. I'll do everything I can."

"You're the best, Arlo."

Arlo put his safety glasses back on and picked up the soldering iron. Madison didn't move.

"Was there something else?" Arlo looked like a bug with his glasses on.

Madison pulled Barrett's phone out of her purse and slid it across the counter.

Arlo set the iron back down and slowly removed his glasses. "Oh right, the drowned cell phone."

"I know. But seriously, what a boring life you would have without me, right?"

"I like boring."

That was probably true. That was why he worked at a little shop instead of solving world financial crises or catching terrorists.

Arlo had taken the phone and was now in the process of taking it apart. He had pulled out a jar of rice and dropped each piece of the dismantled phone into the jar.

"Does that rice thing really work?"

"It's the first line of defense."

"Well, you're still my hero."

Arlo smiled and picked up the soldering iron again. "I'll call you."

Madison walked out of his office. From the second-floor landing she could scan two streets, since he was on the corner. She didn't see any of the surveillance vehicles, and she didn't see any cars at all that looked suspicious. That was good. She did not want to bring them to Arlo's door. Whoever they were.

As she walked down the steps, she wondered if she should be doing more to figure out who was doing surveillance on her. At this point, her only option, if she really wanted to know who they were, was to do counter surveillance on them. Follow them, see where they went, and confront them if necessary. And she didn't have time to do that. She needed to find Barrett.

Madison snagged a parking space directly in front of the Pannikin at 11:55 AM. She'd seen Haley's white BMW parked a little bit farther up the street, so she knew Haley was already there. As she got out of the car she scanned the nearby parked vehicles as well as the ones traversing the busy intersection. She saw the black Ford Fusion parked across the street and down about seven cars. They had figured out that Madison went to the Pannikin a lot; so, having lost her, they decided to leave a car at the Pannikin, and probably one at her apartment. It's what Madison would have done. Smart. She didn't care if they knew she was meeting Haley for lunch, so she didn't bother to hide.

Madison spotted Haley the second she stepped up onto the curb. Everyone else at the Pannikin had spotted Haley as well: her naturally bright blonde hair shimmered in the October sun, and everyone on the patio was staring at her. She wore huge

Jackie O sunglasses, and her long legs were crossed as she read something on her phone. Madison walked up and stood in front of the table.

"I see you're still homely."

Haley set her phone down and sat up straight. "Shut up, sit down, and tell me about your new boyfriend."

This was why Madison didn't normally share personal details about her life.

"He's not my boyfriend," Madison said as she sat down. "He's my client. If anyone is my boyfriend, it's Dave."

"You don't even want a boyfriend. But here you have a dreamy surfer and now some rich client throwing himself at you. Not fair."

"Oh, yeah, and you suffer so. Can we please not talk about men? I need to find this girl. And I need to hear what information you have for me. Let me grab a sandwich and I'll be right back. What can I get you?"

"Get me whatever you're having."

Madison walked up the steps and went inside to wait in line at the counter. When it was her turn, she ordered two chicken curry sandwiches and two bottled waters. She took the waters, some napkins, and the number on the stand back to the table. She set the number in view so the waitstaff could find them with their sandwiches, put her purse on the back of her chair, and turned to Haley.

"Okay. Spill it."

"Okay. Here we go. Do you understand living trusts?"

"Not really," Madison said. "Act like I'm a fifth-grader. A smart fifth-grader, but a fifth-grader nonetheless."

Haley took a sip of water. "Okay. So you hire an attorney to set up a living trust so that while you're alive, and even after you die in most cases, all of your money and assets are contained in the living trust. Think of it like an imaginary storage facility. There is a trustee who you select to be in charge of your imaginary storage facility. And it's a big storage facility. Your house, all the money in your accounts, stocks, bonds, your car, jewelry, etcetera, are all in one place. This imaginary storage facility is actually a document called a living trust, and it lists all of that property and your wishes and decisions about it."

Madison always said she was smart with math, she just wasn't quick with it. Sometimes it took her a while to grasp concepts that had to do with numbers. Or money. Which might explain the state of her bank account.

"Okay, so why would I want to do this?"

A cute waiter with a fauxhawk and eyeliner brought their sandwiches. They thanked him and Haley picked up the top piece of bread from half of her sandwich and looked inside.

"Curry? Yum."

She took a bite and they waited while she finished chewing. She took another sip of water and then spoke.

"There are a lot of reasons for setting up a living trust, one of which is that trusts don't go through probate court if someone dies, like a will does, so it's easier for the beneficiaries to access the money after the holder of the trust dies. And then there are some tax reasons for doing it that I won't bore you with."

Madison finished chewing and set her sandwich down. The sun was beating down on them, and Madison wished that Haley had chosen a table with an umbrella. She was starting to catch on, but she had questions. She put her hand up to shade her face and summarized to see if she was catching on.

"Okay, so there is money and houses and stocks and bonds in this imaginary storage facility, which is really a document called a living trust. In my current investigation, at least two of the couples who died in accidents had these living trusts. What happens to the assets in the trust when the person dies?"

"The trustee is in charge of doing whatever the rules of the trust say to do when the person dies, for example distribute the money to family, pay off debts, or a combination of things. The trustee gets a fee for doing this work, usually a percentage of the assets in the trust."

A wasp buzzed down and landed on Madison's sandwich. She picked up her hands and held them up, out of the way. Haley and Madison were silent, letting the wasp do its thing, not wanting to disturb it or make it mad. The wasp grabbed a tiny piece of chicken in its tiny insect hands and flew away with it. Madison had never seen anything like it.

"What the hell?" Madison said, and they both laughed. "Okay, back to trusts. Let's get specific. Who was the trustee in charge of the Brady family's assets, the couple who died on the road coming down from Big Bear?"

Haley finished chewing another bite. "Oh, the trustee for the Brady family's trust? That's easy, because all three couples had the same trustee for their trusts: Joseph L. Viceroy."

Madison was glad she'd stolen that thumb drive now. She hoped Arlo could get something off of it.

"Viceroy was the trustee for all three couples?" Madison said. "Well, his assistant was the reporting party on the death certificates, so maybe that makes sense?"

"Well, he was the trustee. And yes, if he's in charge of their estate, it's not unheard of to handle all of the arrangements."

Barrett had pulled these death certificates because she saw similarities; at least, that was the theory Madison was going on. One of the similarities was that the reporting party was the same on all six certificates. Viceroy happened to be their attorney. He was probably just handling everything having to do with the deaths, including reporting them. Was this all just a big coincidence?

In a world of cause and effect, all coincidences are suspect.

Madison needed a moment to process this. “I need more water. I’ll get you some. Do you need anything else?”

“Do they have chips?”

Madison stared at her. “How do you stay so thin?”

Haley finished chewing. “Metabolism. Genes. Do they have chips?”

“I’ll see.”

Madison walked back inside the Pannikin. She didn’t see any chips, so she got Haley a blueberry muffin. Not quite the same thing, but she didn’t want to come back empty-handed.

Somehow Viceroy had managed to make himself the trustee for three different couple’s trusts, and at least two of them, maybe three, had no real assets. So why the trust? She walked back out to Haley and set the muffin in front of her.

“What is this?”

“A muffin. They didn’t have chips.”

Haley shrugged and took a bite of the muffin. “Questions before I continue?”

“I have questions, yes. So many. Let’s start with this: so I assume if a husband dies, and the couple has a trust, the trust goes to the wife, and vice versa.”

“Yes, that’s generally how that works. The wife is the beneficiary of the trust and usually the husband is the ‘owner’ of the trust, but there is a fancier word for it.”

Madison was thinking hard. “Okay, so what happens if they both die, like in all three of these cases? Who gets the assets in the imaginary storage vault then?”

Haley had eaten half the muffin before finishing her sandwich. “This is delicious. Okay, so if both the husband and wife die, the assets would go to a *contingent* beneficiary, which is the word we use. Contingency means something that may occur but is not certain to occur—like both spouses dying at the same time. That may occur. A trust asks: What do we do if that happens? The answer is a contingent beneficiary, the person or entity that gets all of the stuff in the imaginary vault if both of the primary beneficiaries die."

"Okay, I get that. So . . . who was the contingent beneficiary in these three trusts? Well, I know one of them was a cancer charity, right?"

Haley set down her sandwich and picked up her Hermès briefcase. Being a fancy corporate lawyer paid well.

"In each of these cases, there were no children. So the couples named a charity as their contingent beneficiary in the event they died at the same time—three different charities."

"Is this just the way Viceroy recommends that his clients handle trusts? Maybe they were all, coincidentally, civic minded and wanted charities to receive their tiny assets?"

Haley had finished eating and was eyeing Madison's plate. Madison took a bite of her sandwich.

"Maybe," Haley said. "But it is a tad unusual to have a charity as the contingent beneficiary on a trust. Not unheard of, but somewhat uncommon. So it is quite a coincidence that all three couples who died had no children and yet didn't name other family members as the contingent beneficiary."

The fauxhawk came back and asked them if they needed anything else. Haley ordered another blueberry muffin to go. Madison raised her eyebrows as the fauxhawk walked away.

"What? It was delicious."

"Okay. So it's weird that all three couples chose a charity to receive the money in their trusts if they both died, especially when there were family members who could've been the contingent beneficiary."

Haley piled her plates on top of each other. "Right. And again with the coincidences, they all chose Viceroy to be a trustee."

"Okay, but this is the question that is still screaming in my mind: they have no money! Why make a trust?"

Haley smiled. "They didn't have any money—until they died."

Madison set her sandwich down. Haley was smiling like the cat that ate the canary.

"They had no money until they . . . what?"

Haley folded the piece of paper she'd gotten out of her briefcase and set it next to her plate. She looked at Madison.

"There was life insurance."

Madison's heart stopped, reset itself, and started again. She had a mild heart condition that caused her heart to beat prematurely, especially when startled, and the heart in its infinite wisdom, realizing it had beat too early, stopped to reset itself, like when you turn your computer off and on to get it to unfreeze. The time between her heart stopping and it restarting again could feel like a lifetime. She'd been checked out and told this was just slightly outside normal, but it was startling at moments like this. She grabbed her water bottle and took a swig. Her heart was pounding in her chest.

"This is the first I'm hearing about life insurance, and I interviewed two of the family members."

"That's because the family members weren't listed as beneficiaries on the life insurance policies."

"Again with the beneficiaries? Don't tell me: the charities were the beneficiaries of the life insurance policies?"

"No, that would be impossible. The trusts themselves were the beneficiaries of the life insurance."

Madison wished she had her whiteboard so she could draw a diagram. "But normally don't you list a family member as the beneficiary of a life insurance policy, like wife or husband or kids?"

Haley was enjoying being the person to drop the bombs. "Not in this case. Each policy listed the living trust as the one and only beneficiary. No other beneficiaries listed. The life insurance paid the money to the trust. That isn't uncommon, and again it is to avoid tax and probate problems."

Madison was wrapping her head around this. "So if only Mr. Brady had died, the life insurance would've paid the trust, and then the trust would've paid Mrs. Brady as the primary beneficiary of the trust."

"Exactly."

Madison was catching on. "But because the primary beneficiaries of the trust died, when the insurance company paid the insurance proceeds to the trust, the only entity left to get the assets in the trust was a charity."

"Yes. The life insurance paid the trust, and since the couples were the only beneficiaries of the trusts and they had died, the trust paid the charities as the contingent beneficiaries."

Madison stretched her arms over her head, and rolled her shoulders back. She moved her head forward, back, and side to side, trying to release the tension in her upper back. This was so hard to grasp.

"Doesn't the insurance company think it's weird that they're paying a charity?"

"No, no, that's the point," Haley said. "All the insurance company knows is that they fulfilled their obligation and paid the money to *a trust*. That was *their* beneficiary, and it's not that unusual. The 'Mr. and Mrs. Brady Living Trust' was the beneficiary of the life insurance, and the insurance company paid the money to that trust. It's none of the insurance company's business who the trust then pays."

Wow. "Okay, so how much was the life insurance?"

"I thought you'd never ask," Haley said.

"Yes? Do I have to do a drum roll? How much?"

"Each policy was worth one million dollars."

One million dollars? Madison was speechless, so Haley continued.

"And that is *each*. Meaning one million for the husband, one million for the wife. Total of two million per couple."

"So the charity that was the contingent beneficiary on the trust got two million dollars when the couple died?"

"Actually, they got more than that. Because the people died in an accident, the insurance paid double. It's an optional coverage that costs extra, and it's added on to the insurance policy. So if the insured dies in an accident, whatever the insurance payout would be, it doubles; the official title is double indemnity."

Madison sat up straighter. "Wasn't there an old movie called *Double Indemnity*?"

"Yes! Great movie. A man and woman having an affair kill the woman's husband to get the life insurance, and because it was made to look like an accident, the insurance company paid double."

Madison's head was exploding. "So you're telling me that each of these charities got *four million dollars*?"

"Yep."

"Any chance Viceroy didn't pay the charities and instead kept the money for himself? He is the trustee in charge of all the assets, right?"

"He paid them. Long story, but I checked. He paid the charities. But he got a hefty trustee fee for each death."

"Well that explains his G-Wagon and his house in Del Mar."

"Yes, it does."

Madison rubbed her forehead. All this money talk was giving her a headache. "Okay, but look: I do work for insurance companies. They don't like paying out money. Didn't the insurance company see a commonality between the three cases? Didn't that make them investigate before paying the money?"

"There were three different insurance companies—one for each couple. The same broker sold the policies, but he placed the insurance policies with three different insurance companies. So to each of these companies, it was just *one* payout of four million dollars, paid to the trust of a couple that died in an accident. A big payout, but hey, it happens, and that is what life insurance is for. Nothing to investigate."

That was smart. If you're going to do something fishy with insurance, don't do it more than once with the same insurance company, or the company will notice and investigate.

"Who was the broker?"

Haley looked at the piece of paper she'd gotten out of her briefcase. "Fred Durant Insurance Brokerage in La Jolla."

Haley read her the address and Madison's head popped up. They were sitting across the street from the brokerage firm. It was in a small office building, and Madison could see the entrance from where she sat.

"Is this why you wanted to meet at the Pannikin? For effect?"

"Hey, I can enjoy some dramatics when I've brought you a smoking gun," Haley said. "This is a smoking gun, isn't it?"

"My God, won't you please go into business with me? You wouldn't be working for me. We'd be partners. We could fight crime together."

"If I did that, who would you come to for information like this?"

"Good point. Okay. So Fred Durant Insurance." Madison looked across the street again. A new player. Was he connected to attorney Viceroy?

"Yes. I wanted to get you more information on the charities, but I couldn't. This was a lot of work and my boss noticed. I had to stop. This is as far as I can take you. Just follow the yellow brick road from here."

"Well, you are Glinda the Good Witch, so yes, I will follow the yellow brick road on my way to Oz."

Haley handed Madison the piece of paper. It had the information Haley had just given her, along with the names of the three charities: Cancer Society of North America, Children's Hope Society of America, and End Hunger Society of the Americas. Madison had never heard of them, but they sounded worthwhile. It was a strange coincidence that these charities had been the recipients of millions of dollars in life insurance payouts from trusts set up by Viceroy, but it didn't necessarily mean anything nefarious. It was just more strings to pull. Madison would call Robyn and ask her to get information about the charities.

Madison looked across the street again. She couldn't keep her eyes off the next place she wanted to check out. She returned her gaze to Haley.

"So what does this tell us? I have an idea forming in my mind, but I want to hear it from you."

Haley leaned back. "Well, if those charities are legitimate, then there were three couples with no children who just wanted to make sure that their hefty life insurance benefits were paid to something worthwhile if they happened to die at the same time. They were financially smart to create family trusts. It was merely a coincidence that each couple's life insurance paid the proceeds to trusts and those trusts listed charities as contingent beneficiaries."

"Okay that is the non-sinister version, and it requires some real suspension of disbelief. What is the sinister version?"

Haley leaned forward. "Those charities are fake, set up for the sole purpose of benefitting someone millions of dollars if both husband and wife happened to die in an accident."

"And whoever runs those charities has recently received four million dollars," Madison said. "And if the charities are somehow connected, the person or persons recently received twelve million dollars."

"Yes."

Twelve-million-dollar insurance fraud. And Barrett had discovered it.

Chapter Sixteen

Wednesday 2:02 PM

Madison sat on the patio of the Pannikin and stared at the front of the building that contained the Fred Durant Brokerage Firm. She was contemplating the gag she would use when she walked into their office. Haley had left, and Madison knew her next step was to walk into the brokerage firm and see what she could learn.

She had texted Robyn with the names of the charities and asked her to get whatever information she could find on them. Each couple had no children; each couple had life insurance that paid out to a trust; each couple had trusts that benefitted a charity.

In a world of cause and effect, all coincidences are suspect.

Madison knew that she was hot on the trail of an insurance fraud ring and likely financial fraud, embezzlement, and who-knew-what-else kind of ring, but where was Barrett?

I tried to warn her, Eddie the clerk had told Madison, and he had signed all six death certificates. Attorney Viceroy's office, in the form of Crystal, was listed on the death certificates as having reported the deaths, and Viceroy had set up the trusts. Fred

Durant had sold the couples the million-dollar life insurance policies. Eddie, Viceroy, and Durant had to be connected.

By the way he had set up the trusts, Viceroy had made sure that those charities benefited from the life insurance policies. Madison recalled her background check on Viceroy, and the fact that he lived well; but he didn't seem to be living twelve million dollars' worth of well. Plus he seemed way too frantic to be running a major insurance fraud ring. Nevertheless, he had to stay on the list of possible masterminds.

She felt she was discovering what Barrett had discovered, but would that help her actually *find* Barrett? Madison sighed. All she could do was keep moving forward, keep pulling the string until she got to the end of it, and hope Barrett was at the end of the string.

Madison switched seats so that she could sit under an umbrella, to avoid the early afternoon sun that was now searing into her cheek. She could still see the front of the building that housed the Fred Durant Insurance Brokerage.

And where were the police in all this? Were they so far behind that they hadn't discovered what Barrett had been working on? Madison had no legal requirement to share her findings with the police, but she wanted as many people as possible looking for Barrett. She took out her phone and texted Tom.

Anything? Did you find out who's handling Barrett's missing person's case?

She waited a few minutes for him to answer. The lunch crowd had left, and the Pannikin was getting ready to close. The waitstaff was cleaning tables, picking up trash from the patio, and closing the umbrellas. Madison realized the Ford Fusion was no longer across the street. Where had her surveillance team gone? Maybe Madison at lunch with a friend was too boring even for them, and they'd left to eat, go to the bathroom, or have a shift change. Being a PI meant making judgment calls and having good luck when you decided to leave a surveillance and come back later. Her team had demonstrated poor judgment. This was her chance: when they came back, her car would be in the same place, and they'd think she'd gone inside the Pannikin.

Madison picked up her purse and walked across the street.

The building was older, probably built in the early fifties. She walked through the passageway off Girard to get to the entrance to the building. She took the elevator, which she quickly regretted since it apparently had not been serviced since 1952, and she breathed a sigh of relief when it opened on the top floor. She turned left and saw a small wooden plaque that read "Fred Durant" in cursive script. It was an office building, so she didn't think she needed to knock, but she wasn't sure. She knocked as she opened the door.

It was a small office with no waiting room. There was a desk, an executive chair, and a wingback chair for guests. The furnishings were expensive, and it was a bit of a shock after the rundown hallway. It was an oasis from the outside world: an expensive area rug filled the entire space, the desk was a treated maple that had been shellacked to a high shine, all of the desk accessories were copper, and along the far wall there was a small fish tank on a credenza that matched the desk.

There was a man sitting in the executive chair, and he smiled and stood upon Madison's entrance.

"Welcome! My name is Evan Reed, and I'm at your service. Please, sit down."

"Thank you, my name is Madison." Madison used her real name just in case she needed to take this gag far and show him identifying information. She sat in the chair. She still wasn't sure what she was going to say. "I was looking for Mr. Durant?"

Evan was affable. "Yes, most people who come here are. They are indeed. I am his trusty servant, and I can help you with all your insurance needs. May I ask, did someone refer you?"

Madison figured that, again, this was an important question, and everything hinged on her giving the right answer. "Yes, Joseph Viceroy referred me."

Madison had chosen well. Evan beamed. "Of course, Mr. Viceroy! I'm happy to assist you." Evan was getting papers and brochures out of the doors of the credenza. "Were you referred to Mr. Viceroy by Kerry at the bank?"

So that was how the young couples were referred to Joseph Viceroy.

"Yes, that's right. Kerry."

"Excellent, and will your husband be joining us?"

Madison knew the building was from the fifties, but she hadn't thought Evan Reed was. He looked to be about thirty-five. So why, in the twenty-first century, was he assuming she had a husband, and more specifically a husband who needed to attend meetings with insurance brokers? Was it because Joseph Viceroy only referred young couples to this insurance brokerage?

"He will come once I've gotten all the information and made the preliminary decisions."

"Excellent." Evan sat back at the desk with his paperwork. "So let's discuss your life insurance options."

Again, this guy was assuming she wanted life insurance because that's why Joseph Viceroy sent clients here. Madison had not said what type of insurance she wanted. Well, at least he was doing all of Madison's work for her.

Madison wanted to see if she could pin him down. "So is it you that has the relationship with Mr. Viceroy? Or is it Mr. Durant?"

There was just the slightest crack in the veneer that was Evan's face. Madison realized she had to be careful: this guy was smart, even though he was acting like a Stepford wife.

"Relationship?" Evan tilted his head to the side.

Madison backpedaled. "I just meant, he referred us here, so I assumed you guys have worked together before?"

Evan had put the fake smile back on. "I see. Well, I wouldn't say 'relationship.' We just like to do business with friends in La Jolla. Do you live in La Jolla?"

"Yes, I do. At Windansea."

"I love that area. Are you in one of the new condos?"

Over my dead body, Madison thought. "Yes, that's right. Steel and cement. Love it so much." Madison tried to think how to steer this conversation to get the information that she needed. This guy was wily, and she had to be careful. "How long have you worked here?"

"Oh quite some time. Do you have children?"

"No, we don't."

"Do you plan on starting a family soon?"

"No, we don't plan to have children."

"I understand. In this day and age, one has to think about bringing children into the world."

And it helps if I don't have any beneficiaries, Madison thought.

"Now, we help Mr. Viceroy's clients a lot, and we know how he likes to do things. So I assume you've set up a living trust with him, and you want that trust to be the beneficiary on the life insurance policy?"

Exactly, Madison thought. "Yes, that sounds right."

"Perfect. It really makes things so easy in a terrible time. God forbid your husband should die, you don't have to worry about the insurance company doing an investigation, or about estate taxes coming out of the life insurance proceeds; the insurance company just pays the trust, and boom it's done."

"What if I need money for funeral costs, or to pay the bills?"

Evan paused. "Well, that's not really my forte, but I assume Mr. Viceroy has explained all that? Once the insurance company pays the trust, you have access to the money as a beneficiary of the trust. The trustee, I assume Mr. Viceroy, gives you whatever money from the trust that you need. I mean, you are the beneficiary to the living trust, right?"

"Right, right," Madison said. *As long as I'm still alive,* Madison thought. *Mr. Viceroy's clients have been having bad luck lately.*

She would realize later that it was at this moment, telling herself that little joke, that the full picture of what had happened began to materialize. She was about to have full understanding hit her like a ton of bricks. In the meantime, she was listening to Evan ramble on with his sales pitch.

"And the same goes for your husband as beneficiary of the trust, should, God forbid, you be the one to die. The life insurance pays the trust, and then Mr. Viceroy gives your husband any money he needs out of the trust."

"I'm so blonde when it comes to financial things."

Evan smiled conspiratorially. "I have to tell you, before I started working here, I didn't understand a thing about life insurance, or trusts, or anything. This has been such an education."

"Yes, it's definitely a learning curve. Usually my husband handles all of this." Madison thought for a moment about how there really were women whose husbands handled all of the financial matters. She had to admit, that would be nice to have.

"And I assume you and your husband are healthy?"

"Yes, we are healthy."

Evan picked up a brochure and opened it, pointing at things as he spoke. "Most of our young couples get one million dollars of life insurance on each spouse. We have reasonable rates, which I'll go over with you. In addition, most of Mr. Viceroy's clients get a rider on the insurance that pays double should an insured die in an accident. It's called double indemnity. It's an inexpensive option, but it can be helpful if, God forbid, there should be an accident that results in a death."

"The accidental death insurance is inexpensive? And yet it pays double? That's surprising to me."

Adding an additional million dollars of coverage to a policy was inexpensive? Madison understood insurance, and that didn't make sense to her. Insurance companies liked their money, and they didn't like to pay a lot of it out without receiving a good sum in premiums up front.

"Well, insurance companies set their rates based on the likelihood that something is going to happen," Evan said. "Everything about insurance rates relies on statistics. And surprisingly, it is unlikely that someone will die in an accident. Strange, right? But it's true: people are much more likely to die of heart disease or cancer. So it doesn't cost the insurance company much to offer this protection, since it is unlikely that they will have to pay out. People don't die in accidents as much as you'd think. Nevertheless, we like to offer it to our customers since it doesn't cost much, and it certainly doesn't hurt to have that extra protection."

That's when it hit her. She couldn't believe that neither she nor Haley had thought of it before. *It was unlikely that someone would die in an accident.* And yet three couples *had* died in an accident, just one month apart. Three couples had died in an accident after putting their money into a trust that benefitted a sketchy charity. Three couples died after being sold life insurance with an accidental death double payout that benefited their trust, which benefited a sketchy charity. Three couples had died in an accident just one month apart. And yet accidental death was so unlikely that insurance companies didn't charge much for the coverage.

Viceroy and Evan and whoever else was involved weren't just committing insurance fraud; they were *murdering* people for the insurance money. How had she and Haley missed this? Madison had been so busy trying to understand what a trust was that she had missed the most important part: these trusts and life insurance policies were all being set up so that the couples could be murdered for the insurance payout. Twelve million dollars was worth murdering for.

Madison's heart was racing, and she had started to sweat. Evan could tell that something was wrong, and there was nothing Madison could do to cover her emotion. She saw the entire scheme: identify the mark, which was young childless couples who came into the bank; send them to Viceroy, who set up a trust with a sketchy charity as contingent beneficiary; then Viceroy sends them to this broker for the insurance that benefits the trust; and then someone—Viceroy? Evan?—sets up a murder that looks like an accident to kill the couple for the money.

The realization of the enormity of the crime stunned Madison, but it was the realization that came right on the heels of it that was causing her to have a meltdown in front of this insurance salesman: Barrett was dead. Barrett had discovered this massive crime ring, and they had killed her because she knew too much. Madison was certain of it. They had searched Barrett's apartment to see if anything traced back to them, like the copies of the death certificates, and either they'd found something or not, but either way Barrett was dead.

Madison had so hoped she would find this smart, pretty girl alive, this girl who lived alone and didn't need a guy, this girl who was independent and brave and didn't stop when an investigation got scary, this girl who reminded Madison so much of herself. Madison was starting to cry, and she couldn't stop. Her grief at the loss of a young life, someone whom she'd started to think of as her friend, and the deaths of six other young people with their whole lives in front of them, was too much for her in that moment.

Sometimes if you start crying you'll never stop.

"Mrs. . . . I mean, Madison, are you okay?"

Madison stood up. "I'm so sorry. I have panic attacks sometimes, it's very embarrassing." She walked to the door. She was having trouble controlling her voice; it was shaking. She hated emotion like this. She turned back to Evan. "They come out of nowhere. All this talk of death. I'm so sorry, I'll have to come back."

She didn't think her story was fooling him. He seemed unnerved. "Of course. Come back anytime."

Madison flew out of the office and ran down the stairs and out of the building. She leaned against a brick wall at the entrance to the passageway and let the tears flow. She put her hand over her mouth and tried to keep the sobs inside. She had hoped this whole time that she would find Barrett alive, but there was no way they would keep her alive if she knew about the six murders to go with the twelve million dollars they stole. *I tried to warn her, but it was too late* Eddie had said. Now she knew why.

And not only that: this meant Madison's life was in danger. The surveillance team that had been following her was suddenly more sinister than she had thought.

"Are you okay?"

Madison turned. A man had stopped just behind her. He was wearing a suit with a tie, carrying a briefcase. Not terribly unusual in laid-back sunny La Jolla, but not that common either. He had gray hair that was cut short and neat, with a kind face that wrinkles had softened even more. He reminded Madison of her dad. The sight of this man caused a sudden need for her father so intense that she felt all the air rush out of her, as if she'd been punched in the stomach. This wasn't her father. It would never be her father again. Her father was only a memory.

"Yes, I'm okay. I just got some bad news." Madison used the bottom of her T-shirt to wipe her eyes and her nose. She was making a spectacle of herself on the street. Her grandmother would be turning in her grave.

The man wasn't giving up on her. "I'm sorry. Can I help?"

"No, thank you." No one could help her now. She had to help herself.

Madison crossed the street to her car. She got inside and locked the doors. It felt good to be inside her space, where she felt safe. She took out her phone and wrote in her notepad everything she had just learned. She drank some water and got a hold of herself. She'd had a blow, but that was it. She still had a job to do.

The best way to avenge Barrett's death was to get her killer or killers arrested. Madison wouldn't stop until she'd done it. And as part of that, she would find Barrett.

"I will find you, and I will bring you home," she said aloud.

But who was the mastermind of this operation? Viceroy didn't seem … organized enough to pull off the intricacies of this operation. Setting up six murders to look like accidents? No. Evan seemed too young, more like a paid minion. But there were certainly young heads of criminal organizations. Eddie had warned Madison, and according to him he'd warned Barrett too, so unlikely it was him. Madison decided she hadn't gotten all of the principals of this operation. It was way bigger than just Viceroy.

Just then Evan walked out of the building across the street. He got into a small Lexus parked at the curb. He backed up and drove south on Girard.

Madison made a U-turn and followed him.

Chapter Seventeen

Wednesday 3:06 PM

Madison wasn't shocked that Evan had driven straight to Joseph L. Viceroy's office, but she was glad. Just further evidence that the attorney and the insurance broker were in this together. Madison parked in the gas station across the street and watched Evan walk up the stairs to Viceroy's office. She could see him through the big windows, and she got out her field glass to see better. Evan stopped briefly at Crystal's desk and spoke with her, and she waved him to the back, to Viceroy's office.

Madison picked up her phone and googled Viceroy's office number. She found the number and selected it on the screen, causing the phone to dial the number.

"Joseph L. Viceroy's office, this is Crystal, may I help you?"

Crystal sounded just as harried as the last time Madison had seen her. It seemed to be a permanent condition. "Hello Crystal. This is Madison Kelly. I was in yesterday and I showed you the picture of Barrett. Remember?"

Madison was looking at Crystal through the field glass while she was talking to her on the phone. Crystal was alone in the office, but she looked around frantically at the sound of Madison's voice.

"I can't help you. You can't call me."

"Where is Barrett? You recognized her photo. What happened to her?"

"I don't know. I don't know her."

"Are you involved in the murders?"

There was silence on the end of the line. Through the field glass, Madison could see that Crystal's mouth had dropped open.

"Crystal?"

"Murders?"

"Yes. Don't you realize that the people who are getting these trusts set up and life insurance policies issued are then getting murdered? Why else did you have to report six deaths within months of each other? You know they're being murdered, don't you? You must. Are you helping to murder them?"

Madison didn't really think Crystal had a direct hand in the murders. But she must know that people were being murdered. Madison was trying to shock her into confronting what she was involved in.

"I don't . . . I haven't . . . I just work here. My dad makes me. He owes Mr. Viceroy money." Crystal was holding the phone in the crook of her neck, and her hands were doing the fluttering dance about her face.

Madison hadn't met such a tragic figure as Crystal in a long time. If Madison weren't so desperate, she would've taken pity on her and left her alone.

"Crystal, I know you're only seventeen. You need to decide what kind of a person you are. Are you the kind of person who lets bad things happen because they are too afraid to act? Or are you the type of person who stops bad things from happening, when you have the power to do so? If you know about these murders and are helping to cover them up, that makes you an accessory to murder. That's a felony. That's a lot of years in prison. You have the power to stop these murders."

Through the field glass, Madison saw Crystal put her head down on the desk. Her voice came out muffled.

"I don't have any power."

"But you do, Crystal. You have power, and with what you know right now, you are not safe. You are right in the middle of a huge crime ring, and you could be the person that brings it to a halt. Or you could be the next person killed. Once murderers start killing, the next murder is easy, and people involved in the crime ring start dropping like flies. All you have to do is walk out right now and come down to my car. You can get in my car and you will be safe. I will protect you. I'm parked across the street in the gas station."

Crystal's head came up off the desk and she looked out the window.

"Do you see the black SUV? That's me. Just walk down the stairs. Pick up your purse, walk out the door, walk down the stairs, cross the street, and get in my car. That's all you have to do. Stand up and walk out the door. Right now. Stand up. Stand up."

"I can't."

"But you can. You can, Crystal. Stand up. Stand up right now."

Crystal hung up the phone.

Madison put her head on the steering wheel. Crystal probably had so much information. And Madison wasn't lying: Crystal wasn't safe. No one involved in this was safe as long as they had information that could expose these criminals.

What now? Madison picked her head up and looked through the field glass. Crystal had walked into the back of the office. To tell Viceroy about the call? Maybe.

She set the field glass in the console and stared through the windshield. Everything was spinning and this case was out of control. Madison felt out of control.

There was a nicely dressed woman pushing a stroller across the street, the old kind where the baby lies flat. It looked French. Nowadays strollers were made so that the stroller could be propped up or laid down, and then altered as the baby got older. This was one that Madison thought of as a perambulator, more like a rolling bed, with silver accents on the sides. Probably expensive and made to look old-fashioned. That was a La Jolla mother thing to do: pay a lot to make something look old. The woman was wearing Lululemon workout wear and Stella McCartney sneakers, so she was definitely a La Jolla mom. She was crossing the busy street to Madison's side, and Madison realized she was holding her breath until the woman and baby made it safely.

Madison wrenched her mind back to the case. She was sure she was missing who the ringleaders were. She had the minions right now, Crystal being the smallest minion. Viceroy was on someone's payroll. Evan was on someone's payroll. Maybe the thumb drive that Arlo had would tell her more. Madison was glad she'd stolen it, and she had no qualms about that now. But Crystal could have told her everything. Madison had to hope that Crystal would think about it and realize it was best to call Madison and tell her everything. Madison had left her card yesterday, so hopefully Crystal had saved it and would call.

The woman with the old-timey stroller was now walking east on Pearl, next to Madison's car. Madison watched as the woman reached down to adjust the baby's blanket; in doing so, she accidentally flipped it back. There was a plastic doll in the pram, not a baby. The doll's arm was sticking up and its eyes were wide open, huge and staring. Madison gasped audibly and put her hand to her mouth. It was like a horror movie. The woman flipped the blanket back and looked up nervously at Madison before increasing her pace and pushing the pram out of view.

The Ford Fusion turned left onto La Jolla Boulevard from Pearl, right in front of Madison. The driver swiveled in his seat as he drove past, staring at Madison.

They had found her again, and now they had added reinforcements.

The Fusion headed south on La Jolla Boulevard, so Madison turned right out of the gas station and headed in the opposite direction. She needed to figure out what she was going to do about this surveillance team, and she didn't want them following her while she was doing her figuring. In addition to the realization that the surveillance team could be dangerous, it had become another string to pull: if she could figure out who was following her or, more to the point, who had paid this surveillance team to follow her, she could find the ringleaders of this criminal organization.

Madison's head was spinning with everything she'd learned, and she was exhausted from her emotional outburst. She decided to drive five minutes to the Cove, a touristy part of La Jolla. It was touristy because it was beautiful. She would walk in the park among all of the sightseers. It would be safety in numbers, and she could look at the ocean and think. And she was already headed in that direction.

Her phone rang and she saw on the display that it was Tom, finally calling her back.

"Thank God."

"That's a nice reception, for once. So you're glad to hear from me?"

The normal banter that she had with Tom was exhausting in the best of circumstances. Now she just couldn't take it.

"Yes, I'm glad to hear from you. Do you have some information for me? Have the police made any progress on finding Barrett?"

"No, not much progress."

"I was afraid of that. Are they even working on it? Or do they think Travis is some dumb boyfriend who has been ghosted, and Barrett just doesn't want to talk to him?"

Madison found a parking space right along the boardwalk. It wasn't made of boards anymore, it was a cement sidewalk, but the term for the path that runs along a beach is still *boardwalk*. On the other side of the path were the bluffs that went down to the beach, a bit too steep to navigate here. Madison was so exhausted that she hadn't been listening to Tom, who had been talking.

"I'm sorry Tom, I got distracted. What did you say?"

"It's pretty hard to make progress on a missing person when the missing person has not been reported to the police as missing."

Madison stared through the windshield at the ocean. There wasn't a cloud in the sky. The difference in the blue between the ocean and the sky was one of perception; where did one end and the other begin? As she replayed over and over what Tom had just said, the scene before her shattered like it was stained glass and Tom's words had hit it with a hammer.

"Are you saying she wasn't reported missing?"

"Yes, that is what I am saying."

"Couldn't the boyfriend have walked in and reported it to a desk officer, and the desk officer didn't take him seriously so didn't take the report?" As soon as Madison said it, she realized that couldn't be the case: when she had seen Travis with his wife and then confronted him at the Pannikin, she'd asked him if the police had given him any updates. He had told her that he had been calling the police and they always told him they had no update for him.

Tom was answering her. "I mean, anything's possible, Madison."

However, Madison had answered her own question. That was not possible. Which meant only one thing: Travis was lying about reporting Barrett missing to the police.

The silver Ford Escape drove slowly past her car. Madison watched it in her rearview mirror, and saw the driver stare at the back of her car. Madison felt hunted.

"Madison?"

"Tom, I might need your help. I'm not sure yet." Anytime she got Tom involved, it was like killing a fly with a sledgehammer. He would come in with guns blazing and she might not find out who was following her. It wasn't against the law to follow someone, something Madison was thankful for since it was her full-time job. He couldn't arrest them for following her. He could, however, scare them, and Madison would never find out who they worked for.

"Okay, what's going on?"

The Ford Escape had continued down the road, and Madison could no longer see it after the road turned. The driver was probably notifying his team member and they would set up to follow her as she left this location. She backed out of the parking space and drove in the opposite direction.

"I . . . I'll let you know."

"What is going on, Madison? This is starting to sound fishy. Who are you working for?"

If Madison answered those questions, Tom would start to take over this investigation. And now she needed to figure out why Travis had not reported Barrett's disappearance to the police, and she needed to decide if *she* was going to report it to the police. Yes, of course, she needed to report it to the police. But she didn't want to do it in an offhand manner. She wanted to go home, compile a report, and submit it to the police so that they would have all the information in one place. Otherwise she would be in an interview room answering questions for hours, instead of looking for Barrett. She was close to figuring out who the ringleaders of this operation were and exposing them. She no longer felt the panic of finding Barrett before something happened to her, since Madison was certain something already had. However, she did need to figure out what was going on before something happened to herself.

"I have to go Tom."

"No you don't. You need to explain to me exactly what is happening, who you are working for, and I want all the information on this girl who is missing."

"That's my other call coming in, I'll call you back."

"No it isn't! You're using that as an excuse—"

Madison used the button on her steering wheel to disconnect the call. Tom was great if you could point and shoot him. He was not great if you gave him information and let him wander. He would completely take over, and Madison was not ready for that to happen.

So the police had not been working on this for a week, as she had previously thought. The only information about Barrett's disappearance, these insurance fraud crimes, all of it, was what Madison had developed. She pulled into a parking garage in the center of the village. It took her down underneath a building. The surveillance team would not find her by just driving by. She picked up her phone and texted Travis:

I need to meet you right now. It's an emergency. At the shack at Windansea.

She sat and waited for him to answer. There would be a lot of people at the beach, many of them surfers she knew. Dave might even be there. It was a safe space for her to meet Travis. If he tried anything he would quickly learn that the laid-back, pot-smoking image of surfers was a mistaken one. And if he tried something in front of Dave, he would sorely regret it.

Why was he lying about reporting Barrett missing? When she'd found out he was married, she'd angrily confronted him; she couldn't afford to do that now. Being married was a minor sin compared to failing to file this report. The revelation made Travis suspect number one in her mind, and she had to be careful in how she approached him.

Her phone pinged. It was Travis.

On my way.

Madison started her car and drove up the ramp out of the parking structure. As she drove through the Village she kept an eye out for the surveillance team, but they must've been down at the Cove, looking for her where they'd last seen her. It wouldn't be too long before they went back to Windansea to see if she'd gone home, but she probably had a few minutes. They had likely seen her with Travis before, so she wasn't too worried about that; however, the big question remained: Were these people dangerous?

The traffic in La Jolla was always bad, but it was now the beginning of rush hour. There was nothing worse than entitled people in Porsche Panameras and Ferraris feeling they were better than the other people at the four-way stop sign. Madison had to control her road rage under the best of circumstances, and she was getting angrier as she got closer to her meeting with Travis. She wasn't going to yell at him, but she was going to find out what was going on, once and for all. Her phone rang, and the display indicated a number she didn't recognize. She pressed the button on the steering wheel to answer the phone.

"Madison Kelly."

"This is Crystal."

Crystal had changed her mind. She was going to tell Madison everything. Madison really needed a break. She was about to cross Pearl, and she could easily turn right and go to Viceroy's office.

"Hi Crystal. You want me to pick you up at work?"

"No. I'm not there. I left."

"That's good! I'm glad you left. Are you at home?"

Madison could hear voices in the background, but she couldn't make out what kind of place Crystal was calling from.

"No, I'm not at home. I can't talk right now. I just wanted you to know—I have to call you back."

"You wanted me to know what, Crystal? Can you tell me something right now? Where is Barrett? Can you just tell me that?"

"I have to go."

"I can pick you up wherever you are. Where are you? I'll come and get you." Madison was saying anything to keep Crystal on the phone.

Crystal disconnected the call.

"Shit."

Madison redialed the number.

"Answer. Answer. Answer."

The call went to a cell phone voicemail: "Your call has been forwarded to an automatic voice messaging system . . ."

Madison yelled and hit the steering wheel. She felt like she was losing her mind. She took five deep breaths, breathing in deep from the lower part of her diaphragm, and letting each breath out slowly. She was going to have to wait for Crystal to call her back when Crystal was ready to talk. At least she had called. That meant she could call again. Patience had never been Madison's strong suit.

There were no parking spaces available in the lot, not surprising considering there were only about ten of them, and it was prime surfing time. She found a spot along the curb across from the boardwalk. She didn't see Travis's car, but he could be parked farther down. Dave's Jeep was in the lot.

She locked the car and crossed the street. She found a spot on a bench facing the ocean and the shack down below. She didn't see Travis anywhere, but he would be able to see her when he arrived. She pulled her legs up onto the bench and sat on them, cross-legged. She took in a huge breath of ocean air, letting it out slowly.

Madison examined the surfers in the water, but she could never tell which one was Dave. They were just bobbing heads and wetsuits, some of them sitting on their boards waiting for a wave, a couple of them riding a wave in. The late afternoon sun was getting closer to the horizon; it always turned the ocean here purple. The wind was chilly as it whipped off the water.

"There you are!" Travis had come up behind her.

Madison stood as he joined her. Dave had told her that while the surfers were sitting on their surfboards waiting for a wave, they could see everything on the beach and up on the street, even if the people on the street couldn't see the surfers well. She knew that Dave had seen her.

"Hi."

Travis chuckled. "Uh-oh. Are we going to have a problem because of what happened last night? Look, I'm an asshole. I'm sorry, I acted out on a feeling. I was caught up in the moment. I swear it won't happen again."

"It's not that. Why did you lie to me about reporting Barrett's disappearance to the police?"

Travis stared at her. He had a blank expression on his face. "Lie to you?"

"I have friends in the police department, Travis. I'm surprised it took me two days to figure out that you had lied. I just hadn't had a chance to speak to my friend. He checked. Barrett has not been reported missing. Can you explain this to me?"

Travis sighed and sat down on the bench. "It was dumb of me to think I could hide that from you. I'm an idiot, as usual."

"Actually, I think I'm the idiot. You have made a fool of me. Why this lie? Did you have something to do with her disappearance?"

Travis threw his arms up. "No! I keep telling you! Why would I pay you to find her if I had done something to her! That's not the reason I lied."

One of the surfers out on his surfboard was waving at her. She waved back. She still didn't recognize him at this distance, but it must be Dave.

"Okay, tell me the reason then."

"Look at me. I'm having an affair with this girl. I'm cheating on my wife with her. I don't want my wife to know; I love my kids, and she's threatened to take them away from me. Now the girl goes missing. If I report her missing to the police, who is the first suspect? Who are they going to look at right away?"

Madison knew he was right. "You, clearly."

"Exactly. Me. And I wouldn't blame them. I would be the most obvious suspect if I walked into a police station and reported her missing. They would think, 'Oh, he's reporting her missing so that we don't think he did it. But he killed her because she was going to tell his wife,' or whatever. I didn't want them to waste time on me. I just wanted her found. So I thought if I hired the best investigator I could find, you, then any time that normally would be wasted on me, would instead be spent trying to find her. And that's why I didn't tell you about being married, either."

Madison had to admit he was right. Everything he was saying was exactly what would've happened. In fact, it was now probably going to happen when she reported this to the police.

Travis stood up. He moved so that he was in front of her, stooping slightly to look directly into her eyes. "I swear to you, I had nothing to do with her disappearance. All I want is for you to find her. I have paid you five thousand dollars. I will give you another five thousand dollars right now. I just want her found. Every moment that is wasted on me is another moment that she could be being tortured or God knows what else."

People were starting to congregate for sunset. It was a Windansea tradition to bring plastic cups with cocktails, wine, and beer down to the boardwalk and watch the sunset in quiet camaraderie with your neighbors. It was one of Madison's favorite parts of living there.

Madison didn't want to tell Travis that she had figured out Barrett must be dead. There would be time for that. If she were completely honest with herself, the truth was that she just couldn't take his emotional reaction to that news right now. She was tired. She could tell him when she had firmed up her theories more and had had a good night's sleep.

A Cadillac SUV pulled up adjacent to the lot and stopped. This particular stretch of Neptune was a notoriously slow drive; surfers often paused there to look at the ocean and see if there were any waves worth surfing, and if so, then they watched the sets of waves in order to time them and work out the best way to surf them. Occasionally, an out-of-towner would honk at a slowed vehicle. Those individuals were told to go up to La Jolla

Boulevard, the large thoroughfare that ran parallel with Neptune, if they didn't like it. As such, Madison's attention was not necessarily pulled to a slowing vehicle. But when the driver rolled down the window and spoke, she and Travis both turned their heads.

"Hey, is that you Travis?"

Travis looked at Madison and then back at the driver. "Hey, what's up?"

"Who's the lovely lady?"

Travis seemed uncomfortable, but the guy just seemed happy to see an old friend.

"My name is Madison Kelly—hi."

"Madison, that's a great name. My name is Randy Lemond. So, Travis, what's new?"

A car came up behind the Cadillac and in true Windansea fashion, just waited. There was a surfboard on the roof of the waiting car, and the driver and passenger were staring at the ocean and appeared to be discussing it. A middle-aged couple with polka dot–decorated plastic cups crossed the street, arm in arm, in front of the Cadillac, strolling over to the beach side, and then stood holding hands in preparation for sunset.

"Not much," Travis said. "Just working hard."

"Okay, well, don't work too hard, now. Nice to meet you, Madison."

"Nice to meet you too."

Randy drove away, but the car with the surfers behind him didn't move, because they were still talking about the waves.

"Not a close friend?" Madison asked.

"He knows my wife. He doesn't know about Barrett. I think he was giving me a hard time because I was standing with a girl."

"I see."

"Look, like I was saying, I just want you to find Barrett. I know that my actions have seemed unusual, but things aren't always what they seem. There can be an innocent explanation."

Madison was silent. Ultimately, it didn't matter, because at this point she was going to find Barrett no matter what. She had played her cards close to the vest with Travis anyway, and she would just continue to do so, not revealing all of the investigation details to him; it was probably better to be that way with clients anyway, to keep them from micromanaging the investigation. Besides, what he was saying was true: he was paying her to find Barrett, which he wouldn't do if he had killed her. His explanation about his lies really did make sense. She would see this through to the end and for the time being take Travis at his word.

Apparently Travis mistook Madison's silence for judgment. He suddenly started yelling.

"What the fuck? What is it about you that makes you so distrustful? I have made mistakes, but I have been dedicated in my desire to find her. Nothing I have done has demonstrated anything other than my wanting to find her. And yet you stand there judging me, wasting time on me, and I'm fucking sick of it!" Travis's chin started to shake.

My God, is he going to start crying?

He had been gesturing wildly with his arms while he spoke. Madison looked out to the water and saw a surfer soaring on a wave, heading toward the shore. As she watched, she recognized Dave's shoulders. He didn't surf over the top of the wave like he would have had he planned to paddle back out and catch another wave. He stayed on the wave as it got smaller and smaller, taking it all the way in to the shore. He was coming to see what was going on.

Madison looked down at the ground. People weren't perfect. People were flawed. In books and movies there were bad guys and good guys, and there was a clear distinction between the two. But in real life, there were good guys who had bad qualities, and bad guys who had good qualities. Everything in real life was on a gradient scale of good and bad. There were no absolutes. Travis was just a good guy with bad qualities.

She looked up at him. "Okay. Okay. Calm down. I believe you. Look, I'm working hard for you. My God I even *stole* something for you yesterday."

Travis stared at her. "You stole something? What did you steal?"

Madison hadn't wanted to share that; it just came out. "Yes, I did. Never mind, I just mean I believe you and I'm doing everything I can to find her."

"Am I going to get in trouble for you stealing something?"

"No, no, it's fine. Really. Forget I said it."

She looked over at Dave's progress. He was pushing his surfboard the rest of the way out of the water.

She continued. "But I need you to tell me right now, are there any other lies? Is there anything else I don't know, right now, that I should know to help me find Barrett?"

Travis wiped an errant tear off his face as if it were a bug that had landed there.

"Considering you found my two lies in two days, no, that's it. There's nothing else. And at the very least it proves that my confidence in you was not mistaken."

"Well, that's true, I *am* really good." Madison laughed.

Dave was making his way up the path dug into the small bluff from years of surfers going from the street to the sand. Madison turned and waved.

"Hey, what's up?" Dave said. He scrabbled up the last bit of bluff holding his surfboard.

"Hey," Madison said. "This is my client, Travis Moore. Travis, this is Dave."

"Nice to meet you," Dave said. "I would shake your hand but . . ." Dave held up his hands to show they were covered in water and sand.

"No problem. Nice to meet you."

"So what's going on?" Dave sounded friendly, but it didn't fool Madison. He was doing an ancient masculinity ritual of checking the current threat, both physical and emotional. If they had been dogs, Dave would've been sniffing Travis's loins.

"Not much," Madison said. "We were just discussing strategy."

Dave had to tip his head back slightly to look up at Travis, which was strange to see. Madison was used to Dave being taller than everyone. Nevertheless, Madison had never met anyone who could take Dave in a fight; in fact, she wasn't sure that person existed. So she wanted to disperse this little meeting before things got any more tense.

She spoke to Travis. "Anyway, I'll give you a call tomorrow."

"Are we good?" Travis said to Madison.

Madison smiled at him. "Yes, we're good."

Travis smiled back, and she felt that now familiar shot of adrenaline. *What* was *that, and why did it keep happening? And right in front of Dave?*

Dave stood silently, watching their exchange. He had the slightest furrow to his brow.

"Will you call me in the morning with an update?" Travis asked.

"Yes. I'll call you."

Travis told Dave it was nice to meet him, and then he walked down the boardwalk, presumably to where he had parked his car.

"So, what's up with that guy?"

"He's okay, he has a missing girlfriend and he's a little emotional."

"It looked weird from the water. Like he was yelling at you."

Madison put her arms around Dave's neck. "My hero."

She hugged him and didn't care that it got her shirt wet. Looking over the top of his shoulder, she saw Travis had stopped and was looking back, watching them. He turned and walked away.

Dave released her and kissed her nose. "What are you doing now? Do you wanna get something to eat?"

Madison shook some sand off her jacket. She was so exhausted from her day that she couldn't think straight. The next thing she needed to do was type up everything for the police; however, first she wanted to see Arlo and get the thumb drive data and whatever he'd managed to recover from Barrett's cell phone. She didn't want to mention Arlo's name to the police, and if she said in her report that she had taken the electronics somewhere, they would want to know where. If she just presented them with the data recovered, she could keep Arlo out of it. She would call Arlo first thing in the morning and see if he'd made progress. And maybe by then Crystal would have called her back and spilled everything, and she would have that to add to the report. After that, if the police questioned Travis, oh well, but they would have a lot of leads to follow up on, leads that were way more interesting than the boyfriend-is-the-first-suspect trope. She could do that much for him.

The sun had set, and her neighbors were turning and walking back home in the twilight. She should go home and at least get started on the report, but she was just too tired. She didn't want to eat, either.

"Would you understand if I wanted to just go home and go to bed?"

Dave wrapped his towel around his waist. "Why didn't you introduce me as your boyfriend to that guy?"

Oh my God. Really? He was going to have a relationship conversation with her right now? And it was so ironic: he was the biggest confirmed bachelor in town. They hadn't discussed not seeing other people, although Madison wasn't, but she assumed Dave felt free to sample the wares of La Jolla whenever he wanted.

"He is just a client."

"Okay, so why didn't you introduce me as your boyfriend?"

"Because I'm not seventeen?"

Madison turned to walk to her car, but his voice stopped her: "There are other women I could see, you know."

Madison turned back. "Yes, Dave, I know that. I'm not seeing him."

Madison could be a jealous person, which was why she cut off that particular emotion and refused to feel it. Dave was probably one of the most sought-after guys in town: family money, champion surfer, and really hot. She was sure there was a long line of girls waiting to take her place. And some were probably working on it right now.

But she wasn't good at talking about her feelings. "We just have to trust each other."

Dave closed the gap between them and reached for her hand. He put his forehead on her forehead.

"When are you going to be done with this case?"

"When I find this girl." She tipped her head back. "You realize that you're whining about me seeing some guy who I'm not seeing, and meanwhile there's a girl that is probably dead, after being tortured for information?"

Dave stepped backward and looked down at their feet. "No, I guess I wasn't thinking of that."

"Okay. So can I just be alone tonight with my thoughts?"

Dave kissed her and turned to walk to his Jeep.

Madison called after him. "Text me later?"

He spoke over his shoulder as he continued walking. "Sure."

Madison stood on the path overlooking the ocean while Dave loaded his Jeep with his surfboard and drove away. The sun was gone and it was dark and cold. She wrapped her flak jacket tighter around her and folded her arms. When that didn't help block the chill she unzipped the hood from the neckline and put the hood over her head. She let the cold wind straight from the ocean blow on her face, making her nose and eyes red.

She walked over and sat on the bench and tried to clear her mind. The neighbors had all gone home, and there were only a couple stragglers in the lot talking about their surf session.

Barrett was dead, Travis was acting weird but she still believed he wanted to find Barrett, and she had a huge criminal organization that was tracking her every move. All in a day's work. She needed to go home and write all of this down and get it to the police. But she couldn't move. She didn't even have the energy to look for the surveillance team.

"A beach girl is always at the beach."

Madison's head flew up and she saw Tom standing next to his Crown Victoria in the parking lot.

Madison smiled. "You know what Tom? You're actually a sight for sore eyes."

Tom walked over and sat down next to her on the bench. His hand accidentally touched her hand, and at first it was awkward. She didn't want to yank her hand away, but she didn't want there to be any confusion in the relationship—like there had been before. He fixed it by patting her hand and then folding his hands in his lap.

"I'm a sight for sore eyes, huh? Why is that?"

When a strong man was kind to her it made her want to cry. A psychologist could probably have a field day with that. Madison thought that probably, because she acted tough and like she needed no one with a chip on her shoulder, a guy could break through all of that by just being steadfast and kind. Was her natural state grief, and she was just meandering through life waiting for a shoulder to cry on?

"I've had a rough day."

"Is this the missing person's case? It sounds hinky. What's the deal? Is she missing or not?"

Madison wanted to tell him the entire story, right now, right here. He was listening, he was in a sympathetic mood, and she could tell him everything. She could hand it over and walk away, her responsibility to Barrett met. She got her five grand, let the police find Barrett. It was so tempting.

But then it wouldn't be her case anymore. And that meant something to her. She wanted to find Barrett. It was beyond professional pride: this was personal. She had made a promise to Barrett and she wanted to keep it. If she told Tom everything right now, the case would be out of her hands immediately. It would be handed out in pieces to the various law enforcement agencies that handled the different aspects of this case: insurance fraud, racketeering, missing persons, and likely homicide. It wasn't that she thought she could do a better job than those departments, it was that she wanted to finish this case because she had started it. And she didn't want to be pulled in twenty different directions over the next week while everybody got her story and began their own investigations, constantly asking her questions along the way, filling out their paperwork, consuming all of her time. If she typed it up in a report, she could keep working on the case while the huge law enforcement machine oiled its parts and got itself into motion. They would have a document to which she could refer them, and she would remain free to investigate her case.

"Yes, it's the missing person's case. Yes, she's missing."

Tom stretched his arms back. His shoulders were huge. "You want to tell me about it?"

Yes, Madison thought. *I want to tell you everything.*

"I will. I just . . . I actually want to write it all down so you have it all in one place. There are a lot of moving parts to this."

Tom patted her on the shoulder. It was brotherly and intimate at the same time.

"Sounds good."

Madison knew he wouldn't say that if he had any idea what she had discovered. But it was only a matter of hours. She would have a report for him by tomorrow afternoon.

She sat forward on the bench and looked back at him. Such a handsome man. His dark hair was slicked back, and his brown eyes were huge. He had dark brown eyelashes that any girl would kill for. But he was married, and there was so much water under the bridge. That ship had sailed.

"Well, I'm going to go home and go to bed."

Tom got a twinkle in his eye, and Madison could tell he was about to say something flirtatious or with an innuendo of some kind. She cut him off by standing up and walking away.

"So that's it? 'I'm going to bed' and you walk away? I don't even get to say goodbye?"

He was kidding, but he sounded slightly irritated, which made Madison think he had been about to try something, and she had stopped it by walking away. Which had been her intention.

She spoke over her shoulder as she crossed the street to her car.

"I'm tired, and you need to get home to your wife."

Tom shook his head. "Always gotta bring up my wife."

Madison opened the car door and got in the driver's seat. "Somebody has to."

She shut the door and started the car. Tom watched from the boardwalk as she drove away.

Chapter Eighteen

Thursday 7:05 AM

Madison opened her eyes. She could tell the time based on the way the sun was slanting through the blinds behind her bed. Her apartment was silent. She could hear the faint sounds of the waves. There were a few creaks from the old building settling. Home.

And then she remembered Barrett. Madison was no longer on a rescue mission; she was on a recovery mission. And the crime ring. Six people dead. She had a lot of report writing to do.

And Dave. She hadn't heard from him after he'd left her at the beach.

She rolled over and texted Arlo.

Any luck? Really need the data from that thumb drive. And the cell phone. You're my only hope, Obi-Wan Kenobi.

Arlo was a *Star Wars* superfan. He had an actual storm trooper outfit and went dressed up to Comic-Con each year. Apparently there was an entire code of conduct for those wishing to dress up as storm troopers. It was a subsection of life with which Madison was not familiar. In any event, she hoped that her *Star Wars* reference would get her some preferential treatment.

She doubted Arlo was up this early, or if he was he hadn't gone to bed yet. He'd get the text when he woke up, and she could start on the report for the police and add the data from the electronics when she got it. As she lay there contemplating life, she wondered whether she should try to call Crystal again. She didn't have Crystal's home number and it was too early to catch her at the office, but she could try to redial the number Crystal had called her from the night before; that might be her cell. Maybe she would call at nine AM. Next thought: Should she call Haley and tell her everything she had learned after their meeting yesterday? She would later.

She got out of bed and went to make coffee. After she had set the coffee maker to brew, she opened all of the windows. Another beautiful, crystal-clear autumn morning in La Jolla. The trees were moving gently in the breeze. When she was little she had wondered if the leaves could feel the breeze, and if so, did it feel good, like when someone tickles your back?

She turned on the local news for background noise and walked over to the whiteboard. She had learned so much yesterday that it would take her a long time to update this board. It would be faster to just type the report for the police. A headline on the news program made its way into her consciousness, and she started paying attention halfway through their announcement.

> *She is estimated to be in her early twenties, and police have no information as to how long she has been dead. This is a developing story, and we will have more for you in the next hour.*

They had started talking about something else, and yet Madison was not moving from her spot on the floor. She had been waiting for this, she had known it was not just a possibility but had become a probability, and yet she still wasn't ready for it. They had found Barrett. It must be. She turned and sat down at her desk. She often got strength from objects, and she put her hands flat on the table that her grandfather had made for her grandmother when they had first gotten married. It had been in Madison's house as a child growing up. So many dinners, so many difficult conversations, so much history, so much life, ingrained like old polish. She turned on the monitor and selected Google Chrome to browse the internet. She searched "body found San Diego" and looked at the search results.

There were many, so she picked one from a local newspaper.

> *The body of a young woman was found last night floating in the water near Fiesta Island. At about 8:00 p.m. a visitor discovered the body and called 911. Police and fire rescue personnel responded and removed the body from the water. Authorities said that little is known about the victim, other than she is a Caucasian in her early 20s. An autopsy will be performed.*

So, it had happened. She'd had her emotional breakdown yesterday at the realization that Barrett was likely dead. She didn't need to have another one. She texted Tom:

I need to talk to you. It's urgent. Please call.

Should she call Travis? No. Let's wait until Tom had confirmed it. It would be a terrible conversation; no point in having it until the identity had been confirmed. Her phone rang. It was Tom. She started talking as soon as she picked up.

"Listen. The news is saying that a body was found in the water off Fiesta Island."

"Yeah. I didn't catch that case, I'm not up." Tom was referring to the fact that the teams of homicide investigators took turns taking cases.

"Okay. I need to know if it's my girl."

There was a pause as Tom grasped what she was saying.

"Right. Your missing girl. Okay. Give me her particulars." It was one thing she appreciated about Tom: he didn't waste time asking stupid questions.

"I'll text it to you. How quickly do you think you can find out?"

"I don't know how much identifying information there was on the body. I don't know what state the body was in or anything. I'm just gonna have to call and see. If they need dental records to identify the body, it's going to be a while."

The thought of Barrett's body being in such a decomposed state that they needed dental records to identify the body made Madison want to vomit. It felt like it was Madison who was waiting to be identified.

"All right. I'll text you."

They disconnected and Madison quickly texted him Barrett's description, the information on her Harley-Davidson tattoo, along with her Social Security number and driver's license number, not that those last two would help.

She set the phone down just as it pinged with a new text.

We're looking forward to seeing you today!

The text was so cheerful that Madison was momentarily taken aback. Then she remembered: her doctor's appointment. Nothing like facing death in the face of death.

She set the phone down and went outside onto her landing in her pajamas. She took a big deep breath of sea air and bent over, placing her palms flat on the landing. She released the muscles in her back, but there was a constricting tightness in her chest where the implants were shoving her pectoral muscles out of place. She concentrated on releasing her pectoral muscles, but they wouldn't relax. Up until now, vanity had won out: she would rather have Barbie boobs than strength and flexibility. She was really starting to doubt that decision.

She stood up and looked out at the water. The Ford Fusion came down the alley from Nautilus Street.

There were two guys in the car this time. They were both looking up at her apartment, and when they saw her looking back they quickly averted their gaze; the passenger looked out the passenger window and the driver looked out the driver's side window. If it weren't for the fact that Madison had started to get nervous about their intentions, it would have been comical.

Madison walked back inside. She didn't know who these people were, and she didn't know how dangerous they were; but given the fact that she was now investigating six murders, chances were they were dangerous. She needed to get the police involved, so that report needed to be written. She texted Arlo again:

You're probably not up yet, but I really need that information.

She didn't know why she'd bothered to text him again; he would answer her when he saw her text, or else when he had information for her.

She decided to get ready for her doctor's appointment. That was about the only thing that was certain in her life today. She took a shower and washed her hair. She put on a black T-shirt with "Listen to Bob" (for Marley) on the front, jeans, and her flak jacket. She laced her Doc Martens, and then she paused and stared at the spot on the floor next to her bed that contained the safe.

She was a firm believer in a citizen's right to bear arms. But with every right comes responsibility. If a person was going to have a gun, they needed to know everything about that gun, how to shoot it, and how to handle it safely. Her father had taught her about guns from a young age, including an adage that she had never forgotten: *There is no such thing as an unloaded gun.* If you treated every gun as if it were loaded, you would never have an "accidental" shooting. Guns didn't go off accidentally: you had to pull the trigger. So you needed to know not to pull the trigger unless you planned to kill someone.

Madison went to the shooting range once a month. She hated the sound of the gun firing. She hated the feel of the gun when it fired. But she had a gun, and so she had to be responsible and keep up her skills. She also had a permit to carry a concealed weapon, which was difficult to get in California. However, just because she had the permit didn't mean that she always carried her gun.

If someone came into her apartment in the middle of the night, she had no problem shooting them and asking questions later. No one should be in her apartment in the middle of the night without her permission; Dave knew better than to sneak up on her. It was easy to decide to shoot a strange man standing over her bed at two AM. However, out in the wild, there were a million decisions that had to be made in a split second: Does this person present an immediate threat to my life? Am I willing to kill this person and take them away from their family and friends? If I shoot this person is there anyone standing nearby that I could hit accidentally, thereby killing an innocent person? All of these questions had to be asked before the gun was pulled out; once the gun was out, she had to have made the decision to shoot. That was also how to prevent "accidental" shootings—don't pull the gun out unless the decision to kill had already been made. But if Madison didn't have a weapon on her, what kinds of decisions would she make instead? Madison had known people who failed to extricate themselves from dangerous situations because they had a false sense of security due to being armed. She would rather use her wits to get out of a situation instead of taking someone's life.

Even though people were dying and she was clearly in the middle of a murder investigation, she still didn't want to carry her gun today. If she found herself confronted with danger, she wanted to use her wits to get out of it. When she had gone to Idaho, she'd known she had to get a teenage girl away from a dangerous man, and she had needed a literal arsenal to help her do that. Today she was going out on a sunny California day and had no plans to confront criminals. She hoped she didn't regret her decision to leave the gun at home.

She grabbed her purse, set the alarm, and headed out the door.

She decided not to lose her surveillance team on the way to the doctor. She was going to an office building in the village of La Jolla surrounded by hundreds of people, so she would be safe. It was still to her advantage to let them think that she hadn't spotted them, and every time she made evasive maneuvers they would suspect that she knew. As she drove north on La Jolla Boulevard, she saw the Fusion two cars behind her.

She got to the office building and parked in the underground garage. As she got off the elevator on the third floor, her phone pinged with a text. It was Tom.

It isn't her.

Madison was so shocked she had to lean against the wall for a second. It wasn't Barrett? Madison had been so sure it would be. She didn't know whether to be relieved or upset. In a way, she supposed she had been hoping she was going to be able to bring Barrett home. Now Barrett was still out there, needing to be found. She paused another moment for a thought for the poor girl whose body had been found, and for the girl's family.

Okay. Good to know. She sent the text to Tom. Then she straightened up and walked into the doctor's office.

"I'm going to need to do a biopsy."

Madison liked her doctor. Dr. Schultz was no nonsense, but managed to have an underlying kindness that pervaded all of her blunt words.

"I figured. But I do have a question."

Dr. Schultz had pressed the button for a nurse to come in the room, and together they were preparing a tray of medical instruments.

"Now is the time. What is your question?"

"If this turns out to be cancer, do the implants have to come out?"

Dr. Schultz came over and put her hands on Madison's knees. Nothing made you feel more vulnerable than sitting in a paper gown on an examination table. Because of Madison's size, the paper gowns never went all the way around her. So not only were they made of flimsy paper, they didn't even cover her. Madison had an urge to just take it off and sit naked on the table.

"Short answer? Yes. It can depend, but in your case I'm going to just get you prepared for the inevitable. Yes, they would need to come out. Doesn't mean you couldn't do some type of reconstruction in the future. But for right now, the answer is yes."

Madison was silent. In a way, it was somewhat of a relief because of her love–hate relationship with the implants. But would she still feel like a girl?

"Can we do first things first?" Dr. Schultz said. "Let's do the biopsy. Then let's worry about what can happen after that. It may be negative for cancer."

"Sounds good."

The nurse handed Dr. Schultz a syringe and needle filled with the numbing agent that would be injected into Madison's skin. Madison looked up at the ceiling so as to avoid looking at the needle. She winced as the needle went in. Madison had a high tolerance for pain, but that didn't mean she didn't feel it. She was strangely sensitive to touch and pain while still being able to take a lot of it. The needle hurt for a few more moments, and then the lidocaine took over and she was numb.

Dr. Schultz added a few things to the tray and then turned back to Madison. "Do you feel this pinprick?"

Madison was still looking at the ceiling in order to avoid eyeing the medical instruments. She had found that if she didn't watch what was happening, it made it a little bit easier.

"No, I don't feel that."

"Okay, I'm going to do the biopsy now."

Madison could feel tugging on her chest, but it didn't hurt because it was numb. It was a strange sensation. She thought about how she had gotten to this point. The first abnormal mammogram. The ultrasound to follow up on the abnormal mammogram. The four punch biopsies, done in the clinic, of suspicious areas inside her right and left breasts. The news that she had to have an excisional biopsy, a real surgery done under general anesthesia, to remove an area of abnormal tissue found in the biopsy. Because they couldn't determine from the initial biopsy if it was cancer, they'd needed to get more tissue out, which required an operation. Each step of the way Madison had had to get used to what it could mean. Doctors never say, "You have cancer"; they tell you, "We found something and now we need to . . ." until you're scheduled for a bilateral mastectomy.

Just before the excisional biopsy, Madison had taken a trip to Palm Springs for the weekend. She had stayed at a resort where there were families with children swimming in the pool from morning until night. She'd been in a huge suite with a kitchen, all by herself. It ended up being sort of lonely, but necessary. She had taken herself to the movies, ending up in an empty parking lot in the middle of a weekday with time to spare before the movie started. The enormity of what she was facing finally hit her, and she'd sobbed for fifteen minutes at the loss of the life she'd known before, and the new one that was to come. There was no more "normal"; there was only new. Nothing would ever be normal again. Once she had gotten on the other side of that realization, things had gotten easier.

She hadn't cried when Dr. Schultz told her the excisional biopsy had shown cancer. She hadn't cried when the geneticist told her she had a gene mutation that had likely caused her mother's death from breast cancer and indicated her own increased chances. She hadn't cried when she decided to have a bilateral mastectomy; she wanted to stop worrying, she wanted to stop constantly looking for changes and recurrences.

It hadn't occurred to her that it could come back.

"All done!"

Her phone pinged with a text. It was Tom.

They found this girl's purse. Her phone was in it. The last person she called was you.

What? For a minute Madison thought Tom was telling her that it was Barrett after all, but Madison had never met Barrett—so Barrett's phone wouldn't have Madison's phone number in it. Would it? Of course not.

Madison texted back. *Who is the girl? Have they identified her?*

"I should have the results for you in a few days. Try not to think about it. I know that's hard, but try and stay busy."

Madison looked up at Dr. Schultz. It took her a moment to understand what she was saying. Right, the biopsy.

"Okay. Yes, I'm busy and that should help. Will you call me either way?"

"Yes," Dr. Schultz said. "I will definitely call you either way."

Madison looked down at her chest for the first time. There was a thick piece of gauze folded over and taped to her chest. A little bit of blood was seeping through the gauze.

"Don't take a shower for twenty-four hours. Don't exercise for forty-eight hours, just because it will start to bleed again. Don't lift more than ten pounds for forty-eight hours. You can take a shower tomorrow and just let the water run over the incision. Then put a bandage on it. But take it easy for a few days, okay? I just cut a piece of you out. It's small, but it's still a surgery." The nurse handed her some large bandages with adhesive around the edges, along with little packages of petroleum jelly.

"Okay, thank you." Madison stood up from the table and the paper covering from the table came up with her, sticking to every spot on her body where she'd been sitting. Apparently she had been sweating. She pulled it off her legs and butt. If Madison ran a medical clinic she would make things less embarrassing for the patients.

Dr. Schultz and the nurse walked out of the room after saying their goodbyes. Madison got dressed, her mind back to what Tom had texted her. Some girl had called Madison, and then ended up dead. Were they sure it was the dead girl's purse and the dead girl's phone? Her phone pinged with a message from Tom.

Crystal Ladessa.

Chapter Nineteen

Thursday 2:21 PM

Madison sat in the driver's seat of her car, in the basement of the doctor's office building. She held her cell phone in her hand, staring at the screen, trying to make it say something different.

Crystal Ladessa.

Madison had gotten Crystal killed. Crystal had called to give her information on the crime ring and someone had discovered it. If Madison had never walked into Crystal's life, she'd be alive right now. Madison had used Crystal because she was the weakest link. She thought she could get Crystal to turn. Instead she had gotten her killed.

Tom texted again. *Do you know this girl?*

Madison thought back to being in the office with Crystal. Crystal frantic, Crystal running around, Crystal being overwhelmed.

I'm only seventeen, she had said.

And now she was dead.

Do you? Tom texted again.

Madison had wanted to find Barrett because she had been hired to do it, and probably because Barrett reminded Madison of herself. And in the course of that she had decided to find and expose the crime ring.

But now, *now*, Madison was going to find these people if it was the last thing she did on this earth. She was going to find these people if she died trying. They would pay for what they had done to Crystal.

Crystal, who was only seventeen.

Tom again. *Madison. Answer me.*

Madison started the car. Her phone went off again.

"Jesus, Tom, give me a minute!" she screamed into the interior of her car. She had to keep it together or she could really lose it right about now.

But the text wasn't from Tom; it was from Robyn.

Call me.

Madison pulled out of the parking garage onto Ivanhoe Street and turned south. The Ford Fusion came in right behind her. They were being bold because they thought they had gotten away with tailing her for several days without her seeing them.

But she was not in the mood.

She made a quick right turn onto Wall Street and then an immediate right into the post office parking lot. The Fusion made the turn onto Wall with her, and when the driver saw that she had parked in the lot for the post office, he pulled into a parking space at the curb in front of the post office door. Madison jumped out of the car and walked quickly into the door of the post office facing Wall Street, right in front of the Fusion. She pretended she didn't see them.

The post office was on a corner, so there were two doors: one on Wall, where Madison had entered, and a door facing Ivanhoe Street. She walked immediately to that door and out of it. She rounded the corner and walked straight for the passenger door of the Fusion. The guy sitting in the passenger seat was saying something to the driver, so his head was turned away from Madison's approach. But the driver saw her and smacked the passenger on the arm. The driver started the car in an attempt to get away from Madison, but there was traffic behind him and he couldn't pull out of the parking space. Madison made it to the passenger window just as the walkie-talkie in the passenger's lap went off.

Abort! Abort! Subject is approaching your car. Abort!

The passenger looked down at the radio in his lap as if it were speaking in tongues. The driver was so startled by the radio transmission that he stopped trying to back up. He put his foot on the brake and stared at the radio in the passenger's lap. They looked at each other with their mouths hanging open.

"Who the fuck are you and who do you work for?" Madison said it so loudly that a woman walking her poodle stopped and stared.

Good, Madison thought. It might be helpful to have a witness so she didn't get herself killed. She had made a rash decision, but she was so angry she didn't care if it was a stupid move.

"Who the hell was that on the radio?" the driver asked the passenger. They were still so startled by the radio transmission that they were ignoring Madison, the person they had been tailing for several days. This was the most humiliating thing that could ever happen to an investigator, but in their confusion they were unfazed by it. Since the radio transmission was what had their attention, Madison figured she'd join in.

"Don't you know who radioed you?" she asked.

She finally had the passenger's attention.

"Look lady, we were hired to see where you went, and report back. We don't want any trouble. We're trying to make a buck, just like you."

Now that she was up close, Madison could tell that these two guys were not dangerous. They were just ex-cops working as private investigators, probably trying to supplement their retirement income. They were both in their fifties, and they seemed like guys she would like to get a beer and trade war stories with. Her anger started to dissipate.

"Okay, so then why are you so shocked that your friends at the other end of the radio told you I was walking up to your car just now?"

"Because we don't have friends," the passenger said. "I mean—"

"Shut up dingus," the driver said. "What he means is, it's just the two of us. We are the only two people on this job."

"What about the silver Ford Escape?"

The two guys looked at each other. The driver spoke. "You know about the silver Ford Escape?"

"Dude, I've known you guys were following me since day one. What, you think I'm an idiot?"

The passenger answered. "Shit. Well, okay. Anyway, I've been driving the silver Ford Escape, and Joe here has been driving this Fusion. The battery was dead on the Escape this morning, so we decided to do—"

"An idiot's two-man surveillance?" Madison used investigator lingo for two men in the same car. Normally, a two-man surveillance is two cars, one man in each car. Only an idiot would put two men in one car.

"Basically, yes," the driver said. "Don't rub it in. The radio is to talk to our boss back at the office, and to each other when we're not in the same car. The point is, we have *no idea who just radioed us* to say you were walking up to the car."

"It's downright spooky," the passenger said, and crossed himself.

Madison stood up because her back was hurting from leaning into the car. She didn't see any likely surveillance people. This meant that she had spotted this surveillance team, but there had been another team, probably including the lady with the doll in the carriage, which this team didn't even know about. And neither did she. Two-way radios, sometimes called walkie-talkies, weren't like cell phones: they were public. They had about a two-mile radius where anyone listening to the radio channel could hear what was being said, and could also listen in and join the conversation. So another surveillance team was following these guys, monitoring *their* surveillance and their communication. She had seen the lady with the doll, but only because the blanket had blown back to reveal a doll in a carriage. There must be people in cars, too, with radios, talking to each other on a different channel, but in this moment they'd switched to this channel to try and warn the Fusion/Escape team that Madison was walking up to the car. And she'd had no idea there was another surveillance team. She didn't feel so smart after all. She leaned back into the car.

"Are you guys the ones that kept sending me that stupid weather report text? The one that locates me on GPS?"

The two PIs looked at each other. The passenger looked back at Madison.

"Hey, lady, we're simple guys. We just followed you when we could and reported back. Then we go home at the end of the day and have a beer. Nothing fancy. No texting."

"I don't even have a smartphone," the driver said.

"Then how did you keep finding me after you'd lost me?" If these guys hadn't sent the text, they weren't the ones receiving her GPS location.

The driver looked at the passenger, and his eyes got really big. He turned his attention back to Madison. "There's a new guy in the office. We would report to the office that we'd lost you, and he would radio us back with a location to check. And you were always there. He started the day we got this job."

"I knew there was something funny about that guy." The passenger crossed himself again.

"This has gotten way too weird," the driver said. "We don't go for any of this funny stuff. What have you gotten yourself messed up in lady?"

Madison's phone, which was in her hand, pinged with a text message. Tom again.

What is going on? Call me.

Madison stood up and rubbed her forehead and ran her hand through her hair. It was hot with the sun beating down on her face. She had heard of this type of investigation before, but she certainly didn't think she would ever be the subject of it. There was a team of investigators hired to follow her and report on her activities; that would be the Escape and the Fusion. Then there was *another team* of investigators hired to follow the first team, without the first team's knowledge, for a couple of reasons: first, to make sure that Madison didn't spot the first team or follow them; second, to make sure the first team was honest about reporting what Madison was doing. This was a large operation.

Her phone pinged again.

In case I wasn't clear, I really need to talk to you.

This time it was Robyn. Madison felt pulled in a million different directions. And the lidocaine was wearing off; the part of her chest that wasn't numb from the mastectomy was starting to hurt. It was a deep ache, like down into the muscle.

She leaned back down and looked inside the car. "So, who is your client?"

The driver answered. "Look, lady, you're not getting this. We're the hired help. They don't tell us shit. 'Follow Madison Kelly, she's a fucking giraffe with blonde hair, report back where she goes and who she sees.' That's it. That's what we did. I don't know who the client is and I don't care. I just want to cash my paycheck, and even that isn't feeling worth it right now."

Madison sighed. "Okay, welp, you're burned. Game over. Go tell your boss you need to be reassigned and I'm too smart to assign new investigators to, so they should just give up."

The passenger looked at her with what could only be described as a pout. "You're not that smart, you didn't know about the second team either."

"Oh my God, go home."

Madison turned and walked back to the sidewalk, heading toward her car in the parking lot.

The Fusion backed out of the space and pulled away, the guys leaving with their tails between their legs. Madison got in her car, started it, and headed toward home. She needed to recharge. She needed to think. Her phone rang and the display indicated it was Tom. She pushed the button on the steering wheel to answer the call.

"I was at the doctor, Tom. Jesus."

"Okay, so how do you know Crystal Ladessa?"

"It is such a long story, Tom. Yes, I need to tell you, I need to report everything I've discovered to the police. But I would like to do it in an orderly fashion. I don't want to be questioned like a suspect."

"And what do you consider an 'orderly fashion'?"

"A fashion in which I write a report that contains all of the information, all of the names of the people involved, their addresses and contact information, something that every law enforcement officer involved in this case can read, so that I'm not stuck in an interview room being questioned by an endless number of cops who each need to hear my story in full for the aspect of the case that they're handling."

"What aspect? This is a homicide."

Madison was tired deep within her soul. "There is so much more, Tom. So much more."

Madison crossed Pearl on Girard and saw Dave's Jeep parked in front of the Pannikin. She pulled into a parking space across the street.

"Just tell me how you knew the dead girl."

"Tom, I need to do this my way. I will have a report for you by the end of the day."

Madison disconnected the call and got out of the car. She didn't like the way she and Dave had left it the night before. She crossed the street and scanned the patio tables, but she didn't see Dave.

She walked up the steps into the cottage and saw him sitting in the back on the banquette. With a tall blonde that Madison didn't recognize.

Does he have a subscription to Blondes 'R' Us or something? Madison thought.

They were sitting next to each other and were mid-laugh as Madison approached.

"Hi," Madison said.

Dave jolted at the sound of her voice, and when he saw her his face froze. However, he quickly recovered his aplomb.

"Hey! Madison. What's up? This is Tammy."

The girl beamed a set of really white teeth at Madison. She was about twenty-three. Her words came out in a giggle. "Hi, nice to meet you."

Madison put on her winningest smile. "Nice to meet you too! Well anyway, I'm going to head out."

Madison turned and walked back to the door and down the steps. She could walk quickly when she wanted to, and she made it to the sidewalk before Dave caught up with her.

"Maddie! Wait up. What's the matter?"

"Nothing is the matter. I've got a lot going on. I thought I would stop and say hello when I saw your Jeep. I didn't know you were busy. I need to go." Madison started across the street to her car.

Dave followed her. "If I were going to have some hot date do you think I would bring her to the Pannikin? That's like taking out a front-page ad in the *La Jolla Light*. This is the center of the La Jolla universe. If I were trying to hide something from you I wouldn't bring her here."

Bring her.

Interesting verb choice, Madison thought. She made it to her car and opened the driver's door.

"I don't care, Dave. I understand that you might want to test-drive a new model in case this one is totaled."

She got in the driver's seat and sat down. This is why she didn't want to label herself a *girlfriend*. The girlfriend got cheated on. The girlfriend got hurt. The girlfriend got broken up with. She didn't want to be the girlfriend.

"Oh my God," Dave said. "'New model'? Did you seriously just compare yourself to a car?"

Madison looked down at her lap. She spoke softly, almost to herself. "Why are there so many girls, Dave?"

"Why are there so many guys?"

She looked up at him. "What guys? You mean my client? My client who tried to kiss me and I wouldn't let him?"

Dave clenched his teeth and the muscle in his jaw popped out. "He . . . what?"

"Do not get all macho on me after you were sitting there laughing with that blondini. My point is that I didn't go for it."

"Gee, thanks."

Madison shook her head. "Dave, we always come back to this. I don't see other people. But I'm not sure about you."

Dave looked down at the asphalt. He was wearing flip-flops. He hitched up his jeans, which were always falling down his slim hips.

"What happened at the doctor?"

Madison was thrown for a second by the change of subject. "Oh. Yeah. We'll know in a few days."

Dave nodded. "Am I your boyfriend?"

You're my one and only, Madison screamed inside her head. *You're the only person who would look for me if I were lost.*

"I can't define it," she said.

Dave turned and walked away. Madison watched him cross the street, back to the Pannikin, back to . . . the blonde girl du jour. She contemplated going after him. She contemplated saying, *text me later* or something like that, so they didn't leave each other angry.

She shut the door and started the car.

She backed out of the parking space and headed north toward home. She didn't think this day could get any worse, but she didn't want to say that out loud and jinx it, thereby making something worse happen. But she didn't see how it could.

It was then that her phone started making a strange sound, some sort of alarm that she hadn't heard before. She drove a couple of blocks and pulled over to examine it.

It was the camera in Barrett's apartment, chiming an alarm to tell her that there was motion detected. It felt like a year ago she'd placed the hidden camera in Barrett's apartment: she had forgotten all about it. She pulled up the app and expanded the video feed so that she could see what was triggering the camera. It was a man, going through the bureau drawers. He backed out of the camera view, and then walked into frame again as he picked up things from the coffee table and looked at each one.

It was Cornell.

Cornell, the editor from Barrett's work. Cornell, who said he didn't know Barrett outside of work but was in a photo from her Mexican vacation. Cornell, who said he knew nothing about Barrett's private life or her disappearance. The guy who Madison gave every benefit of every doubt to because she didn't want to falsely accuse him of something.

Madison made an illegal U-turn in the middle of Girard and raced out of La Jolla. If she hurried, she could make it to Barrett's house in twelve minutes. She would follow Cornell to see where he went next.

Chapter Twenty

Thursday 3:14 PM

Madison sat unmoving in the driver's seat of her car, one block from Barrett's apartment. She had made it in eleven minutes. She was watching the video feed from the camera. Cornell was standing in the middle of the room, looking around. As she watched, he turned and walked in the direction of the front door, and then he was out of view.

Madison didn't know which vehicle Cornell had come in, or if he had come in a vehicle at all. She could see the front of Barrett's home from her location, and she would see him walking out onto the street. She could decide how to follow him when she learned his mode of transportation.

It had been three minutes since she'd seen him walk toward the front door on the video feed; where was he? It didn't take three minutes to walk down the path to the garden gate. She got her field glass out and looked at the exit to the garden, waiting for him to appear. Nothing. She looked back at the video feed, and it was empty. She put the field glass back up to her eye and scanned the street and the front of the garden. Then she saw him.

He was standing up against a tree that bordered the garden, silent and still. As she watched, his face turned slightly in her direction. She gasped and put the field glass down.

Calm down, he can't see you a block away, she said to herself.

She raised the field glass again. He was turning his head this way and that, slowly, just slightly, scanning the street. She could barely make out his form standing right up against the tree, in the shade. Apparently satisfied, he jogged out of the darkness into the bright sunshine. His clothes were no longer the stylish ones she'd seen at the newspaper office: they were black running clothes and black sneakers.

Cornell increased his speed as he got onto the sidewalk, sprinting to a blue Honda Civic parked at the curb. The car was facing Madison's position. That was unfortunate, given what she would have to do if he drove straight in her direction. He jumped in the driver's seat and had the car started and moving within seconds. He drove straight in her direction.

Madison fell like a tree over onto the passenger seat. She had to listen for his car to drive past her so she'd know when to sit back up. When it passed she sprang up, started the car, and looked in her side-view mirror to see what his next move was. She didn't want to flip a U-turn directly behind him, because he could see that and become concerned that someone was following him. He was driving really fast. He made a right turn at the next street.

Madison made a U-turn and gunned her V-6 engine up to sixty miles an hour. She couldn't lose him. She made it to the corner, checked for traffic, and made the right. She saw him up ahead in the right lane. She was able to drive the speed limit while keeping him in view.

Cornell. This was such a twist in her mind that she could barely think with it. Was he involved in the crime ring? That would make sense: he would have known that Barrett was getting too close to something, because he was involved in it; he could have alerted the others. He was so young that Madison had a hard time believing he was a mastermind in this twelve-million-dollar, six-murder crime ring. But Madison had been wrong before. Whether he was the mastermind or merely a minion, clearly he was involved. And Madison was going to see where he went next. Maybe he would lead her to the rest of the ring. Or to wherever Barrett's body was.

He lined up at the red light for a left turn at Laurel. The traffic was just beginning in San Diego. As soon as school started letting out in the afternoon, traffic picked up. Madison couldn't afford to get too far away from him on city streets, or she would lose him at a red light. As such, she was forced to sit right behind him at the stoplight. He was looking in his rearview mirror furtively. Madison put the sun visor down and turned her head, pretending to look for something in her purse.

Normally she wouldn't be too worried, because no one expects her to be a private investigator. If they're looking for someone following them and they see Madison, generally they're not concerned. However, Cornell had met her. If he recognized her in his review mirror it was all over. There was nothing she could do; she had to wait for the light to turn green.

She had not been prepared for surveillance. She didn't have her duffel bag with all her surveillance items in it. However, her car was littered with things she could use. She reached into the back and found a baseball cap. She wouldn't put it on right now while he was looking in his review mirror, but as soon they started moving she would.

She glanced at him and he wasn't looking at her anymore. The light turned green, and they both made the left onto Laurel. Madison's phone rang, and she saw from the display that it was

Robyn. She couldn't talk while she was tailing someone through city streets, so she hit the "Decline" button on the steering wheel.

She gave Cornell a little distance, letting another car come between them. Now when he looked behind him he would see some random Chevrolet and not her car. But at every block there was a stoplight, and with a car between them Madison risked Cornell making a green light while she got stuck as it turned red. It was hard to do a one-person surveillance in the city. Cornell moved to the right lane and put on his signal to turn right onto Fourth Avenue; he paused, waiting for some pedestrians who were crossing the street. The car in front of her kept going straight, so Madison was going to be directly behind Cornell again. To fix that she slowed down and pulled over to the curb and stopped. As soon as the pedestrians cleared the intersection and he turned, she would zoom to the corner and make the right. But before that could happen, another car arrived and sat behind him, waiting for him to turn right. Cornell turned, but the light turned red right at that moment, and the car behind him stopped at the red, thereby blocking Madison from being able to make the right turn after Cornell.

There was no way Madison was losing Cornell. She jumped into the left lane, putting the stupid car that had gotten in her way on her right. There were pedestrians crossing the street in front of them, as well as traffic heading south on one-way Fourth Avenue, the direction Cornell had just gone. She looked over the top of the car to her right, but Cornell was completely out of sight.

"Get out of the way!!" Madison screamed at the pedestrians, waving her arms and inching forward into the crosswalk. A man stopped right in front of her car and put his hands on his hips.

"Fuck you!" he screamed at Madison.

Madison drove across the double-yellow line to her left into oncoming traffic. She maneuvered around the angry pedestrian and made the right turn onto Fourth. Several people screamed at her and two cars honked furiously.

"I know! I know! You'll get over it and go on with your lives."

Madison punched the gas, frantically looking ahead for the blue Honda. She started playing checkers with the cars on the street in front of her. In and out, weaving back and forth, racing to catch up with Cornell before she lost him completely.

She finally saw him as he drove under the freeway overpass. He was lining up to turn left on Cedar. She pulled to the curb at the right and waited until the light was green for him, so that she didn't have to sit behind him at the red. Her heart was pounding out of her chest, the adrenaline coursing through her veins. The light changed, Cornell made the left, and Madison jumped across three lanes and made the same left turn after him, outside of his view. The light was green at Fifth Avenue, the street that ran one way in the opposite direction of Fourth, the street they had just come off of, and Cornell turned left. He was now heading back to where they'd started. Had he seen her? Was he now taking her on a wild goose chase? They were making a square: south on Fourth, east on Cedar, and now north on Fifth. What was going on? She realized what was happening when he jumped on the 5 freeway south. He had just been getting to the freeway on-ramp.

"Thank God," Madison said. It was much easier to follow someone on the freeway than it was on city streets.

However, Cornell took this opportunity to up his game. He quickly achieved speeds of over ninety miles an hour, racing across five lanes to get into the far-left lane.

Madison couldn't follow him to the left lane immediately or he would notice her. She didn't want to anyway. All she had to do was stay on the right side of the freeway and wait for him to move in front of her when he saw his exit approaching. However, it was harder to keep him in sight from the right, where the slower drivers congregated, at the speed he was driving. At least with her SUV sitting up high she could keep an eye on him.

Madison stuck to seventy-five miles an hour and was able to follow him from the right, frequently passing cars that were going more slowly. Her speed wasn't that high for a San Diego freeway with a speed limit of sixty-five miles per hour, but she could still get pulled over. Hopefully it would happen to Cornell first since he was going way faster than Madison.

As she got into a rhythm with this tail she had a moment to think. She now wondered what Robyn had to tell her. Robyn had been looking into the charities, and obviously she had found something and wanted to tell Madison about it. But Madison had tried talking on the phone one time when she was tailing someone, and she had lost them. She'd have to call Robyn later.

Madison tried to keep her attention on the scenery. She had noticed that when she was tailing someone, if she put her attention on the back of their head, they would look in their rearview mirror at her, or start turning their head to look for whoever was staring at them. It was similar to what happens when you stare at someone in a restaurant and they feel the stare and turn their head. So when tailing, Madison tried to look at things along the road, buildings, trees, the car in front of her, and not pay too much attention to the subject of the tail, in this case the driver of the speeding blue Honda Civic, on whom so much depended.

She had really underestimated Cornell. Just when she thought she was so smart about people's personalities and being able to spot liars, something like this happened and showed her she didn't know much at all.

Cornell started moving over to the right side of the freeway, and Madison slowed down so that he could get in front of her, while still leaving space to obscure his view of her in his review mirror. It looked like he was lining up to get off at National Avenue. She could see Cornell's braids turning this way and that; he was looking for a tail. As they got closer to their destination, Madison had to be extra careful. If he was already looking for a tail on the freeway, when he took her wherever he was going he was really going to be searching. She wished she had someone else that she could trade off with, like the team that had been following her.

And that reminded her: this entire trip she hadn't looked behind her even once. She was so focused on Cornell and what was in front of her. She looked in her rearview mirror but didn't see the Fusion or the Escape, but that didn't matter; those guys had either given up or traded in their cars for different ones that she wouldn't recognize. And also, what about the surveillance team that she had never spotted? The ones that were following the Fords? She was going to have to let that take care of itself; she had to see where Cornell was going.

Cornell exited the freeway, drove to the end of the off ramp, and stopped at the red light in the left turn lane with his signal on. Madison drove into the right lane and smoothly turned right, the opposite direction to where Cornell was headed. She turned her head away from him as she passed him, glancing back at the last moment just before she turned. He was searching his rearview mirror, watching for vehicles following him off the freeway. Well, he would not see her. She drove half a block, made a U-turn, and drove past him as he waited at the light. As soon as she had cleared the intersection she pulled over to the curb and waited.

She kept him in her side-view mirror as his light turned green and he made the left turn. He passed her, still searching in his review mirror for someone following him. She was right next to him and he didn't even see her. She let one more car go by and then pulled into traffic.

She didn't have far to go. He drove just a few blocks, made a U-turn, and parked in front of a coffee house. Madison pulled over to the curb, watching his movements from across the street. He got out of the car and walked into the coffee house.

"Well that was anticlimactic," she said.

The possibility existed that he was inside the coffee house, with its huge windows facing the street, looking out to see if anyone had followed him. That's what Madison would have done if she had wanted to see if she had a tail: go into a store or restaurant with big windows and watch the street.

The phone rang and Madison saw that it was Robyn. She hit the button on the steering wheel to answer the call.

"I'm on surveillance right now and I might have to hang up on you if my guy comes out. What's going on?"

"My God, I've been trying to get a hold of you."

"I know. I've been . . . you have no idea Robyn. You have no idea what I've been. Anyway, what's going on?"

"Okay. It was really difficult to track down these charities, but I've done it. There were so many shell companies, convoluted ownership statuses, one company owning another company, it was like those Russian dolls where one fits inside of the other and you pull one out and open it and there's another doll inside."

Madison had experienced that kind of thing before, when she'd done background investigations into companies where the owner did not want anyone else to know that they owned or had some sort of financial interest in a company. Most investigators would give up after a while, but she knew Robyn would not.

"Well, that's why I pay you the big money."

"Yeah, and my bill is going to be big, believe me. Okay, so first of all, they aren't actually charities, so let's get that out of the way right off the bat. The names make them sound like charities, but they are not actually 501(c)(3) organizations, which they would need to be to be considered a charity by the IRS. So, I will continue to call them 'charities,' but realize I use the term loosely. They are for-profit entities, okay? They were formed to make money and keep it as a profit."

"Got it."

"Good. Next: I found that after you get to the bottom of all the corporations and limited liability companies that are hiding each other, there is just one individual who is the principal of all three charities."

That made sense to Madison. The charities were formed to receive the millions of dollars from life insurance policies on couples with no children who were murdered. So she figured that the charities were fake, and whoever was behind the charities was getting those millions. She was afraid Robyn was going to tell her it was the attorney Joseph L. Viceroy, since a lot of people put a registered agent down for a corporation instead of the actual principal who was getting the money. And usually they would put an attorney as a registered agent. She really didn't think Joseph L. Viceroy was the head of this operation. She felt like he was a paid minion.

"Is it Joseph Viceroy?" Madison asked.

"No. It's one guy, but not Joseph Viceroy. I don't think you've mentioned this guy's name to me."

Probably the head of the operation didn't trust anyone, especially Viceroy, to be in charge of the company that received twelve million dollars.

"Oh. Okay. Then who is it? Who is the owner of these so-called charities? Because he's a multimillionaire and a murderer."

"His name is Randy Lemond."

Madison got a shot of adrenaline so strong that for a second she was lightheaded and saw stars. She gripped the steering wheel.

"Randy Lemond," she whispered.

"Do you know him? He lives in San Diego."

Randy Lemond was the name of Travis's friend, the one she'd met at the beach. The one in the Cadillac SUV who stopped to talk to them. The one who made Travis really uncomfortable.

How did this fit together? Randy was the mastermind? Did Travis know this? Did Randy become friends with Travis because Travis was Barrett's boyfriend? But Travis said Randy didn't know about Barrett. What was happening? Madison was so confused. She couldn't make it make sense.

"I know of him," Madison said. "Randy is friends with my client. I don't get it, Robyn."

"Okay, I don't know a lot about the case that you're working on, but I don't think this is good."

"No, it is not good, Robyn. It is not good at all."

Cornell walked out of the coffee house.

"I have to go Robyn. I'll call you later."

Madison hadn't turned off her car, so she waited to see which direction Cornell would drive. But he didn't get in the car. He stopped at the edge of the sidewalk and looked up and down the street. Madison leaned back on her seat so that the darker glass in the back of her car would obscure her. He didn't seem to notice her. He looked down at the ground, and then lifted his head and walked slowly across the street. A huge cement building with boarded-up windows was across from the coffee house. The building looked like it had been built in 1942; it had the name of a metal works company on it. It had been abandoned long ago, and there was a huge sign on the side, yellowed with time, that said it was for lease.

Cornell stood in front of the old building and again looked up and down the street.

"What are you doing?" Madison whispered. She hadn't had a second to process the information she had just received from Robyn. She didn't know what any of this meant, but she had to go where the investigation took her. She needed to see what Cornell was up to. She could figure out the rest later.

Cornell jumped up onto the six-foot fence surrounding the parking lot and was over the top of it in seconds.

Madison put her phone in her coat pocket, hid her purse under the front seat, and flew out of the car. She hit the alarm on her key fob as she ran to the fence. She slowed as she got closer. It was a chain-link fence with green plastic strips threaded through the links, surrounding a big empty parking lot that belonged to the abandoned building. Putting her face up to it she could see through. There was no sign of Cornell. There was a door to the building and no other exit from the parking lot.

Madison hadn't been great at chin-ups or rope climbing before her pectoral muscles had been sliced through for her operations. Not only that, she had basically just had surgery on her chest that morning. But nothing was going to keep her from figuring out what Cornell was doing. She put her hands on the chain-link as high as she could reach and pulled herself up.

Her Doc Martens were too big to fit into a toehold on the chain link, so she had to rely almost completely on her upper-body strength. She almost screamed from the pain in her chest with each pull of her arms. If there were people in the coffee shop looking out the window, they would probably wonder what she was doing. She'd have to move fast and hope they didn't notice.

She got up to the top of the fence and swung her leg over. She held the top of the fence and used her feet to slide as far down as possible, stretching her arms out and again creating searing pain. She felt blood dripping down her chest from where her wound had opened up. When her doctor had said no exercise for twenty-four hours, she probably didn't think this would be on the agenda. Madison dropped to the ground on the other side.

She ran to the door of the building and tried the knob. It was locked. There were no windows on that side of the building. She was standing in an empty parking lot in front of a locked door.

She stood and thought for a minute. It was the kind of door that locked automatically when it shut. And yet Cornell had gotten in. Did he have a key? There were two strips of gravel on either side of the door. Possibly there used to be plants there when the building was in operation. Now it was just sparse gravel, some rocks, dirt, and pieces of trash. As Madison stared at the gravel she noticed a rock that was a different color than the others. She reached down and picked it up. Turning it over, she saw it wasn't a real rock; there was a compartment in the rock. It was a Hide-a-Key made to look like a rock. She opened the compartment and pulled out the key. It had probably been left there when the building was for sale, long forgotten by a fired real estate company who couldn't get rid of a wartime manufacturing building that was no longer of use to anyone.

Madison figured the key would fit. But now she had to make a decision. She was contemplating walking into a building, by herself, to confront a possible crime ring that was murdering people. She was afraid she was going to find Barrett's dead body, but she was also afraid she wouldn't. She needed to bring Barrett home. Should she call Tom? By the time she convinced him that what she was doing was important and that he should come join her, Cornell could have left. No. But she didn't have to be a complete idiot. She picked up her phone and texted Tom.

I'm at a building across the street from Café Moto in Barrio Logan. A suspect in the case I'm working just went into this deserted building. It's the old metal factory. I'm going to go inside. If you don't hear from me in fifteen minutes you better send out the cavalry.

She put her phone on silent and put it back in her pocket.

Then she put the key in the lock. The knob turned. She opened the door.

She barely opened it a crack and slipped inside, using her body to close the door gently behind her. She was in a cavernous room that was lit only by the indirect light coming from the boarded-up windows at the front. She smelled dust and motor oil. The building was silent and huge. She waited for her eyes to adjust, and she listened.

There were stairs to her right. She could hear soft voices coming from above. The stairs were the sturdy kind that you find in government buildings: cement with a linoleum overlay, each stair wide enough to accommodate lots of people at the same time, with fraying rubber strips along the edge. She walked over and stood in front of the stairs, listening. She couldn't make out words. She put one foot on the stair to test it, gingerly adding weight to it to see if it made a sound. It was silent.

She slowly walked up to the first landing. The voices got louder. She couldn't make out how many, or if they were male or female, although she assumed one of them was Cornell. She paused on the landing and strained to hear.

What was she doing? She had no idea who was upstairs with Cornell, and she could be confronting the actual crime ring right now by herself with no weapon. She cursed herself for not bringing her gun.

She lay down on the next set of stairs and slowly crawled her way toward the top. There was a half wall on either side of the opening to the stairwell, so that she could only see what was directly ahead. And there was nothing directly ahead. The voices were coming from the right. She got to the top of the stairs by crawling on her stomach, and peered around the wall.

There were a few metal folding chairs set up in a circle. There were a couple of sleeping bags on the floor, empty fast-food containers, cups, and an overflowing trashcan.

Cornell was sitting, facing Madison's direction, on one of the folding chairs. There was another man, approximately Cornell's age, sitting on a metal chair next to him. He was Hispanic, heavyset, wearing a Denver Broncos T-shirt and jeans. They were across from a girl, who was sitting with her back to Madison in one of the folding chairs.

Madison decided to use the element of surprise in her favor. She got to her knees, and then onto her feet while still crouching down. She stood suddenly and spoke.

"Hey guys, what's up?"

Cornell dropped the cup of coffee he'd had in his hand and leapt backward and up over the top of the chair. The guy sitting next to him allowed his jaw to drop open and stay there. The girl jumped up and turned to Madison.

It was Barrett.

Chapter Twenty-One

Thursday 4:07 PM

Madison felt like the wind had been knocked out of her. She braced herself against the half wall around the stairs. Barrett was alive.

"Get the bags," Barrett shouted to Cornell, and suddenly the whole room was in motion.

Cornell started stuffing things into a gym bag. The other guy started grabbing the sleeping bag and folding it. Barrett stood stock-still and watched Madison.

"No, no," Madison said. She'd suddenly realized that they thought she was working with the bad guys. "No! I'm not here to take you."

"Keep moving," Barrett said to the men.

She was just as Madison had imagined her. She had a presence about her, a strength that made you feel like although she was a nice person, you'd better not mess with her. She seemed older than her twenty-four years. She was wearing a tank top that showed off her Harley Davidson tattoo, jeans, and Chuck Taylors. Madison had the same pair of shoes.

Madison tried again. "Seriously! I'm alone. I'm not going to tell anyone you're here."

Cornell stopped moving and looked at Barrett. The other guy stood and waited. Barrett eyed Madison. "I don't believe you."

Madison shook her head. The shock of seeing Barrett was too much, and she couldn't get her thoughts together. How could she assure them?

"Look. Travis hired me to find you. He said he was your boyfriend."

"I don't know anybody named Travis."

And there it was. That thought had been forming since Robyn had told Madison that Randy was behind the fake charities, but she hadn't been sure until now.

"Okay, yeah, I'm figuring all that out, give me a minute to catch up," Madison said. She moved into the room and hovered near a chair. "Can I sit down? I've had a shock. I thought you were dead."

Barrett hadn't moved. She stood with her legs hip-width apart and her arms loose at her sides. Like she was getting ready to fight.

"I'm not dead. I'm hiding from you and your people."

This wasn't going to be easy.

"I'm not 'my people'! I don't have people. I'm my own person. I make my own decisions. Just five minutes ago I started to figure out that things weren't as I'd been told."

"Like what?"

"Like the fact that Travis isn't your boyfriend. Well, I wasn't sure of that until just now. And that he might be involved in the crime ring you were investigating."

Something about Madison or what she was saying seemed to be getting through to Barrett. Or at least she was calming down.

She motioned with her hand, telling Cornell to put the bags down. Then she indicated the chair.

"You can sit."

Madison sank into the chair. Her mind was racing. Randy, Travis's friend, was in charge of the charities. Which meant he had recently gotten twelve million dollars. Had he killed those six people? Likely, yes. Did Travis know?

"So, you've never even met Travis?"

Barrett looked at Madison like she was thick, and shook her head. "No."

Okay. Travis wasn't Barrett's boyfriend. So Travis and Randy were in this together. Travis hired Madison to find Barrett. Why? So he could kill her for what she knew. That was obvious. And Madison had happily trotted along finding his victim for him. It made her sick to her stomach. She had never been so wrong in her life.

"I've made a terrible mistake. This guy Travis hired me to find you, and I now realize that he was hiring me to find you so he could kill you. That is the bad news. The good news is he doesn't know where we are right now, and I kept most of my investigation close to the vest, so I haven't told him much."

Barrett and Cornell looked at each other. "What do you think, babe?" Cornell asked.

Babe? *Wow, okay, that really was him in the photo in Mexico,* Madison thought.

She suddenly remembered Tom and the text she had sent him. Her phone was on silent, so she wouldn't know if he had responded.

"You guys. Let me just text someone that I'm okay."

"Wait! Who are you texting?" Barrett's voice echoed in the cavernous space.

"Don't worry, I'm not going to tell anyone that you're here."

"That's not what I asked you."

Madison paused. She was not used to someone talking to her like that.

"I know that you are in the middle of a serious situation. But I'm here to help you. I need to text someone that I'm okay or there is going to be a whole shitload of cop cars here in about fifteen minutes. You can come read over my shoulder." Madison picked her phone up and looked at the screen. There were several texts from Tom. Barrett moved in behind her and read the texts with her.

What you mean?

What suspect?

What are you doing? Don't go into a building by yourself.

Call me right now or I'm heading over there.

The last text was about two minutes before. Madison texted Tom. *Everything is okay, it was a misunderstanding. I'm fine. I will call you in a bit.*

Madison waited a moment and Tom's answer came: *Ok.*

"That was a cop?"

"Yes. He's a good guy. But we don't need him right now." Madison rubbed her face and pushed her hair back off her forehead. Her eyes settled back on Barrett and stayed a beat too long. Barrett got uncomfortable, and her lips hardened into a line. Madison spoke quickly; she didn't need Barrett getting tense again. "I've been walking in your footsteps for the past week. I feel like I know you."

That seemed to work. Barrett's chin relaxed and when she spoke she sounded interested. "What did you find?" Barrett moved over to a chair and sat opposite Madison.

"You were investigating those six deaths. The couples who died in accidents, right?"

"Yes," Barrett said. "I'm surprised you figured that out. What did you learn?"

"Probably more than you, at this point. They died in suspicious accidents, but they got no autopsies because a clerk at the County Recorder's Office, Eddie, signed all of the death certificates and said they didn't need autopsies. Someone paid him to sign them and avoid autopsies, since he's been throwing money around lately."

"Right," Barret said. "I noticed the similarities between the death certificates: how weird it was that three couples had died in accidents, all reported to funeral directors by the same attorney, all the death certificates signed by Eddie. It was like playing the card game Concentration. Have you ever played that card game?"

"Remind me."

"You take the whole deck and spread the cards out in rows, facedown. You play with another person. On your turn, you're allowed to flip over a card. You want to find pairs, or four of a kind is even better. So you turn one card over and see what it is. Then you try to guess where its pair is, and flip that card over. If you're right, you put the cards in your pile and continue your turn. The object is to get all of the cards in your pile. If you're wrong, you turn the card back over, and it's the other person's turn."

"Yes," Madison said. "I remember I used to play that game a lot. I was good at it as I recall."

"Me too. The best. So on your next turn, you remember where the cards were that you've seen in your previous turns and in other people's turns as well. It's called Concentration because you have to concentrate and remember where all the cards were when they got turned over and then put facedown again."

"Okay, yes, I remember."

"It was like that with the death certificates. I was just looking at them as they came in each day, looking for a story. And I remembered seeing the name 'Crystal' as the reporting party, because the name reminds me of a chandelier. And the fact that it was two death certificates, a husband and wife. So I went back and I found the two earlier certificates. I thought it was weird, and I made a mental note. And then the third set came in. That's when I asked Eddie."

"Did he admit anything to you?"

Barrett got up and grabbed a water bottle out of a plastic bag. She offered one to Madison, but Madison waved that she was fine.

"Not at first. I worked on him a bit. Finally, in order to keep me from reporting him, Eddie told me someone had paid him. But he wouldn't tell me who."

"Probably Randy. Or Travis," Madison said.

"Hello? Is anyone going to introduce me?" It was the other guy who everyone had been ignoring.

"I'm sorry," Barrett said. "Madison, this is Javier."

"Nice to meet you."

"And you," Javier said. That done, he took the other metal chair and settled in.

"By the time Eddie admitted someone had paid him, I had already been to interview the sister, Judy, of one of the victims." Barret pulled her legs up to the seat of the chair and sat cross-legged.

"I found your tape recorder with your interview with her."

"Wow," Barrett said. "I'm surprised that was left after they tossed my apartment looking for stuff."

"If a guy is looking for something, hide it in your makeup bag."

Barrett laughed. "Exactly. But they found the death certificates I'd copied and took those. I asked Cornell to get them for me but they were gone."

So that is what they'd been looking for. Madison had been right. And they'd found them. So all that was left was to kill Barrett to keep her from telling what she knew.

"I called and spoke with Crystal," Barrett said. "She's the girl listed as the reporting party on the death certificates. She works at a law firm that specializes in trusts, and—"

"Please spare me more discussion of trusts," Madison said. "I know enough about trusts to last me a lifetime." Madison didn't want to tell Barrett that Crystal was dead. She'd find out eventually, but it could wait.

"Okay, okay, so you've heard about trusts. Maybe you can fill *me* in, because I'm still not sure what I was onto. Eddie warned me I was in danger, but he didn't tell me much. I met him at Balboa Park, and he told me that there were some bad guys that had realized I was looking into them, that they were making millions of dollars doing something involving trusts or insurance or something like that, and they weren't going to 'let a little girl send them to prison.' Eddie told me I had to drop out of my life right then because the bad guys had demanded all of my personal information: my address, phone number, where I worked, even my Social Security number. Eddie can get that kind of stuff, and he had to give it to them, or they would've killed him."

So then they'd needed a PI to find Barrett, because she'd disappeared and they couldn't find her. That's where Madison came in.

"I see," Madison said.

"So I threw my phone in the fountain and walked out of my life."

"I hate to bust up this reminiscence, but I need to get to the newspaper office," Cornell said. "I was just stopping by to make sure you were good. So do we believe her?"

Barrett looked at Madison. "Yes, we believe her."

"How did you find us?" Cornell still hadn't recovered from seeing Madison pop up from the stairwell.

"I followed you here. From Barrett's house."

Cornell looked at Barrett. "Sorry," he said.

Barrett sighed. "That's okay. But I did tell you to make sure that no one was following you."

"I thought I had. She's good." Cornell turned to Madison. "Look, I'm sorry I lied to you about not knowing where she was or anything about her. She made me promise. She said if anyone is asking questions, pretend you barely know me. She was in danger, and I had no way of knowing who you really were or who you were working for."

Madison was ashamed to admit that they'd been right to lie to her: if Cornell had told her where Barrett was, she might've told Travis before she understood the situation. And Travis would've had Barrett killed . . . or killed her himself? Did Travis do the killing, too?

Cornell kissed Barrett goodbye, and then he and Javier shook Madison's hand and walked down the stairs.

"Let me tell you the rest of what I've figured out," Madison said. "Travis has a friend named Randy who is the recipient of twelve million dollars in life insurance payouts, because he arranged for three couples to list fake charities as their contingent beneficiary on their living trusts. And when the couples died at the same time, the life insurance companies paid the living trust, and the living trust paid the fake charity, and Randy Lemond got four million dollars each time. It was all set up through that attorney Joseph L. Viceroy, and an insurance brokerage called Fred Durant, just a little criminal ring they have set up to murder people and take their insurance payout."

"Wow, you've discovered a lot."

"And Travis hired me to find you, saying you were missing. That guy should get an Academy Award for best performance by a pretend concerned boyfriend."

"They really wanted to find me, didn't they?"

"Yes. Even more has happened, but those are the basics. We can take all this to the police and get the people involved arrested, I'm sure of it."

Madison paused before continuing.

"I thought you were dead."

They were quiet for a moment, and then Barrett spoke.

"Can I get you some leftover French fries?"

Madison laughed. "I'm good."

Barrett stood up and walked over to the windows at the front of the building. The glass was leaded and beveled so that you couldn't see through, but the light from the street lamps dispersed into the room. It had gotten dark while they'd been talking.

"I have been in this room for over a week. I want to be with the outside people."

"Can we walk over to the coffee house together? Or do you not leave here at all?"

Madison's phone lit up in her lap and she saw that she had a text from Dave.

Hey.

Madison smiled. That was their way of getting over a fight.

Barrett had walked back over to the chair and rested a knee on it. "I go over to the coffee house occasionally, if there is someone with me. We're so far from my stomping ground; I don't worry too much that people will find me here."

That made sense to Madison. San Diego was a big place. It had fully separate ecosystems and weather patterns throughout the county, with insects, plants, and animals that were unique to each area, almost like it was in a different country. There were human ecosystems as well: people who lived inland were completely different from the people who lived at the beach; North County was completely separate from South County; and Hillcrest was a lifetime away from Barrio Logan, where they currently found themselves, and never the twain shall meet.

"Can we head over there? This place is giving me the willies."

"Totally." Barrett put a couple of things in her pocket, and they headed down the stairs. Madison had her phone in her pocket; she could use her Apple Pay to buy stuff. That reminded her she needed to answer Dave's text, so they could be over their fight.

They got to the bottom of the stairs and Barrett put her hand on the doorknob as Madison took her phone out of her pocket to text Dave back. That was the last normal thing that Madison remembered for a long time. The door exploded inward and two huge men rushed them. They had predetermined their actions so that it was as smooth as a choreographed dance: one of them went straight for Barrett, putting a black hood over her head, while the other did the same thing to Madison. Madison didn't have a chance to kick or punch. She was completely overpowered, and her arms were pinned to her sides. The guy picked her up like she was a doll. He threw her over his shoulder and carried her outside, which caused her phone to fly out of her hand and go skidding across the parking lot. She yelled "Call 911! 911!" as her father had taught her as a child: always yell instructions to bystanders instead of just screaming. But the man pulled a cord at the base of the hood tight until it cut off her air supply. She stopped yelling. He loosened it so she could breathe.

Never get in a car.

Let them kill you right where you are now.

It's not going to get better wherever they are taking you.

She had studied how to survive a kidnapping. No matter what you are being threatened with, never get in a car. Taking you to a secondary crime location means that they can do things to you without witnesses.

But she was helpless. Almost six feet tall, stronger than a lot of men, and she was rendered helpless by a much larger man who had pinned her arms to her sides. He shoved her into the back of a large vehicle. The car smelled new. They must have cut the lock on the gate that Cornell and Madison had jumped over, in order to get a car into the parking lot. As the other guy threw Barrett inside, she landed half on Madison, and Barrett's elbow got Madison in the chest. She felt the warm blood trickle down into her armpit as the wound opened again. The man rolled Madison over onto her stomach and zip tied her wrists behind her. Then he rolled her onto her back again. Suddenly they were in silence as the back of the vehicle was shut. It felt final. The car started, and they were in motion.

It had taken thirty seconds to kidnap two grown women in broad daylight.

Fourth right. Fifth left. Speed increase means the freeway. Twenty minutes on the freeway now. Darkness. Time.

Madison knew how to slow down her body to preserve energy and strength. She did it all the time when she was on surveillance, putting herself into a Zen-like state while she waited for her subject to move. Now she was doing it in order to preserve her strength and her oxygen for whatever lay ahead for them.

She was also keeping track of their turns and speed changes in order to map in her mind where they were going. At first, no stop signs and longer stops with cross traffic meant they were on National Avenue, a bigger street. A right turn and an increase in speed meant they'd gotten on the 5 freeway north. It was just a short hop from the building where they'd been kidnapped, and she recognized the motion of the car. She knew it was a freeway because of the sudden increase in speed; if they had gone south, it would have been a straight entrance onto the freeway, without the big hairpin turn.

Madison and Barrett didn't speak. The car was loud, and there was nothing to say. They both seemed to instinctively realize that speaking could get them in trouble: they didn't know how close their captors were, or if what they said could be heard. So they were silent.

Madison knew every inch of San Diego from her years of driving for her career, and her knowledge was being put to the test. This test could have a really painful final exam. Once they got wherever they were going, knowing exactly which way to head to get to civilization and toward people who could help them, if they could escape, could mean the difference between life and death.

I didn't answer Dave's text. He's going to think I'm still mad at him.

These are the things you think about.

She didn't know who had ordered their kidnapping, but she figured it must be Travis or Randy. She'd given up thinking Viceroy was anything more than a hired hand. Why not just shoot them and kill them in a deserted building in Barrio Logan? Why kidnap them? The only reason to take them somewhere was to torture them or get information out of them. Or torture them in order to get information out of them. And then kill them. Like Crystal had been killed.

Madison had to face the fact that she had probably brought them to Barrett's door. This must be the second surveillance team, the ones Madison had never been able to spot. The lady with the baby carriage, and whoever else was with her. They must've been following Madison in case she found Barrett. And she had.

The car was slowing. They'd only been driving on the freeway for about ten minutes. Madison estimated they were somewhere between downtown and the Midway district, where the 8 freeway crosses over the 5 freeway. Madison didn't feel a turn; they must've hit traffic. They were still headed north.

She pictured Dave walking away from her at the Pannikin. His gait was distinctive. She saw the future in the promise of his walk. And that might be the last time she'd ever see it.

The traffic picked up again. They were back up to freeway speeds. Fifteen minutes and counting.

Her mind was racing with the meaning of this kidnapping, who was behind it, what she could do about it. But the fact was she couldn't figure anything else out without more data. She needed to see where they ended up, and who was waiting for them when they got there. Until then, she had to get her mind onto something else.

Dave. Her mind kept going back to Dave and the fight they'd had.

She'd known Dave for ten years. Ten on-and-off, crazy, magical years. She'd just moved to Windansea, and someone at the beach had invited her to a party on a yacht docked on Shelter Island, right next to downtown. When she had gotten there everyone was already drunk, and Madison had stood against the railing looking out to sea, wishing she'd stayed home. She heard a commotion when Dave arrived, lots of high fives and people offering him drinks and girls offering themselves. Dave spotted her immediately and walked toward her across the deck.

It was like the old-fashioned movies where they put gauze on the camera to make it look dreamy, everything except the hero fading out. She'd stood, frozen, but had managed a smile.

"Hey," he'd said.

She had never experienced that feeling before or since: sure, she had felt animal magnetism with Travis, having to do with her attraction to criminals most likely, but with Dave it had been love at first sight.

He had walked up and poked her in the hip, which she had teased him about ever since. *Really?* she'd say. *My hip?* "You were so pretty," Dave would reply, looking away.

A few hours after they'd met they'd been walking down the boardwalk on Shelter Island, looking at the boats moored there.

"Pick a boat," Dave had said.

"What?"

"Pick a boat."

Madison hadn't answered, and Dave had turned and walked down a private dock.

"What are you doing? This is private!" she'd stage-whispered. The good-girl Madison had been horrified, but she had followed.

Dave ended up at the edge of a cuddy cabin boat. "This one looks good!" he'd said, jumping on board and reaching his hand over to help Madison.

"No! This is illegal."

"We're not going to hurt anything. I promise."

The car jolted to the side suddenly, and Barrett rolled over onto Madison, smacking their heads together. They both exclaimed in pain. The car righted itself.

"Shut up," the driver said. Madison and Barrett were silent. The vehicle continued through the night.

Madison on Shelter Island with Dave: she'd been drunk enough that she'd agreed to get on the boat; it seemed harmless but naughty at the same time. She'd accepted his hand and stepped onto the deck. Dave got a credit card out of his wallet and used it to open the cabin door. Suddenly they were inside a little house.

Madison had thought Dave was pretty skilled to get her into a bedroom within a few hours of meeting her, without having to pay for a hotel room. However, he hadn't tried anything—to a fault. They'd lain down on the bed and looked through the skylight at the stars. They'd talked about their lives, their hopes, and their dreams, never running out of things to talk about. Five hours later, as the sun was coming up, Madison had finally asked the question she'd been wondering about for hours.

"Are you ever going to kiss me?"

"I thought you'd never ask." He'd put his hand on her back and it had felt like he'd set her on fire.

Barrett coughed, and it brought Madison back to the present. The awful, unbearable present. She wanted to tell Barrett that she was sorry. She had brought the bad guys right to Barrett's door. But she didn't want to speak and have someone overhear her and somehow use what she was saying later, when they were being tortured.

When she'd been on the boat with Dave it had been like a time out from her life, because the circumstances were so unusual. She'd known she would regret the one-night stand as soon as she got off the boat and reality hit. It was funny to think of the ten years of "one-night stands" they'd had since then, showing how off Madison's prediction had been. After six hours on the boat they'd stepped onto the private dock in full daylight. Nothing like the sun to shed light on the sins of the night before. Madison had jogged to the end of the private dock, pushing open the gate and getting back on the boardwalk as quickly as possible. She'd thought Dave was right behind her, but when she turned, she saw he had gone back to the boat for some reason.

"Hurry up!" Madison had said under her breath. She'd searched frantically to see if there were any early morning joggers who would see them in their clothes from the night before, standing on a dock that didn't belong to them.

Dave had been looking at the front of the boat for some reason but then had run back, bare feet tottering on unfinished wood, and pushed through the gate to join her.

"I had to get the name of the boat!"

Madison realized then that she had met a guy who was more romantic than she was.

"What was the name?"

"The Courageous."

Barrett and Madison rolled to the right as the vehicle made a wide turn. They were getting off the freeway. Madison returned her attention to concentrating on where they were headed. They had been on the 5 north for twenty-five minutes at least. They were now into North County San Diego. Maybe Sorrento Valley, maybe as far as Del Mar. They had certainly passed the exit for La Jolla. She didn't know how much it would help to know where she was when they got out of the car, but it made her feel like she was doing something.

The car stopped briefly, as if for a stop sign, and then turned left. Then there were a couple of quick jogs, right, left, and then they must've been on a big street because the speeds went back up to about sixty miles an hour. North County had a lot of open space, and it was nighttime so there wouldn't be traffic.

Then they were turning into a driveway. Madison could feel the SUV rock as it went over the separation between the street and some type of uplift in the pavement. Then they kept driving, so it must've been a parking lot. And then the car stopped. They were at their destination. And now it would begin.

Chapter Twenty-Two

Thursday 7:34 PM

"You need to stand up."

The man in charge of Madison had tried to pull her out of the SUV, but her wrists were tied so tightly that her arms had gone to sleep on the ride. She couldn't shimmy down to the edge of the tailgate, and she was big enough that the guy couldn't pick her up from that angle.

"I can't. My arms are tied too tightly," Madison said from underneath her hood. There was sweat dripping down her face, and her breath was hot and sticky as she spoke.

"Jesus Christ." The guy rolled Madison onto her stomach roughly, and then used some instrument to cut the zip tie. He rolled her onto her back and yanked her arm to pull her out of the SUV. She made it to her feet. "Start walking."

Madison stumbled forward blindly with the hood on and the guy guiding her.

"Step up." Madison did so, and then she must have crossed the threshold into a room of some kind because the air changed.

The man pushed her further into the building they were in, and then he turned her and shoved her in the stomach so that she bent. He pressed on her shoulders and she sat down in a chair.

He ripped the hood off of her head and she took a huge breath of beautifully fresh air. The artificial light was bright compared to the darkness she'd been in, and it was hard to focus at first.

She was in some type of industrial space that was small. There were no windows, just a rolltop door, like the kind that is used to load and unload a storage facility, and on the other wall a heavy door that was currently standing open, utilizing a little kick stand at the base of it. There was a key in the lock attached to a long strip of wood, like the bathroom key they give you at the doctor's office when they don't want the key lost. The outer room had a desk and a chair, but that's all that Madison could see from her chair.

Madison and Barrett were facing each other on folding metal chairs. Madison thought Barrett would look afraid, but instead she just looked angry.

The guy was coming at Madison with duct tape. The other guy spoke to him.

"Where are the zip ties? They work better."

"I left them in the car. Don't worry, I'll tape her up good."

Madison put her hands together in front of her, with her wrists touching and her fists pointed outward.

"Good. Cooperation. Things will go better if you cooperate."

The guy taped Madison's wrists together with the duct tape.

Barrett shook her head and looked away. Disappointed in Madison.

"Get their phones."

Madison's guy reached into her pocket. "We lost my phone when you grabbed us, remember?"

"Oh yeah."

The guy walked over to Barrett.

"Touch me and I'll bite your dick off."

Wow, Madison thought.

The guy ignored her and reached into Barrett's back pocket and got her phone. Then he yanked on the zip tie to make sure it was secure.

"You better tie me up," Barrett said. "Otherwise I'll kick your fucking ass you fucking piece of shit."

The guy chuckled and Madison raised her eyebrows. Barrett sounded like Madison—well, how Madison would sound under normal circumstances.

"You better keep your trap shut, or I'll put tape on your mouth."

The two men then set about duct taping their ankles so that they were effectively hobbled.

"So, what is the plan, guys?" Madison asked.

"That is for us to know and you to find out."

Seriously? This guy sounds like he's in a Raymond Chandler novel. Madison took the opportunity to size them up. They were clearly the muscle of the operation, not the brains. Neither one of them seemed to have a neck, and their upper bodies were massive. They had overdeveloped pectoral muscles, which caused their shoulders to roll forward, giving them that hulk effect that bodybuilders liked, but Madison recognized as failure to strengthen their upper back muscles. Madison liked shoulders, but not these kind. The men looked so similar that they could have been twins. Madison suddenly realized that they probably were.

"Are you guys twins?" She knew that talking helped to humanize her to her captors. When captors thought of their prey as human, it was harder for them to torture and kill them.

"Shut the fuck up."

"I was just wondering; you look a lot alike. I think twins are cool."

Barrett was shaking her head at Madison, in disgust. She didn't understand what Madison was doing, so she thought Madison was being submissive.

The floor of the room they were in was cement, as were the walls, other than the rolltop door. Madison wondered if it was an actual storage unit. However, they had walked straight from the car inside, and normally you have to take an elevator or walk down hallways in a storage facility.

"Where are we?" The possibility existed that they might answer one of her questions. If not, at least she was talking, trying to sound human.

"Like we're going to tell you that."

The guys finished taping their ankles. Barrett was glaring at them. Madison thought she'd give it another shot.

"Seriously, just give us a hint about what's about to happen. Why are we here? Or do you not know? What do you think the plan is?"

"We don't get paid to think."

That's a good thing, Madison thought.

The guys headed for the door that was still standing open.

"How long are we going to be here?"

Her question was ignored, and the door slammed with a finality that Madison didn't like. The doorknob was shiny silver, with no keyhole or lock mechanism on the inside. Barrett was looking down at her lap, but suddenly her head flew up and she spoke.

"Seriously? I thought you were the big bad Madison Kelly. And you offer up your wrists?"

Madison put her lips together and mimed the sound for *shh.* She wanted to see if she could hear what the guys were saying. Even though the door was heavy, she could hear sounds through it.

Mumble mumble when he gets here we can ask him.

Mumble mumble mumble yeah you do that and see how that works out.

She's fine. He won't care. Mumble mumble.

Mumble mumble that's what your mother said.

Hey fuck you man.

Laughter.

Then the men stopped talking. Barrett was glaring at her. Madison needed to think. She had some things in her favor: Barrett certainly wouldn't shrink away from a fight, that was clear. But Madison needed a plan, and for that she needed more information. Why were they there? Why hadn't they been killed instead of kidnapped, and now that they were in a quiet unobserved place, why weren't they being killed? There had to be a reason for it. If Madison could figure out the reason, perhaps she could keep them alive.

Barrett mouthed the word *plan?* and raised her shoulders. Madison mouthed back *I'm thinking.* She had brought the bad guys right to Barrett. It was the biggest mistake she had ever made in her life. Maybe if she hadn't been worrying about foobs, or Dave, and had instead been thinking about her job, she wouldn't have put them in a situation where they were likely both going to be killed.

She was racking her brain for everything she knew about what a person should do if they were kidnapped. She'd already done some of it: she wanted to give the captors a false sense of security. Talking to them and making them feel like Madison and Barrett were human was another aspect. But Madison needed to figure out how to get them out of a cement room while they were tied up. She wasn't Houdini.

She whispered as quietly as possible to Barrett, hoping that she would be good at reading lips. "They want something. Otherwise we would be dead. What do they want?"

Barrett shook her head and shrugged.

Madison and Barrett had already figured out that her apartment had been trashed because they were looking for the copies of the death certificates she had obtained. But they had gotten those. Now what did they want?

The men in the other room were talking again, this time about what they had done the night before. It was harder to make out the words because they had lowered their voices, and anyway it was meaningless jabber.

Madison heard a car pull up and stop in front of the structure they were in. Barrett heard it too; she turned her head suddenly, and then went back to Madison with big eyes. It was the sound of a big car, like an SUV or truck. They stared at each other in silence, both listening. An outside door opening. The scrape of the captors' chairs as they stood up. Three voices talking, the new one deep.

Are they tied up?

Of course.

Did you ask them?

No, we figured you would want to do that.

And then the sound of the key in the lock, and the squeak of the hinges as the door slowly opened.

Randy Lemond walked in the door. He was taller than the other two guys, but wiry. Madison had only seen him sitting in his Cadillac SUV. He was wearing an expensive suit and had neatly cut short brown hair and brown eyes. His shoes were some type of expensive dead animal. He pulled up a metal chair and sat down. He looked serious, as if Madison and Barrett were in trouble with the boss at work. The other two guys stood with their backs against the wall, hands clasped in front of them, at ease.

"I suppose you're wondering why you're here?"

"Fuck you," Barrett said.

"The thought had crossed my mind," Madison said. He looked like a normal guy. Madison wouldn't have guessed that he was the head of a criminal organization. His eyes were keen and smart, but they moved back and forth between Madison's left eye and her right eye, constantly. Like he was amped up on something. And his words came out slightly breathless. His pupils were pinpoints, and the room was not that bright.

He turned to Barrett. "You have caused us so much trouble."

"Good," Barrett said.

Randy clenched his teeth and Madison could see the muscle on the side of his neck tense. She decided to jump in. "What do you need from us?"

He regarded Madison. "Yes, what do we need . . . that is the question."

"Are you and Travis in this together? Partners?"

Randy seemed to consider before answering. "Yes, we're partners. But the bad news for you is that he is the nice one."

Madison knew that he was going to kill them. That had to figure into any plan she could come up with. He never would have walked in, shown his face, made it clear he was their kidnapper, and then let them go. So he planned to kill them, no matter what information they gave him, no matter what they did, he was going to kill them. She had nothing to lose; might as well see if she could get him to talk.

"Oh, you're the mean one? So you were in charge of getting rid of the couples who bought the life insurance?"

Randy seemed pleased. "Oh yes, I was in charge of it. Travis is too weak to make decisions like that."

"The couple heading down from Big Bear. How did you do that?"

"Oh, that one was easy." Randy was proud. "A leak in the brake fluid and the power steering fluid. Halfway down the mountain the brake fluid ran out and they couldn't stop. The rain was cooperative and added to the swiftness of the accident."

Madison wanted to keep him talking.

"And what about the airplane?"

"GHB in the water bottles provided with the plane. So simple. They drank, he went unconscious, boom right into the ocean. And of course, no autopsy." Randy smiled.

"And the couple on a harbor cruise? All you had to do was push them over, right?"

"Like taking candy from a baby."

"But why Crystal? She was only seventeen."

Randy's hands wrapped around his knees and he squeezed. "She was calling you. She was going to tell you everything. She had to go." His hands released. Then squeezed again.

Madison felt like he was reliving strangling Crystal. Madison didn't know how she was ever going to forgive herself. But right now she wanted to keep Randy talking.

"So, whose idea was it to set this whole thing up? To have Kerry at the bank refer people to Viceroy for their trusts, and then get referred to the broker for life insurance? Who set up that system?"

"I have to admit, that was Travis. He's always had a head for business."

Travis, who had almost kissed her. Travis, to whom she'd been attracted. Travis was a murderer.

"But how did you get the couples to agree to make your charity the contingent beneficiary for the trust, the entity that got all the money if they happened to both die?"

"Oh, don't be silly," he said. "They didn't agree to it. The minute they left his office Viceroy just changed the contingent beneficiary. He'd talk to them to find out what kinds of charities they supported, just so that it would make sense to the family. Then we made a charity that sounded like it, Viceroy changed the beneficiary in the paperwork, and boom we're in the money. Of course they had to die, but that was always going to happen anyway."

"What do you mean 'always going to happen'?"

"People die. That's what happens. No one lives forever."

Well, that's one way to justify murdering people, Madison thought.

"And why are we here? What is it that you want from us?"

"I think you know. Since you stole it."

Madison at first didn't know what he was talking about. But the word *stole* stuck with her. Her first thought was that she'd never stolen anything in her life. And then she realized she had: the thumb drive. The thumb drive that was with Arlo right now.

At first she panicked, thinking they'd followed her to Arlo's place. But if they had, they would have the thumb drive and wouldn't need Madison and Barrett. So they didn't know where it was. Madison had made sure no one was following her when she took the thumb drive to Arlo. Even though she had been unable to spot that second surveillance team, she had gone to great pains that day not to be followed by anyone: she had driven into a small residential area and pulled over, waiting for any vehicles to follow her into the neighborhood. No one had. Only once she was sure no one was following her had she gone to see Arlo. That's why they didn't know where it was.

"Stole? I don't steal things."

"Oh, but you do. Yes you do. You told Travis you 'stole something for him.' You stole a memory stick from Viceroy's office. We followed you there, and then the stick was gone. You never did spot my surveillance team, did you? Just Travis's team."

"Travis's team?"

"Yes, Travis said he'd take care of the surveillance, but I knew he'd hire idiots. I needed to know the minute you found this girl, so we could grab her. And I was right: you spotted Travis's team. You didn't spot mine."

"The woman with the baby carriage. That was yours."

"Well, yes, she's fired. Women investigators." Randy made a scoffing sound. "The guy who asked you if you were okay when you were crying on the street in La Jolla—what was the matter, anyway? That was one of mine. And there were others. And they followed you straight to the girl."

"Well, bully for you. You hired great investigators. Leave me their numbers and maybe I'll hire them someday."

Randy laughed, and it was the first time Madison could see that he was crazy. His laugh made "yuk yuk yuk" sounds like Jim Carrey in Pet Detective. For a second she thought he was putting it on, but no, that was the way he laughed when he found something funny. He made sounds with his mouth with a complete absence of mirth. Suddenly he stopped and leaned forward until he was just two feet from Madison's face.

"The memory stick. It has important information on it. I need it back. So, just tell me where it is and we will let you go."

Of course that wasn't true. They would never let them go. They would keep them alive only until they had retrieved the thumb drive.

"I threw it out. It was password protected, and I couldn't get any information off of it. So I threw it out. I only took it on a whim, I didn't know there was anything important on it."

Randy stood up, and as he did so, his coat jacket caught on the back of the chair. Before he freed it, Madison saw a .45 caliber handgun in a holster under his arm. He began to slowly circle the room. "You know what I don't like, Madison Kelly?"

"Women?"

Barrett laughed. A cloud passed over Randy's face and then was gone.

"Good one. Yes, I've heard you're funny. Unfortunately, humor is not going to get you out of this. No, I like women just fine. What I don't like are liars. And you're lying to me. You didn't throw it out. We went through your trash."

Madison had done a lot of dumpster diving in her day. It was a common practice for investigators who needed to get more information about the subject of their investigation. What kind of food they ate, the entertainment they liked, receipts showing stores and restaurants they frequented, sometimes documents that people even in this day and age didn't shred. So she was sure he was telling the truth when he said that they'd gone through her trash.

Randy stopped his journey in the small room and looked down at Madison. "Try again."

"I gave it to the police. My friend, Tom. I gave it to him."

"No you didn't." He said it with such certainty. Madison wasn't sure how he knew, but he knew she hadn't.

"Well—"

Randy swung his arm back and smacked Madison across the face. He had a ring on his hand that cut her cheek, and she felt warm blood trickle down underneath her chin. Tears sprung to her eyes from the pain. She had never been hit in the face before.

Randy turned and looked at the thugs. "Have we gone through her place yet?"

Thug One answered. "The guys are on their way now, boss."

"Good. And don't forget her surfer boyfriend's place."

Madison wondered how that would go. Dave could fight anyone, but he preferred when the fight was two or three against him. It was boring otherwise. If he came home and found men searching his apartment, the men would sorely regret it. She wondered if Dave would know she was missing. Right now he just thought she hadn't answered his text and was probably mad at him. If he found someone searching his apartment, he might call her, but she wasn't sure. He had pride, and he'd already reached out by text; he might not reach out again until she answered him. And she was not going to be answering him anytime soon.

Randy bent down until his face was three inches from hers. "I have a meeting to go to. They are going to search your place and your boyfriend's place. If they don't find it, I'm coming back. And you're going to tell me where that thumb drive is, or things are going to get a lot worse for you guys. I'm going to start on the girl. You're gonna watch her experience severe pain until you tell me where that thumb drive is."

Randy turned and walked out, and the two bruisers followed him, shutting the door behind them.

Madison was trying not to cry. Her face hurt so badly, and it was still bleeding. She couldn't put her hand up to her face because her hands were tied.

Sometimes if you start crying you'll never stop.

Barrett mouthed, *Do you know where it is?*

Madison nodded. Then she mouthed the words, *As soon as I tell them, they will kill us.*

Barrett looked down at her lap.

Another car. This one smaller. Madison would recognize the smooth tuning of a BMW V-8 engine anywhere. That was Travis's car.

Barrett was watching Madison's expression. Madison knew that her face was clouding over with anger. The outer door opened and shut, and they could hear the three men greet the newcomer. And then the door opened.

Travis looked nervous, almost apologetic. He walked in speaking. "I can explain everything—"

And then he saw Madison's face, and the blood that was quickly drying from the cut just under her eye.

"It wasn't supposed to happen this way," he said.

"Really? How was it supposed to happen?"

"You're mad. Don't be mad."

Was this guy serious? "I'm sorry, Travis, how am I supposed to be? Explain it to me because I'm a bit tied up right now."

That made Barrett laugh.

"No, that's not what I mean," Travis said. "I had a team following you because as soon as you found Barrett, I was going to talk to her before Randy got to her. I didn't know he had a surveillance team following my surveillance team."

"You guys are like the Keystone cops. You were going to 'talk' to Barrett? Really. What were you guys gonna talk about? Her preferred method of death?"

Travis rubbed his forehead and ran his hands through his hair. Madison felt nostalgic for when she thought that was cute.

"I was going to get her to understand that she couldn't talk to anyone about what we were doing, because Randy is a lunatic and would kill her. But then you stole the thumb drive and it was out of my hands. I didn't think he would kidnap you guys though."

Madison wondered if Travis believed the things that came out of his mouth. As long as he didn't pull the trigger, he could say it had nothing to do with him. Madison thought people like Travis were more dangerous than people like Randy. You knew what you got with Randy. You knew to steer clear of him. Travis caused destruction quietly and in secret, by giving evil the oxygen to thrive.

Randy walked in, and his arm shot out and grabbed Travis by the collar and yanked him into the other room. Thing One reached in and pulled the door shut.

Travis and Randy were yelling at each other, making it easy to hear what they were saying.

"You need to shut the fuck up. That has always been your problem. You talk too much."

"Why do so many people have to die?"

"You didn't mind the money, did you?"

"We never agreed to kill people."

"How did you think we were going to get the life insurance money? Wait for them to die of old age?"

There was silence, and then Randy laughed. "Exactly. You knew I was going to arrange for them to be killed. There was no other way to get the insurance money. You just don't like getting your hands dirty, and you don't like knowing the details. Because when it comes down to it, you're a coward."

There was silence. And then Randy spoke again. "Hey, Travis, why don't you make yourself useful and go search that bitch's apartment."

There was a moment of quiet, and then Travis spoke. "Okay, but let me take your Escalade."

"Nice try. You want my car parked at her apartment. No, you can take your BMW and park it a few blocks away and walk."

The voices quieted down, and Madison could no longer make out what was being said. She could hear them moving, the creak of a chair as somebody sat down, and then the outer door opening and closing. Travis's BMW started up and drove away.

Madison and Randy had one thing in common: they both thought Travis was a coward. He could have saved them. But instead he drove away so that he didn't have to see what was about to happen.

Chapter Twenty-Three

Friday 2:03 AM

Madison and Barrett had been sitting in silence for hours. One of the goons in the other room had started to snore, until the other goon kicked him and he protested loudly. Then the snoring had quickly resumed. If it hadn't been for the fact that Madison was incredibly uncomfortable, she would've almost been in a meditative state. She had started by trying to figure out how to get them out of this room, but she had come up with nothing. So now she was just sitting. She and Barrett had stopped trying to talk.

Even if they could somehow get themselves untied, they had no weapons. Madison knew that despite what they put in movies and in some books, there would never be a fair fight between a man and a woman. The upper-body strength of a woman was no match for the upper-body strength of a man. No matter how much she worked out. And given Madison's compromised pectoral muscles, she was even less of a match.

The blood had dried on her biopsy site, and it was itching. The cut on her face was itching, too.

Barrett was falling asleep. She was leaning back in her chair, and her chin was resting on her chest, almost. As she would fall asleep, her head would bob down and it would snap her awake. Finally she tipped her head to the side and was able to sleep that way.

Madison felt apathetic, and she wondered if Barrett's falling asleep indicated her apathy as well. They wouldn't find the memory stick in Madison's apartment, certainly not in Dave's, no matter how amusing the thought of them running into Dave while searching his apartment might be, and so they were going to come back and torture Barrett in front of Madison. And Madison knew that she would tell them immediately where it was. She might be brave when it came to herself, but she couldn't watch someone else get hurt.

And then Arlo would get hurt as they got the thumb drive from him, and then they would kill Madison and Barrett. But at least Madison wouldn't have to watch Barrett get tortured before they died. They were going to die either way. Maybe the best bet was to try to negotiate for a swift death.

Madison couldn't believe that she had worried even for a second about losing her foobs. As she sat here and looked at what was likely the end of her life, she cared about some things, but she did not care about fake boobs made out of plastic bags with toxic chemicals inside, placed under her long-suffering pec muscles, all so that she could "look like a girl." She couldn't believe that she had worried about that, instead of worrying about whether she was going to die of a recurrence of cancer.

As she sat on a metal folding chair with her hands tied in front of her, a result of the worst mistake of her life, facing the worst decision a person could ever have to make, she realized that somewhere along the line she had lost the willingness to fight. And it had started before they'd gotten kidnapped.

It didn't happen all at once, at least that's not what happened with her. She didn't decide *I don't want to live anymore.* It was more like she didn't want to fight anymore. Getting through her bout of cancer the first time had required a fierce determination to live, a willingness to go through hell in order to remain alive. But when she saw there was a possible recurrence, a part of her just . . . gave up. It wasn't so much *If I have to lose my foobs then I don't want to go on.* It was more like *I give up.* Which was why she had been concentrating on the loss of her foobs rather than fighting death. Worrying about her foobs became a substitute for confronting the fight for her life. Because the fact was, she didn't want to fight anymore.

Ironically, she was in a situation now where if she didn't put everything she had into fighting for her life, she would die. In racing parlance, this was the moment when the rubber hit the road. Did she want to live, or didn't she?

She looked at Barrett. Barrett was about ten years younger and reminded Madison so much of herself at that age. Even ten years ago, Madison had felt like her whole life was ahead of her. Lately she had been feeling like anything good that had happened was in the past.

Life was a bunch of little decisions to survive. Wear your seatbelt. Don't drink and drive. Eat better. Don't cheat on your spouse because they might put glass in your soup. Put on comfortable shoes for work. You don't realize that with each little decision you're deciding to live. Until something big happens. Like a possible recurrence of cancer. And the removal of something that makes you feel like a girl. The surgery hurts and the recovery hurts. The chemotherapy makes you feel sick and makes your hair fall out. And you're lying in your bed, unable to get up and make food even if you wanted it, and your cute sometimes-boyfriend is the only one you have to help you because your parents are gone and didn't see fit to give you a sibling. Do you want to keep going if you're facing that? It takes effort. Life has to be *worth sticking around for*. It's easier to just give up.

Madison didn't know what happened after a person died. She liked Betty White's attitude: anytime someone died her mother would say, "Well, they know the secret now!" Science answered many questions, but when it came to the human spirit, science was lacking in clinical trials. Madison wasn't religious, but she liked the eastern religions, the ones that looked at life as a stream, not as something that ended and you were gone and that was it. After a certain point, Madison would want to see what came next. She'd want to know the secret. But was this that time? All she had to do was give up, right now, and she would die.

And maybe, if some of those religions were right, she would see her parents. She missed them so.

Haley and Arlo and even Tom were her friends. They would miss her, sure, but their lives would go on. Dave would be upset. And being a man, he would feel that he should've protected her. And the last thing they'd done was have a fight. He would have to live with that fight being the last time they had spoken.

It would be the same if Dave died and left Madison. She would be devastated; if he'd had a chance to save himself and hadn't, she'd think she hadn't been worth sticking around for.

Barrett stirred and looked up at Madison. There was sorrow in her eyes. She knew they weren't making it out of here. She closed her eyes again; better to sleep than to think about what came next.

Madison had to get Barrett out of this. She had to. She realized that was something, right there: Barrett was worth sticking around for. And so was Dave.

And Crystal. If Madison didn't stick it out and bring these people down, Crystal's death would be meaningless.

What kind of example would Madison be setting for other people if she gave up? Giving up in this cement room, sure, people might understand that; but it would still affect them in an *It's a Wonderful Life* kind of way, that ripple effect where everyone's life affects everyone else's. But giving up by refusing cancer treatment was different. That was where you were telling people that they weren't worth sticking around for.

Madison's father had been a man of the world and of languages, and he'd always had the right word at the right time. He had a saying for when Madison was feeling sorry for herself: *porbrecito.* Spanish for "poor little thing."

Her father would never have allowed her the kind of self-pity she'd been demonstrating.

But Daddy, I have cancer again!

Porbrecitooooooo, she could hear him say.

Responsibility. Never giving up. Having the constant willingness to fight back against the slings and arrows of life because other people were watching you to see what you do, and those people were worth sticking around for. And maybe, at the end of the day, even she was worth sticking around for.

Madison suddenly stood, which woke up Barrett. She balanced carefully so that her tied-together ankles didn't cause her to fall. She reached her arms up as high as she could, getting them to about chest level. Barrett's eyes got wide, not knowing what Madison was doing. With her arms lifted, Madison spread her fingers out to tense her forearm muscles, making them as big as possible. Using every last shred of strength in her altered pec muscles, she brought her arms down fast and hard while pulling them apart, making an "ahhhhh" sound with the exertion. The duct tape split in two, right down the center between her wrists.

Her arms came to rest at her sides, untied, the duct tape hanging in pieces from her wrists.

That's why you present your hands in front of you when you're being tied up.

The sound Madison had made was loud. Madison and Barrett froze for a moment to see if the guys outside had heard. They hadn't; one of them was still snoring.

Madison looked down at her ankles. They hadn't searched them, they had just wanted their phones. But she didn't carry anything in her pockets anyway. Maybe Barrett did? She mimed scissors or a knife, and Barrett nodded and pointed her head at her right pocket. Madison took a deep breath and let it out, calming her racing pulse. The concrete floor was now in their favor: no creaking of old boards, just a few silent hops over to Barrett.

Madison reached into the pocket that Barrett had indicated and felt something small and metal. She pulled it out and discovered a tiny Swiss Army knife. Madison raised her eyebrows at Barrett, and Barrett shrugged.

Madison opened the pocket knife and pulled out the little scissors. First, she cut the tape on her own ankles, still listening to the snoring in the other room. Barrett and Madison worked in silence, not even having to whisper to each other. Madison hoped this was a good omen for the minutes and hours that would follow: good team members didn't have to discuss what they were doing, they just knew what the other was thinking instinctively.

When Madison got the tape off her own ankles, she went behind Barrett and examined the zip tie holding her wrists together. She selected the scissors again, thinking they would be the most effective on the plastic zip tie. She was right: the zip tie snapped right off.

Barrett's shoulders slumped forward. Her arms were asleep and wouldn't move. Madison began massaging her arms, trying to get the blood flow back into them. As the arms started to wake up, Barrett grimaced and started breathing harder with the pain. Finally, she was able to take the knife from Madison and use the scissors to cut through the duct tape on her ankles.

Now they were untied, but they had to figure out how to get out of a cement room with two huge jailers sitting right outside.

Madison was hurt. Something in her stomach. She cried out, but there was only silence. She tried again.

"Help me!"

The sound of chairs scuffling on the cement floor came from the other room. A disembodied voice through the dust and grime and the thick metal door.

"What's the matter with you?"

"I need help!"

"I think she's really sick," Barrett said.

The sound of the keychain in the lock, the smooth silver doorknob turning. Madison and Barrett stared at each other, mind melding their thoughts and actions. Words were impossible, but they were unnecessary.

The door opened and Thing One came through. Madison waited until Thing Two had cleared the door frame behind him, the first guy looking confused when he didn't see Madison sitting in her chair. He was walking farther into the room to stand in front of Barrett, still seemingly tied up, to figure out what was going on. From behind the door Madison kicked Thing Two in the side of his left knee as hard as she could with her hard-soled

Doc Martens. She heard crunching and breaking as he screamed and went down.

Thing One turned to see what had happened to his friend, and Barrett leapt up from her chair onto his back, stabbing him deep in the ear with her pocketknife. He bellowed and put his hand to his ear, which was now spouting blood, and went down to one knee, with Barrett still on his back.

Barrett jumped off, leaving him writhing on the floor, and joined Madison as they ran out the door, Madison kicking up the kickstand with her foot and pulling the door shut behind them, locking the two bruisers inside. Madison put the key in her coat pocket.

They ran outside, and Madison took a huge breath of fresh air, so happy to be alive and not in a cement room anymore. She realized that she knew exactly where they were: a business park in Sorrento Valley, just north of San Diego. Sorrento Valley was for the most part a business district, but in a rural setting. Wide open spaces with occasional large office buildings and office parks. Lots of chaparral and large, empty roads. This particular business park was more on the industrial end of things, and it had rows of one-story buildings used mostly as shops or studios. The rows of buildings were accessed by small streets, more like alleyways, that divided them. It was just off a large main road that was empty in the middle of the night. This was a business area and would be deserted after about seven PM. Madison estimated it was approximately two AM. The place was completely quiet and lonely. They were five miles from any type of civilization: a gas station, a Jack-in-the-Box, or any type of home or human being.

Each of the shops or studios in the lot had a front door with a big window next to it and a bay door at the back. The spaces were generally used for manufacturing or servicing machinery.

"We are going to have to walk for miles to find help."

Barrett hit her forehead. "My phone! They have my phone in their pocket."

"I don't know about you, but I didn't feel like going through the pockets of a man who could strangle me in less than a minute."

"Okay, that's true."

The back of the business park was a long alley that bordered a hillside. The front of the business park sat on the large, lonely road that they would have to walk down to get to any type of human being.

Madison started walking toward the front of the business park. She and Barrett had been held on the north side; they walked west toward the exit. As they got to the edge of their row of buildings, they paused to peek around the corner.

An SUV was heading down the road, slowing ahead of the driveway with its turn signal on. There was no one else on the road. Madison recognized the vehicle by the headlights, a game she used to play with her friend from grade school. She loved her Barbies and dolls, but she might have loved cars even more. They would sit on her friend's stoop at night for hours playing "name that model," just by the headlight shape. Another useless piece of trivia; until now, when you recognize a Cadillac Escalade being driven by a bad guy.

"That's Randy's car."

Since he was at the front of the complex, they ran toward the back. A few more moments and they would have stepped in front of the building, in full view of Randy. Madison was happy that Barrett could run as fast as she, and they made it to the back of the complex in mere moments. They turned to the right instinctively, and soon they were presented with the next row of buildings. Turning right, they were now walking in the alley parallel to the office they had been held in. They could hear Randy's SUV pull up in front of the door where the goons were locked in. Randy would know in moments that they had escaped and that they couldn't have gotten far. He would be out in a flash to try to track them down. Madison was glad they hadn't gotten out to the road before Randy had appeared; it was a long, open highway and they would have been deer in his headlights.

Madison tried each door as they passed it. She lucked out with the third office down: the door opened and they stepped inside.

It had been some type of stereo and alarm installation and repair place. There was a plate glass window that shed a tiny bit of light from nearby security lighting onto a floor littered with trash. It was a mostly empty space with pieces of wiring, broken motherboards, and odd metal pieces lying around. The walls had posters with advertisements for alarm systems and car stereos. There was an old clock on the wall, like the kind that was used in classrooms.

Also on the floor was a leftover camp of some kind: a makeshift stove with an old pot, some kindling, and some matches. An old army blanket, rank with mildew, was piled next to it, along with some bloodied cotton balls. From the smell it appeared they had been cooking meth, not dinner. At least there was a fire extinguisher in a glass case, hanging on the wall above the shop sink.

Barrett and Madison moved to the back of the space, as far from the plate glass window as they could get. Nevertheless, they were sitting ducks. Anyone walking by would be able to look in and see them.

"This is not a good hiding place."

"Agreed," Barrett said.

"We kept the key, but he will be able to talk to the no-necks through the door and find out what happened. It is a toss-up whether he searches the business park or goes out to the road to look for us. The road is open and there's nothing for miles. There's an office building across the street, and the possibility exists there's someone in there this late, but it's doubtful. So what do we do?"

Barrett thought for a moment. They had been free for only five minutes.

"Let's go down this alleyway to the end and look at the street and see what we think. I don't know what other options we have to get away."

Without further discussion they went out the door, turned right, and walked to the end of the aisle. They looked around the corner. The parking lot was empty. It could be presumed that Randy's Escalade was still parked in front of the office where they had been held. Maybe he was figuring out what to do, too.

Madison looked across the street at the office building. There was one light on the top floor.

"Cleaning person or someone forgot to turn the light out?" she whispered.

"No way to tell."

The minute they stepped away from their building they would be out in the open for miles. No other people, no other movement. Randy could pick them off easier than a target at a shooting range. It would be like a fun video game for him. Madison looked at Barrett and shook her head. They turned in unison and walked back to the empty office. They didn't speak until they got inside.

"The first place he's going to look is the road, and he would spot us in less than five minutes. At this point, I think he'll just shoot us or run us over with the car." Madison put the bolt across the inside of the door. It was at least some protection, but the plate glass window put them on display.

"Agreed," Barrett said.

They walked to the back of the space, as far from the window as possible, and sat on the floor, leaning against the wall.

"He knows how long we've been gone, Tweedledee and Tweedledum will tell him. So he'll be able to estimate about how far we would have gotten on that street. All he has to do is drive one way, make a U-turn and go back the other way, and when he doesn't see us, he's going to know we are somewhere in this business park."

"Agreed," Barrett said.

"Feel free to make a suggestion, rather than just saying 'agreed.'" Madison was on edge, which increased her natural impatience.

"Sorry, I thought we were just outlining the situation, and we hadn't gotten to the suggestion part yet. I have a suggestion: let's go back in time, and you don't bring the bad guys to my hiding place."

Madison was silent. Barrett was right, and it stung to hear it out loud. But they weren't going to get anywhere fighting with each other, they had to be a team.

Madison took a deep breath and let it out.

"I deserved that. Okay. Here is the bottom line: we need other human beings to help us. That means calling 911, or jumping in someone's car that happens to drive by, or knocking on someone's door and having them open it."

Barrett nodded. "So we need either a phone, someone friendly in a car, or someone behind a door that will open it for us."

Madison looked at the ceiling as she thought of Mutt and Jeff's SUV that had carried them to this place. What were the chances they had left the key in the car? Not good enough to risk going back over there to check.

She put her gaze back on Barrett. "That about sums it up. And we are in the middle of nowhere. During the day this is a fairly active area. But at night we might as well be in the Sahara Desert. No businesses that are open, no gas stations, nothing. Chaparral and trees. There might be a random person or two, maybe some cleaning people, in an office building across the street, but we can't get across the street without risking Randy seeing us."

"Agreed—I mean. . . yes, that's true, let me think."

Madison smiled at Barrett's correction. "Okay. So. We need to bring human beings to us."

Barrett studied Madison, trying to see if Madison had an idea. Madison didn't. She was just reasoning out the situation. They needed to bring humans to them. Why do humans come to you? If there is an emergency. This was definitely an emergency. But they didn't have any way of calling human beings to tell them there was an emergency, with no telephones. So what brings humans somewhere without you calling them?

"Fire," Madison said.

"What?"

"Fire. Fire brings human beings to a place without calling them."

Barrett stared. "You want us to set these buildings on fire? I'm desperate too, but I don't want to . . . what is that? A felony?"

Madison stood up and started scouting the floor. "First of all, we are trying to save our lives from murderers. Any possible crimes we might commit while that is being done would be taken into consideration. Second of all, I don't want to set the buildings on fire, not because it's a felony, but because it is massive destruction that could spread down the street and kill plants and animals."

Barrett stood up, but she didn't know what they were searching for. "But you said *fire.* You said fire brings people. So I assume you're going to start a fire?"

Madison found a dirty plastic bag that had been crumpled and thrown in the corner. She opened it and began putting the detritus from the floor into the plastic bag.

"Yes, we're going to start a fire. But we're going to start a small fire that smokes more than it flames. In order to do it properly, we need to be in an open area where someone might see it, but where we are not risking plants or buildings."

"What are you looking for? I'll help you, but I don't know what we want."

"We want things that don't burn well. Things that smoke rather than burn. Like plastic, rubber, things like that."

Madison picked up all of the cotton balls, even the ones with blood on them, which normally would have grossed her out so much that she would have retched, but desperate times and all that.

"I read a lot, and I collect a lot of useless information. In this case, my useless information works in our favor: when someone is lost in the woods, this is how they ask for help. We want the smoke to be black, because then it is clearly a fire and not someone's barbecue or campfire. So that is why we want things that don't burn well but make black smoke: oily things, things made of rubber or petroleum."

Barrett found her own plastic bag, and was filling it with trash from the floor. "Plastic lids to soda cups?"

"Perfect. Anything plastic."

Now that they had a plan, they were working fast. "Randy won't expect us to go to the back of this facility. The back is a place to get trapped. He's going to be looking for us at the front, and along the street, and ultimately inside these offices. I don't think he'll look at the back. So that's where we're going to go."

Barrett stopped for a moment, holding the plastic bag down at her side. "So we're going to go to the place where he can trap us?"

Madison kept searching the ground and didn't look up to answer. "Exactly."

The last thing Madison did was grab the matches that were on the ground by the makeshift stove and put them in her pocket. She looked at the blanket and thought for a moment. She didn't want to pick it up.

"I wish I had gloves. God knows what I can catch touching this; I might even be able to get pregnant from it."

Barrett laughed and Madison picked the blanket up. She carried it to the back where the sink was, and doused it with water. She put it over her arm and stood in front of the glassed-in fire extinguisher.

"You don't think an alarm goes off if I break this glass, do you?"

Madison didn't think an alarm would go off, but she didn't want to be the only one making the decision.

"No, I don't think it will. It's not hooked up to anything."

Madison used the little hammer hanging from the side to break the glass, and then carefully reached in and grabbed the fire extinguisher. She turned to Barrett.

"Ready?"

"Ready."

Madison opened the door and stuck her head out, looking both ways, up and down the alleyway. It was quiet. She wondered if Randy had driven out to the road to look for them.

Madison turned left and ran to the back of the property. It was only about sixty yards, but she felt like it was ten miles.

They got to the back and Madison saw two old tires thrown against a building. She pointed and Barrett grabbed one while Madison grabbed the other. They rolled them over to the middle of a small parking area set up for about ten cars in a row. The parking spaces were along a retaining wall, and on the other side of the retaining wall was pure vegetation. They would start the fire in between the building on the right and the retaining wall on the left. It wasn't ideal, but nothing about the situation was ideal.

Madison piled up the cotton balls, which would catch on fire easily, and the other plastic items they had found, and then went over to a small tree that was hanging over the retaining wall.

"I'm sorry, tree, I have to take one of your green branches. I hope this doesn't hurt. It's for a good cause. Thank you for your service."

"Jesus," Barrett said.

Madison tried to pull the branch off, but he didn't want to give it. It was a small branch, just part of a sapling, but it didn't want to break.

"Can you come help me please?"

Barrett came over and they yanked on the branch together. Finally it gave way and came off the tree.

Madison's senses were on high alert. She was listening for any vehicle that could be coming down one of the rows of buildings. Any flash of light from the streetlamps reflecting something on the ground caused her head to jerk in that direction. They had so little time to get this done before Randy started driving up and down the rows of buildings. In doing so, he would naturally come to the back in order to turn and go up the next row.

Madison found some duct tape and a couple of oily rags and added them to the pile. Then she remembered.

"It needs to be in a *V*."

"A *V*?" Barrett asked.

"Yes, that is the universal sign for *need help*."

That's when they both heard the SUV. It was coming from the direction of the space where they'd been held. Both of their heads snapped up and they stared at each other. Without any discussion they turned and ran the sixty yards back to their hiding space. They ran through the door and Madison threw the bolt. They scooted to the back of the shop and sat on the floor.

"How can we set this fire to summon help when he is driving up and down these aisles looking for us?"

Madison put her head in her hands. As she did that she touched the cut and what must be a massive bruise on her face.

"I don't know."

They were like rats in a maze, trying to get away from something that was chasing them and could appear around every corner. If he had already been out to the road, he would know they hadn't started walking, and therefore they were in these sets of buildings somewhere.

Madison stood up and looked down at Barrett. "I got you into this. I am going to go set that fire and you are going to wait here."

"No! I know I said that to you earlier because I was mad, but it's not your fault. Ultimately, I'm the one that started all this because I discovered their secret first."

"It's nice that we are in a 'take responsibility' circle, it's good for our mental health, but this is not the time for it. I'm older than you are and I'm pulling rank. You are sitting here and waiting. You run slowly anyway."

Barrett laughed, and surreptitiously wiped away a tear. "I do not."

"Yes you do, you're going to slow me down. Stay inside, against this wall. If I don't come back in ten minutes he got me. And that means he's going to be busy. He's going to be trying to get me to tell him where you are. So you will have time to get away. So in ten minutes, you open that door and you run as fast as you can out to the road. Turn left, not right, because you will reach civilization sooner that way. And just run as fast as you can. I will do everything in my power to keep him busy so that you can get away. Agreed?"

Barrett had put her head down, and Madison could see tears dropping onto her knees. "I don't want you to go."

"I have to."

Barrett looked up, her face streaked with tears. "I don't usually cry. I'm just tired."

Yep, just like Madison. Didn't want to seem weak by crying.

"Oh, are you crying? I didn't notice. I thought it was the dust in here."

Madison put her fist out and Barrett bumped it with her fist.

"You got this, grasshopper. Ten minutes, and then you run."

"Ten minutes, and then I run."

Madison walked to the door, opened it, and ran.

Chapter Twenty-Four

Friday 3:32 AM

As Madison ran, she listened. She could hear Randy's car at the far end of the property, rows of buildings away. He was driving up and down them, looking for Madison and Barrett. If she were in his position, she would start over again when she got to the end.

She got to the pile of fire starter and resumed putting it into a large *V*. She set the wet blanket to the side. She used the matches to light a twig she had found, and then paused. She didn't know whether to light the bottom of the *V* first, or one of the sides of the top.

"I don't know," she said and lit the bottom.

The cotton balls took immediately. She could hear Randy's car two buildings away. The cotton balls caught the plastic lids on fire, and they melted and started to smoke. The plastic lids caught the rag on fire, and it started to smoke. Madison fanned the smoke with her arms, and then searched and found a piece of cardboard that she used instead. She had to make sure the fire was really going before she went back to Barrett.

It was hard to get the branch to catch fire because it was green and moist. The leaves started, and it hurt Madison's heart to think that she was killing a piece of the plant kingdom. She knew it was not the time to worry about things like that, but it was part of her nature. Madison set each item on fire, using the twig. Now most of the *V* was smoking, black smoke from the petroleum items, and white smoke from the plastic. Madison picked up the wet blanket and put it partially on some of the flames. This caused the flames to go out and the smoke to get thicker. Madison coughed as some of it got in her face.

Randy's car was one aisle away. Madison had a built-in clock, and she knew it had been about eight minutes. In another two minutes Barrett was going to run out to the street. If Madison hadn't finished, but she hadn't been caught by Randy, he would see Barrett running and go after her. Madison was now wondering about the wisdom of her plan: she hadn't considered that maybe she wouldn't finish in time, but Randy still wouldn't see her. He would then get Barrett when she came out of her hiding place, while Madison was still at the back of the building.

The smoke was now rising up above the building. Madison saw it swirling in the streetlamps, plumes of smoke against the night sky. It smelled horrific. Madison hated the destruction of fires, not for what they did to man-made things, but what they did to vegetation and animals. This fire was far enough away from the hillside that it shouldn't catch, but nevertheless she was worried. She had the fire extinguisher with her in case it looked like there was going to be too much fire, but she was still terrified of destroying plants and animals. The flames were still close to the ground, and for the most part it was generating a lot of smoke. A helicopter would for sure see it, assuming someone called the fire department. In order to save their lives, someone had to see this fire, call the fire department, and the trucks had to come out. There were a lot of "maybes" in this scenario. But it was the best she had.

About one minute to go. She couldn't hear Randy's car; had he stopped somewhere? Madison turned and ran back to their hiding place. As she got to the door, Barrett had just opened it to step outside. Randy's Escalade was at the top of their aisle, and Madison could just see the nose of it. He hadn't completed the turn. Madison shoved Barrett backward, and she flew and hit the ground.

"What the—"

Madison shut the door and bolted it, and ran to the back of the shop, grabbing Barrett's arm and pulling her with her. They sat down against the wall and waited.

"Why the violence?"

"He's at the end of the aisle," Madison whispered. She didn't know why she was whispering since he was in a car and wouldn't be able to hear them inside. It just seemed like the right thing to do.

"It's pretty dark in here," Barrett said. "Do you think he's going to see us as he drives by?"

"I think if he's driving he's not going to see us. And now he's going to notice the fire at the back of the property and that's going to draw his attention. But I think we better just sit here and not move."

They sat in silence. Madison touched her face where the cut was and gently pressed her cheekbone. It hurt. She looked over at Barrett, whose face was streaked with grime. Madison realized her face must be filthy as well. If she didn't get shot by a madman she would die of an infected cut on her face.

She looked down her shirt. The taped gauze had long since fallen off her biopsy incision, and it was red and swollen. Another infection starting. She shook her head and dropped her shirt back down.

Madison realized that in the last twelve hours the appendages on her chest had served no purpose, and had actually hindered her ability to survive. Granted, the last twelve hours had not been normal, but the point was the same: they were useless.

Madison could smell smoke. She looked at Barrett, who'd gotten the scent at the same time.

"Let's hope there is someone, somewhere, who can see that smoke and will call the fire department."

"If it was a cleaning person, or someone working late across the street, they would see it."

"And it is high enough now that people a mile away can see it. People from the freeway could for sure see it. There should be a lot of 911 calls coming in. We just have to sit here and wait."

That's when Randy appeared in the window.

He cupped his hands around his eyes and put his face up to the glass. His tie was off, and his dress shirt was untucked. He had removed his jacket and left it somewhere. Before, he had looked like a businessman. As his suit became disarrayed, his appearance became more crazed. Now he looked more like the madman that he actually was. Madison and Barrett had frozen at the sight of him, and it took a minute for him to make out their silhouettes in the darkened shop. But he saw them.

He threw back his head and laughed.

He walked over to the door and tried it. Madison and Barrett stayed on the floor where they were. They were sitting ducks. There was nothing they could do. Madison realized that she had taken the one weapon they had, the fire extinguisher, and left it out by the fire. She could have at least had a chance of hitting him with it, or spraying him with it, but now they had nothing. They stayed on the ground because there was nothing left for them to do.

Randy threw himself against the door, trying to break it down. The bolt was strong. He stopped trying to break the door down, and returned to the window, cupping his eyes to see them again. Contemplating. Assessing. If he could break the window, he could get at them. Madison thought that she and Barrett together might have a shot in hand-to-hand combat, but he would use his gun. He could shoot through the plate glass window, but that would be a wild shot, unlikely to hit one of them, and result in just a small hole in the glass. Madison figured all of these things were going through his head. He stepped out of view.

Barrett and Madison stared at each other. If this was the end, this was the end. They'd tried. And then, Madison started to hear something. It was faint. She was afraid she was imagining it. Then Barrett cocked her head the way a dog does, changing the position of the ears so that the reception of sound moved from one ear to the other. She heard it too. Sirens.

Randy appeared in the window again. He had a tire iron. He swung back and hit the window.

The window didn't break at first. It cracked. Madison thought it must be made with some inner material so it wouldn't shatter. Polycarbonate film, she remembered, was put in between panes of glass to keep store fronts from being easily accessible to criminals. There were cracks appearing, shatters of light spiraling out from the impact point, reflecting light onto the floor of the shop like it was shining through crystal.

The sirens were getting louder. Randy swung again. *SMACK.* Another crack.

Madison and Barrett were standing now, still backed up against the wall. Randy swung and hit again. Another crack. Then he stopped and tilted his head. He heard the sirens. He, too, knew that meant rescue for the girls, and the end for him. He took another swing, this time harder. The glass shattered but remained in place. Randy was getting desperate. He had to kill them and get away before the fire engines got there. Timing was everything. If he didn't get to them right now, he might be able to kill them, but his car would be seen leaving the scene of a crime and he would be caught.

Another swing and the inner pane of glass shattered. Madison and Barrett cowered and covered their faces, but no glass sprayed at them. It stuck to the polycarbonate film. Randy dropped the tire iron and took the .45 caliber gun out of his waistband and shot through the remaining glass, but the shot went wild and missed them. Barrett and Madison threw themselves on the floor, making themselves as flat as possible. The sirens were deafening now. Randy aimed again.

Madison looked up just as Randy was bathed in a red glow from the fire engine that had turned the corner and was headed down their alleyway. Randy saw the fire engine. He put his head back and roared. It wasn't a scream. It was something primitive. They couldn't hear the sound because of the sirens, but with his mouth open, the flashing red made his face into something horrifying, something satanic. He suddenly ran out of view and Madison and Barrett jumped up just as a fire engine raced past the window. They ran to the door, and Madison opened it and looked outside. Randy's Escalade was blocked in by three fire trucks at one end, and by the fire and more fire trucks at the other. Randy had climbed into the driver's seat to get away, but he was unable to do so now that the fire department had arrived. He was sitting in the driver's seat, bellowing and hitting the steering wheel.

They were safe.

Chapter Twenty-Five

Friday 5:07 AM

"Ouch!"

Madison and Barrett sat next to each other on the tailgate of the paramedic unit. They had blankets around their shoulders. Barrett didn't really need any attending to, but tell that to a paramedic brought to a violent crime scene. Madison, on the other hand, needed to get the cut on her face cleaned.

"Seriously, that hurts." Madison waved her hand in front of her face so that the cute paramedic boy couldn't touch her. "Can I just do this at home? I know how to use hydrogen peroxide."

"It hurts because it's infected."

The paramedic reached for her face again and she backed away from his hand.

"Oh my God let him do his job," Barrett said.

Madison relented and the paramedic started cleaning again. "It helps that you're really cute," she said.

The paramedic laughed. Madison wasn't sure why she had said that; she was punchy.

Madison looked in the direction of the alleyway where Randy's SUV had been parked. He had been put in the back of a police car and taken away already. Madison and Barrett had explained to the first officer on the scene what had happened, and then they had explained it a few more times with each arriving higher ranked officer. Randy was a felon in possession of a gun, so they were able to arrest him just for that. Everything else would be sorted out later. He would certainly be charged with kidnapping, not to mention the murders of those couples and Crystal. Thing One and Thing Two had been taken away in a large police wagon. Madison doubted they'd fit in the back of a regular police car.

A Crown Victoria pulled up behind the fire engines at the back of the property and parked. Madison watched as Tom got out of the driver's seat. The paramedic finished with Madison and moved to the cab of his truck to do paperwork.

Tom made his way over to them. There were still emergency personnel putting out the last of the fire, and officers were getting statements from the cleaning people who'd seen the fire from the building across the street and called it in. Tom stepped over the electrical cables that were lighting the scene and the hoses from the fire trucks. Madison smiled as he approached.

"You didn't call me back," he said.

"I was busy," Madison said. It was good to see him.

"Somebody hit you?"

Madison put her hand up to her cheek, which now had a clean white gauze bandage over the cut. She hadn't wanted to tell the cute paramedic about the biopsy incision on her chest that definitely needed to be cleaned.

"You should see the other guy," she said. "How did you know we were here?"

"When you didn't call me back I called and texted and you didn't answer. So I decided to head over to Café Moto, where you said you were. There were cops there. Some people at the coffee house heard a commotion and saw a big SUV tear out of the parking lot of what they thought was an abandoned building. I may be dumb, but I can put two and two together."

"I probably should've waited for you to get there before I went in."

"Yeah, you shoulda." Tom shook his head. "And then I found your phone in the parking lot, so I knew someone had taken you. You have me as an emergency contact on your iPhone? That's sweet."

"Whatever," Madison said.

"Thank God I saw that before the battery died." He handed her the phone. It was scratched and dinged, but the plexiglass screen cover had saved it. She put it in her pocket.

"Anyway, I've been trying to figure out who had you ever since. Then I heard this call come in and someone said your name on the radio."

"My name on the radio? You mean I'm famous?"

Tom didn't laugh at Madison's attempt at humor. He looked over the top of her head, and then down at the ground.

"Don't do that to me again, Maddie."

"I'm sorry I worried you. I am."

Barrett jumped in, sticking out her hand. "Hi. I'm Barrett."

They shook hands and Tom turned to Madison. "So, you found your girl?"

"That's why they pay me the big money."

"Yeah, so, I got most of the story from the guys on the scene while I was on my way over here. You seem to have blown apart a massive insurance fraud and murder ring."

Madison looked at Barrett. "Honestly, she's the one who first noticed something weird about these deaths. All I did was follow in her footsteps in order to find her."

"Well, either way, good job. There is a lot of unwinding that needs to occur. There'll be various agencies connected with this and you guys are gonna be telling your story for a long time."

"Yes," Madison said. "And they need to find Travis Moore. He was in on it too, but he left before all the fun started here."

"So, about that—" Tom began.

"Dave," Madison said. "Tom. My cell phone is dead and I need to call Dave. Do you have a charger?"

Tom paused a moment. "I thought he was just a surfer."

That threw Madison. "What do you mean? He is just a surfer."

"No, I mean . . . does he have some sort of specialized training?"

Madison was now completely perplexed. "You need to tell me what you're talking about because I am seriously confused. Specialized training in what?"

A police detective walked over and interrupted them. He and Tom knew each other, and they exchanged greetings. Then the detective turned his attention to Madison and Barrett. "I'm going to need to get your statements, and it's going to be a long night. Is there someone that can bring you clothes? We can get food on the way to the police station."

Madison and Barrett looked at each other. Neither one of them had someone at home who could bring them clothes. This is what it meant to be alone. Madison could ask Dave, but they didn't really have that kind of relationship, and their last conversation had been an argument. He'd be glad to know she was okay, but he might not even know that there was anything wrong. Madison figured Barrett would say the same thing about Cornell. Cornell! Madison had forgotten all about him.

"Hey, Barrett, what about Cornell?" Madison said. "Don't you need to call him? He probably came back from the newspaper office and you weren't there and the police were, and he's freaking out."

"Shit. You're right. This is a new thing with us. It only really started for real after I went into hiding. I'm not used to having someone I need to report to."

A woman after my own heart, Madison thought. "Do you know his phone number? Or is it in your phone?"

"He's probably waiting at the newspaper office. I can call him there."

The detective handed Barrett his cell phone. Madison stood up and her thighs screamed. She was going to be sore tomorrow from all of the exertion; just sitting for twenty minutes had caused her to stiffen up.

"Tom, a minute?"

Madison pulled Tom to the side, away from Barrett's telephone call. The way Tom had been talking, it made Madison concerned that Dave had been arrested for something, coincidental to this mess. Dave generally tried to stay out of trouble, but he was sometimes arrested for getting in a fight.

"Why did you ask me about Dave?"

"Okay. The good news is we have Travis Moore in custody already."

"Wow, that is good news. How did you manage that?"

"He went to your apartment to search it. I guess your friend Dave . . . is that all he is? A friend?"

"Continue," Madison said.

"Okay, well your friend Dave had been wondering about you and he showed up and walked up your stairs, and this guy Travis was trying to pick your lock."

Barrett handed the cell phone back to the detective and walked over to where Madison and Tom were standing. "Cornell is bringing me some clothes. I'm having him bring an extra pair of sweatpants and a sweatshirt; they should fit you."

"Cool. Tom is telling me that they caught Travis. Or someone did. I haven't mentioned Dave to you, he is my . . . he is my something, I'm not sure what. Anyway, I guess he showed up as Travis was trying to get into my apartment to search for the memory drive."

"What memory drive?" Tom asked.

"Later," Madison and Barrett said in unison, and then laughed.

"So what happened?" Madison said.

"I guess Dave asked what he was doing, and he didn't like Travis's answer. So he kicked Travis in the face, knocking two of his teeth out, and then kicked him in the chest and knocked him over the railing into the alley."

Madison threw back her head and laughed. Barrett didn't know how to react at first, then she too had to laugh.

Madison wanted to give Dave the biggest hug she'd ever given him. But she was a little confused about why he had kicked Travis. Normally Dave liked to punch people, at least when they deserved it. He had a black belt in kung fu, so he was certainly capable of kicking people, but normally he punched them. Whatever, it had created the desired result: Travis on his back in the alley with teeth missing.

"And then," Tom continued, "your neighbor Ryan called the police. And the paramedics. Travis broke his shoulder blade with the fall, but surprisingly, other than his two missing teeth, he's okay."

"So, is Dave at the police station? Is he under arrest?"

"Yes, for the time being," Tom said. "You can't really knock someone over a railing into an alley and not get arrested. But I'm sure everyone will consider the fact that he took a bad guy into custody for us. Well, not exactly custody, but he was lying in an alley, broken, and we just had to sweep him up with a broom."

Madison smiled. It was always timing with Tom. She gave him a light punch in the arm. "Thanks for being here."

"Well, I had to make sure these guys were doing their job."

"Can you call the station and have someone tell Dave that I'm okay?" Madison figured that Dave was probably worried.

"I will. He'll be there when you guys get there."

Tom's cell phone rang, and he looked at it. "I need to take this; I'll be right back."

Tom walked away, and Madison and Barrett were left standing alone.

"That detective said he would be back in a minute and we'll be going to the police station soon," Barrett said.

"Cool."

"So . . . Dave, huh?"

"Yeah, Dave."

"It sounds like Dave needs an action figure."

Madison laughed. "Yes, that he does."

A woman in track pants and a hoodie approached them. "Hi, I'm Lyndsay from the *San Diego Union Tribune*. I wanted to set up a time to talk to you guys about what happened. I'd like to do a series on this criminal ring that you discovered, and how you exposed them."

Barrett started to answer, "Sure—"

"Actually," Madison interrupted, "Barrett is a reporter and she's going to be doing an exclusive for the *Hillcrest Holler*."

Lyndsay looked confused. "I'm not familiar with that . . . is it a newspaper?"

"It is. You may not have heard of it because it's up-and-coming. But it should be much more popular once Barrett begins her series. I'm sorry, but she works for them and it needs to be an exclusive."

Lyndsay seemed to be catching on. "Well, let me give you my card. We may be able to work something out where we publish your articles on the same day or just after they appear in your paper. I might just ask for an additional reporting credit, but I'm thinking it might be nice for you to get some exposure, and we likely have a bigger circulation than the *Hillcrest . . . Hokey*."

"Holler!" Madison and Barrett said in unison.

"Right, right, *Holler*." Lyndsay smiled. She handed Barrett her card and they agreed to be in touch.

"Thanks," Barrett said to Madison as Lyndsay walked away.

"You're gonna be famous."

"I'll take being successful. Hell, I'll take making a living."

"You will."

Barrett kicked at a little piece of gravel on the ground. "So . . . are we going to be friends?"

Madison looked at the activity around them: fire trucks, police, paramedics, cables and hoses everywhere; the flashing red strobe light from the fire engines bathed it all in a red glow. The stench from the burning rubber and plastic was infused into everything. They had been through a war together. She had met Barrett less than twenty-four hours before, and yet it felt like they'd known each other their whole lives.

"Yes, Barrett, we are going to be friends."

One week later, 5:30 PM

Madison sat on the beach at Windansea under the shack. She searched through the surfers sitting on their surfboards out past the breaking point of the waves. Dave had told her to meet him at the beach at sunset. His Jeep was in the lot, so she knew he was in the water.

She hadn't gotten home until late in the morning after the fire. They had released Dave long before that, a couple of the cops patting him on the back as he walked out. Sure, on the surface it might appear like he had committed battery, but once all the paperwork was filed, it would be clear that he had been placing Travis under citizen's arrest, and when Travis resisted, Dave was forced to use self-defense. Wink, wink; nudge, nudge. As the police investigation into Travis and Randy continued, the charges against them were mounting. They were both being held in county jail without bail pending their court appearances, and they wouldn't be getting out. They were going to prison for a long, long time.

Sitting on this beach, looking out at the waves, her mind was taken back to her father's last days, as it often was in this spot. Madison was a daddy's girl. She worried that her mother had envied her relationship with her father, because her mother was the best mother a girl could have, and Madison didn't want her to feel slighted. The feeling of family her mother had created had died with her, but Madison hadn't felt truly alone until her father died. He'd been diagnosed with a brain tumor, the kind that is aggressive and kills quickly. They'd rented a condo right here on Neptune, and they had lived there for a glorious two weeks before he'd had to go into a hospice center for twenty-four-hour care. They'd sat on the patio for hours, barbecuing, watching the waves, her father with his binoculars spying on the dolphins playing in the surf. It had been the best time of their lives. She would always have those days in her memory; it was a treasure she had with her all the time, where she could sit with him, hear his voice, laugh at their shared jokes, and visit with him when she was lonely.

Travis was already talking to the DA in an attempt to get a better deal. He told them the entire scheme, including the part that Viceroy and Evan at the insurance brokerage had played, everything. The memory drive that Madison had stolen apparently had all of the accounting on it, showing how much money all of the players received from the insurance payouts. It was a running tally that they shared between them, keeping track of the spoils since none of these criminals trusted each other.

Viceroy and Evan must be shaking in their boots; it was just a matter of time before there was enough evidence gathered to charge them and put them away as well. Madison had laughed when Tom told her that Travis was turning on his partners: *Of course he is,* Madison had said. *He has no honor, even among thieves.*

There were a couple of surfers that had caught a wave. Was Dave the one flying and soaring over the wave, unidentifiable, intangible? Madison thought of the night ahead and what they might do, and she realized it didn't matter. She just wanted to sit by him. There was no one in the world whose quiet company she enjoyed more.

One of the insurance companies victimized in the fraud ring had called Madison earlier that day. They wanted to talk to her about a reward for discovering the fraud, and also about hiring her for another investigation. It had been nonstop for a week: when she had gotten her phone charged, she'd discovered twenty-five messages: from the other insurance companies involved and from news outlets, everyone wanting to talk to her, get her story, and offer her money. It looked like she was getting another fifteen minutes of fame.

She put the hoodie of her sweatshirt over her head and wrapped her arms around her knees. The sun was going down and it was getting chilly. Then she suddenly recognized Dave in the water: he was riding a wave in to the shore. As he got closer to the beach, he jumped off the surfboard and walked it in. Just before he got out of the water he kneeled down, tipping his head back to wet down his hair and get it out of his eyes. He waved at her and walked the rest of the way in.

Madison stood up as he approached. "I forgot to ask you something." She had to shout over the waves as he approached. "Why did you kick him? Why didn't you punch Travis?"

Dave kept walking toward her, shaking his head as he got closer. He waited until he was within speaking distance so he didn't have to yell.

"I didn't want to touch him. He was gross."

Madison laughed and wrapped her arms around his neck. He was soaking wet, and his wetsuit drenched her sweatshirt. She didn't care.

"The doctor called," she whispered into his neck. "It wasn't cancer."

Dave exhaled. She heard the air whistle past her ear. He backed away from her and stood with his surfboard next to him, looking out at the water.

"I knew it wasn't."

Dave had been scared, Madison realized. Her life affected other people.

"I have to keep watching. It's the price I pay for staying alive. Constant alertness."

Dave nodded. Madison was anxious about the next thing she had to say. He was a nice guy, and he would never say anything to hurt her feelings. But she didn't know how he truly felt.

"I don't want them anymore."

Dave looked at her, not sure what she meant. He searched her face, wanting to figure it out without having to ask. Madison kept talking.

"These." She pointed at her chest. "They hurt my back. They make my pec muscles weaker. They're toxic. I didn't realize that the manufacturer requires me to have an MRI every three years to make sure the implants aren't leaking and sending toxic silicone through my body. The doctor said the red marks could be a reaction to the silicone or the other chemicals in them."

Dave was looking out at the water, not saying anything. Madison hoped he was really thinking about what it would mean. She wanted his honest reaction. It wouldn't change her mind, but it might change their relationship.

"I'm not even judging other women who want them. There's millions of women who have them, and they seem to be doing just fine. But it turns out I'm not. I'm really sensitive to things, and maybe that's why they bother me and not other women."

Madison looked down at the sand and saw a tiny bit of peach color peeking out from underneath a rock. She reached down and picked it up: a shell. She thought for a second about the little guy that used to live inside of it. She put it in her pocket.

She looked up at Dave's face, wanting him to understand.

"They reduce my power," she said. "They're my kryptonite."

Dave looked down at her. He brushed a hair away from her forehead, and tucked it behind her ear. He bent his head and kissed her.

"Breasts are overrated," he said.

Madison smiled. He always knew the exact right thing to say.

"Let's go swimming," she said.

Madison pulled off her sweatshirt and sweatpants to reveal a one-piece bathing suit underneath. The sun had set, but there was still a strip of purple light along the horizon. It was chilly, but the water would be warm, having held on to the heat from an especially hot summer. She ran to the water's edge and Dave followed, after setting his surfboard against one leg of the shack.

She dove into the water and swam out, diving under the waves as each one approached. The waves at Windansea broke close to the shore, so she didn't have far to go to get just past the breaking point. She then swam south. Dave caught up to her quickly, being the stronger swimmer. They swam next to each other for a bit, and then when a wave started just behind her, Madison caught it and bodysurfed it for a bit. She swam over the top and let the wave continue on to the shore. Dave had bodysurfed it with her, and he let the wave go when she did. They paddled in place for a minute in the flat water between wave sets, and Madison floated over onto her back, gazing up at the purple and pink sky with a few wisps of clouds here and there.

"Madison, look," Dave whispered.

She sat up just as two dolphins swam past them, only ten feet away. A wave was coming, and Madison eyed it to see if she should ride it in or dive underneath it. It looked to be an easy wave. She glanced back at the dolphins and figured out they were waiting for the wave too. Dolphins were notorious surfers, but she had only ever watched them from the shore.

"Let's go!" Dave said.

She kicked to get up to speed, and the wave came up behind her, pushing her. Out of the corner of her eye she could see the dolphins leaping up and then back down as the wave propelled them forward. She was bodysurfing with dolphins.

She swam over the top of the wave and was once again floating in still water. The dolphins swam away, farther out to sea, playtime with the humans over.

"Seriously amazing," Dave said.

She kicked her way over to him, and he grabbed her and they held each other. The last line of light dropped below the horizon, and the first evening stars appeared overhead.

This is worth sticking around for.

Acknowledgments

"Music gives a soul to the universe, wings to the mind, flight to the imagination, and life to everything."

—Plato

Thank you to Taylor Swift. And Seal. And Sade. Alanis Morissette. Bob Marley. Mozart. Yo-Yo Ma. Lin-Manuel Miranda. Sara Bareilles. And to so many other songwriters and musicians who are poets and have made my mind soar into an aesthetic space where I can call upon the muse at any time because they've infused my life with a soundtrack that's always playing.

Danielle is my sister-in-law, my beta reader, and my friend; thank you so much to her and to my brother, who always helps me when the chips are down.

Thank you to Kristen Weber, editor and friend, always willing to lend an ear, and to Kathy Lazzaro, the quintessential fairy godmother.

Thank you to my Crooked Lane family: my editor, Terri Bischoff, for knowing Madison so well, and to Melissa Rechter, Madeline Rathle, and Rebecca Nelson for getting Madison out into the world; and of course to Matt Martz, for giving Madison and me a home.

Contrary to popular opinion, a literary agent's real work starts *after* they get you the book deal: thank you to Abby Saul of the Lark Group for talking me off the ledge on the regular.

Thank you to Analise for being my best friend.

No one in a county building would accept a bribe, nor would I try to pay one; but it makes for a good story. There is no Rosie at the County Admin building, and in fact I created the character based on my friends Sue and Maria's pug, who had the exact same attitude as Rosie in the book: she was in charge and she let you know it. RIP Rosie the Pug—you will never be forgotten.

As always, there is no Tom Clark, so any errors in police procedure are all mine (and possibly intentional!).

To booksellers and librarians who get excited about books (you mean you're not in it for the big payday?) and have championed my story of Madison and recommended it to readers, thank you for your support and encouragement.

To the readers who message me that they love Madison and that her losses have given them a chance to deal with their own, thank you. I try to write compelling mysteries that keep you on the edge of your seat but that also have moments of poignancy and hope. Thank you for letting me know when I've hit that target. I love hearing from you guys (www.elizabethbreck.com).

And finally, to all of us living through a pandemic with aplomb: we're gonna be in the history books, you guys! Just have courage, keep the faith, and don't lose hope that one day we'll look back on all of this and say, "Remember what a terrible time that was? I'm so glad it's over."

Elizabeth Breck
San Diego
April 2021